Brides fo...

Eligible rakes v...

A friendship formed at ...
leads three bachelors through the trials of
war, mystery and love!

A major, a marquess and a captain reunite
in London to celebrate Britain's peace with
France—only to find society life has many
more exciting things in store for them! They
are thrown into a mystery of jewellery theft
and fraud, and they all find themselves
unlikely suitors to some of the *ton*'s
most captivating ladies!

Will these eligible bachelors
finally meet their matches?

The Major Meets His Match

Available now

Look for the next two stories in the trilogy

Coming soon!

Author Note

Welcome to the first of my Brides for Bachelors trilogy!

I'm really excited about this trilogy as it's the first time I've written a series of stories with connected heroes on purpose! I often get heroes or heroines from one story to walk across the pages of another—just for fun. And sometimes a secondary character has taken root in my imagination and grown until I've had to give him or her their own story. But when I pitched the outline for *The Major Meets His Match*, and described its opening scene, my lovely editor pointed out that the men involved all had stories of their own to tell, and asked why I hadn't thought about writing a linked series from the outset. The minute she suggested that it was as if a light bulb had gone on in my head. I couldn't wait to start writing!

I do hope you enjoy this first in the mini-series as much as I enjoyed writing it, and that you will want to find out what happens to Major Jack Hesketh's friends next.

PS If you are already one of the group of readers who enjoy spotting heroes from my other stories wandering across the pages of books that aren't theirs, then I hope you enjoy the cameo role I've given the hero of my very first publication for Mills & Boon…and have a little giggle at Aunt Susan's predictions about the kind of bride he is likely to marry.

THE MAJOR
MEETS HIS MATCH

Annie Burrows

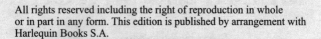

Published in Great Britain 2017
by Mills & Boon, an imprint of HarperCollins*Publishers*
1 London Bridge Street, London, SE1 9GF

© 2017 Annie Burrows

ISBN: 978-0-263-92600-2

Our policy is to use papers that are natural, renewable and
recyclable products and made from wood grown in sustainable
forests. The logging and manufacturing processes conform to the
legal environmental regulations of the country of origin.

Printed and bound in Spain
by CPI, Barcelona

Annie Burrows has been writing Regency romances for Mills & Boon since 2007. Her books have charmed readers worldwide, having been translated into nineteen different languages, and some have gone on to win the coveted Reviewers' Choice award from *CataRomance*. For more information, or to contact the author, please visit annie-burrows.co.uk, or you can find her on Facebook at facebook.com/AnnieBurrowsUK.

I am really grateful to Aidan
for brainstorming with me when I got stuck with
this one. And for reminding me what kind of heroine
I first imagined in Lady Harriet.

Chapter One

Lady Harriet Inskip tilted back her head and breathed in deeply. She could still smell soot, but at least this early in the day it wasn't completely blotting out the more wholesome odours of dew-damp grass and leather and horse. It didn't matter that it was still barely light enough to see the trees and flowers, or the curve of the Serpentine. She hadn't come here to admire the decorous landscape, after all.

She leaned forward and patted her horse's neck.

'Come on, Shadow, let's have a good gallop, shall we? While there's nobody to tell us we can't.'

Shadow snorted and pawed at the gravel path to indicate she was just as eager for exercise as her mistress. And then, with just the slightest tap of Harriet's heel against Shadow's flank, they were off.

For a few glorious minutes they flew through the dappled dawn, both revelling in Shadow's power and vitality. For those few minutes Harriet was free. Free as any wild creature that lived purely by instinct. Unhindered by the fetters with which society restricted the movements of young ladies.

But then her peaceful communion with nature was shattered by a sound that made the hairs on the back of her neck stand up and Shadow to falter mid-stride. It was the neigh of another horse. From beyond a stand of chestnut trees. A neigh so high pitched in outrage, it was almost a scream.

Harriet slowed Shadow to a canter. 'Easy, girl,' she murmured as her mount twitched her ears and rolled her eyes. But Shadow kept fidgeting nervously. And Harriet could hardly blame her when she reared up at the precise moment a black stallion burst from the cover of the trees as though it had been shot from a cannon.

At first she thought the black horse was a riderless runaway. But as it came closer, she could see a dark shape huddled on its back and a pair of legs flailing along its flanks.

'What an idiot,' she muttered to herself. For the man clinging to the stallion had not put a saddle on it. Perhaps there hadn't been time. Perhaps he was attempting to steal the magnificent, and no doubt very expensive, animal. The horse certainly looked as if it wanted nothing more than to dislodge the impertinent human who'd had the temerity to ride him without following the proper conventions first. The stallion had just galloped through the trees as if it had been an attempt to scrape the interloper from his back, to judge from the way he began to buck and kick the moment he got out into the open.

'The idiot,' said Harriet again, this time a bit louder, as she saw that the runaway stallion was now heading straight for the Cumberland Gate. There wasn't much traffic on the roads at this time of day, but if that horse, and the idiot on board, got out into the streets, who knew what damage they might inflict on innocent passers-by?

'Come on, Shadow,' she said, tapping her mare on the flank with her riding crop. 'We're going to have to head off those two before they get into real trouble.' Shadow didn't need much prompting. She loved racing. However, rather than attempt to pull alongside the snorting, furious stallion, Harriet guided Shadow into a course that would take them across his current path. For one thing, even if they could catch up with the runaway horse, any attempt to snatch at the reins to try to bring him to a halt was bound to end in disaster. Though Harriet took pride in her own skills in the saddle, she couldn't imagine being able to lean over far enough to grab the reins without being unseated. Not whilst mounted side-saddle as she was. In fact, only a trained acrobat would be able to accomplish such a feat with any degree of confidence.

For another thing, she knew that no horse would run directly into another, not unless it was completely maddened with terror. And the black stallion, though furious, did not look to be in that state.

Just as she'd hoped, after only a few yards, the stallion did indeed notice their approach and veered off to the left.

It was just a shame for its rider that it did so rather abruptly, because the man, who'd clung on through all the stallion's attempts to dislodge him thus far, shot over its shoulder and landed with a sickening thump on the grass.

Harriet briefly wondered whether she ought to go to the rider's aid. But the man was lying crumpled like a bundle of washing, so there probably wasn't much she could do for him. She could, however, prevent the magnificent stallion from injuring itself or others, if she could only prevent it from reaching the Gate. To that end, she repeated her manoeuvre, pulling sharply to the left as though about to cut across the stallion's path. Once again, the stallion took evasive action. What was more, since it wasn't anywhere near as angry now that it had unseated its hapless rider, it didn't appear to feel the need to gallop flat out. By dint of continually urging it to veer left, Harriet made the stallion go round in a large, but ever-decreasing circle, with her on the outside. By the time they'd returned to the spot where the man still lay motionless, the stallion had slowed to a brisk trot. It curvetted past him, as though doing a little victory dance, shivered as though being attacked by a swarm of flies and then came to a complete standstill, snorting out clouds of steam.

Harriet dismounted, threw her reins over the nearest shrub and slowly approached the sweating, shivering, snorting stallion, crooning the kind of nonsense words that horses the country over always responded to, when spoken in a confident yet soothing tone. The beast tossed his head in a last act of defiance before permitting her to take its trailing reins.

'There, there,' she said, looping them over the same shrub which served as a tether for Shadow. 'You're safe now.' After tossing his head and snorting again for good measure, the stallion appeared to give her the benefit of the doubt.

Only once she was pretty sure the stallion wouldn't attempt to bolt again did Harriet turn to the man.

He was still lying spread out face down on the grass.

Harriet's heart lurched in a way it hadn't when she'd gone after the runaway horse. Horses she could deal with. She spent more time in the stables than anywhere else. People, especially injured people, were another kettle of fish.

Nevertheless, she couldn't just leave him lying there. So she squared her shoulders, looped her train over her arm and walked over to where he lay.

Utterly still.

What did one do for a man who'd been tossed from his horse? A man who might have a broken neck?

Two answers sprang to mind, spoken in two very diverse voices. The first was that of her aunt, Lady Tarbrook.

'Go and fetch help,' it said plaintively, raising a vinaigrette to its nose. *'Ladies do not kneel down on wet grass and touch persons to whom they have not been introduced.'*

She gave a mental snort. According to Lady Tarbrook, Harriet shouldn't be out here at all. Since she'd come to London, Harriet had learned there were hundreds, nay, thousands of things she ought never to do. If Lady Tarbrook had her way, Harriet would do nothing but sit on a sofa doing embroidery or reading fashion magazines all day.

The second voice, coming swiftly after, sounded very much like that of her mother. *'Observe him more closely,'* it said, merely glancing up from the latest scientific journal, *'and find out exactly what his injuries are.'*

Which was the sensible thing to do. *Then* she could go and fetch help, if the man needed it. And what was more, she'd be able to say something to the point about him, rather than voice vague conjectures.

She ran her eyes over him swiftly as she knelt beside him. None of his limbs looked obviously broken. Nor was there any blood that she could see. If she hadn't seen him take a tumble, she might have thought he'd just decided to take a nap there, so relaxed did his body look. His face, at least the part of it that wasn't pressed into the grass, also looked as though he were asleep, rather than unconscious. There was even a slight smile playing about his lips.

She cleared her throat, and then, when he didn't stir, reached out one gloved hand and shook his shoulder gently.

That elicited a mumbled protest.

Encouraged, she shook him again, a bit harder. And his eyes flew open. Eyes of a startlingly deep blue. With deep lines darting from the outer corners, as though he laughed often. Or screwed his eyes up against the sun, perhaps, because, now she came to think of it, the skin of his face was noticeably tanned. Unlike most of the men to whom she was being introduced, of late. He wasn't handsome, in the rather soft way eligible Town-dwellers seemed to be, either. His face was a bit too square and his chin rather too forceful to fit the accepted patrician mould. And yet somehow it was a very attractive face all the same.

And then he smiled at her. As though he recognised her and was pleased to see her. Genuinely pleased. Which puzzled her. As did the funny little jolt that speared her stomach, making her heart lurch.

'I have died and gone to heaven,' he said, wreathing her in sweet fumes which she recognised as emanating, originally, from a brandy bottle.

She recoiled. But not fast enough. Oh, lord, in spite of appearing extremely foxed, he still managed to get his arms round her and tug her down so she lay sprawled half over him. She then only had time to gasp in shock before he got one hand round the back of her head and pulled her face down to his. At which point he kissed her.

Very masterfully.

Even though Harriet had never been kissed before and was shocked that this drunkard was the first man to want to do any such thing, she suspected he must have a lot of experience. Because instead of feeling disgusted, the sensations shooting through her entire body were rather intriguing. Which she was certain ought not to be the case.

'Open your mouth, sweetheart,' the man said, breaking the spell he'd woven round her.

Naturally, she pressed her lips firmly together and shook her head, remembering, all of a sudden, that she ought to be struggling.

Then he chuckled. And started rolling, as if to reverse their positions. Which changed everything. Allowing curiosity to hold her in place while an attractive man obliged her to taste his lips was one thing. Letting him pin her to the ground and render her powerless was quite another.

So she did what she should have done in the first place. She wriggled her right arm as free as she could and struck at him with her riding crop. Because he was holding her so close to him, it glanced harmlessly off the thick thatch of light brown curls protecting the back of his head. But she had at least succeeded in surprising him.

'Let go of me, you beast,' she said, interjecting as much affront in her voice as she could. And began to struggle.

To her chagrin, though he looked rather surprised by her demand, he let go of her at once. Even so, it was no easy matter to wriggle off him, hampered as she was by the train of her riding habit, which had become tangled round her legs.

'Ooohh…' he sighed. 'That feels good.' He half closed his eyes and sort of undulated under her. Indicating that all her frantic efforts to get up were only having a very basic effect on his body.

'You…you beast,' she said, swiping at him with her crop again.

He winced and rubbed at his arm where she'd managed to get in a decent hit before overbalancing and landing flat on his chest again.

'I don't enjoy those sorts of games,' he protested. 'I'd much rather we just kissed a bit more and then—'

She shoved her hands hard against his chest, using his rock-solid body as leverage so she could get to her hands and knees.

'Then nothing,' she said, shuffling back a bit before her trailing riding habit became so tangled she had to roll half over and sit on it. 'You clearly aren't injured after your fall from your horse, though you deserve,' she said, kicking and plucking at her skirts until she got her legs free, 'to have your neck broken.'

'I say, that's rather harsh,' he objected, propping himself up on one elbow and watching her struggles sleepily.

'No, it isn't. You are drunk. And you were trying to ride the kind of horse that would be a handful for any man, sober. What were you thinking? You could have injured him!'

'No, I couldn't. I can ride any horse, drunk or sober—'

'Well, clearly you can't, or he wouldn't have bolted and you wouldn't be lying here—'

'Lucifer wouldn't have thrown me if you hadn't dashed across in front of us and startled him.'

'No, he would have carried you on to a public highway and ridden down some hapless milkmaid instead. And you would definitely have broken your neck if he'd thrown you on the cobbles.'

'I might have known,' he said with a plaintive sigh, 'that you were too good to be true. You might look like an angel and kiss like a siren, and have a fine pair of legs, but you have the disposition of a harpy.'

She gasped. Not at the insult, so much, but at the fact that he was gazing admiringly at her legs while saying it. Making her aware that far too much of them was on show.

'Well, you're an oaf. A drunken oaf at that!' She finally managed to untangle her legs and get to her feet just as three more men came staggering into view.

'Good God, just look at that,' said the first of the trio to reach them, a slender, well-dressed man with cold grey eyes and a cruel mouth. 'Even lying flat on his back in the middle of nowhere, Ulysses can find entertainment to round off the evening.'

Since the man with the cruel mouth was looking at her as though she was about to become his entertainment, Harriet's blood ran cold.

'I have no intention of being anyone's entertainment,' she protested, inching towards Shadow, though how on earth she was to mount up and escape, she had no idea. 'I only came over here to see if I could help.'

'You can certainly help settle the b-bet,' said the second young man to arrive, flicking his long, rather greasy fringe out of his eyes. 'Did he reach the C-Cumberland Gate b-before Lucifer unseated him?'

'It was a wager?' She rounded on the one

they'd referred to as Ulysses, the one who was still half-reclining, propped up on one arm, watching them all with a crooked grin on his face. 'You risked injuring that magnificent beast for the sake of a wager?'

'The only risk was to his own fool neck,' said the man with the cold eyes. 'Lucifer can take care of himself,' he said, going across to the stallion and patting his neck proudly. From the way the stallion lowered his head and butted his chest, it was clear he was Lucifer's master.

Harriet stooped to gather her train over one arm, her heart hammering. At no point had she felt afraid of the man they called Ulysses, even when he'd been trying to roll her over on to her back. There was something about his square, good-natured face that put her at ease. Or perhaps it had been that twinkle in his eyes.

But the way the one with the cruel mouth was looking at her was a different matter. There was something...dark about him. Predatory. Even if he was fond of his horse and the horse clearly adored him in return, that didn't make him a decent man.

He then confirmed all her suspicions about his nature by turning to her with a mocking smile on his face. 'It is hardly fair of you to reward

Ulysses with a kiss,' he said, taking a purpose-ful step closer, 'when it is I who won the wager.'

She lashed out with her riding crop and would have caught him across his face had he not flinched out of her way with a dexterity that both amazed and alarmed her. Even in a state of inebriation, this man could still pose a very real threat to a lone female.

Keeping her eyes on him, she inched sideways to where she'd tethered Shadow. And collided with what felt like a brick wall.

'Oof!' said the wall, which turned out to be the third of Ulysses's companions, a veritable giant of a man.

'You got off lightly,' remarked Mr Cold-Eyes to the giant, who was rubbing his mid-section ruefully. 'She made a *deliberate* attempt to in-jure me.'

'That's prob'ly 'cos you're fright'ning her,' slurred the giant. 'Clearly not a lightskirt.'

'Then what is she doing in the park, at this hour, kissing stray men she finds lying about the place?' Cold-Eyes gave her a look of such deri-sion it sent a flicker of shame coiling through her insides.

'She couldn't resist me,' said Ulysses, grin-ning at her.

'She d-don't seem to like you, th-though, Zeus,' said the one with the greasy, floppy fringe.

'Archie, you wound me,' said Zeus, as she got her fingers, finally, on Shadow's reins. Though how on earth she was to mount up, she couldn't think. There was no mounting block. No groom to help her reach the stirrup.

Just as she'd resigned herself to walking home leading her mount, she felt a pair of hands fasten round her waist. On a reflex, she lashed out at her would-be assailant, catching him on the crown of his head.

'Ouch,' said the drunken giant of a man, as he launched her up and on to Shadow's saddle. 'There was no call for that.' He backed away, rubbing his head with a puzzled air.

No, there hadn't been any call for it. But how could she have guessed the giant had only been intending to help her?

'Then I beg *your* pardon,' she said through gritted teeth as she fumbled her foot into the stirrup.

'As for the rest of you,' she said as she got her knee over the pommel and adjusted her skirts, 'you ought…all of you…to be ashamed of yourselves.'

She did her best to toss her head as though she held them all in disdain. As though her heart wasn't hammering like a wild, frightened bird within the bars of her rib cage. To ride off with dignity, rather than hammering her heels into Shadow's flank, and urging her mare to head for home at a full gallop.

She wouldn't give them the satisfaction.

Chapter Two

Harriet urged Shadow into a gallop, as soon as she was out of their sight. They'd thought she was a lightskirt. That was why *Ulysses* had kissed her, and the one with the cold eyes—*Zeus*—had looked at her as though she was nothing.

That was why the giant had lifted her on to the horse without asking her permission, too. Even though he'd meant well, he hadn't treated her with the respect due to a lady.

Because she'd stepped outside the bounds set for the behaviour of ladies.

Damn her aunt for being right! She dashed a tear away from her cheek. A tear humiliation had wrung from her. She wasn't afraid. Just angry. So angry. At the men, for treating her so…casually. For manhandling her, and mocking her and insinuating she was…

Oh, how she wished she'd struck them *all* with

her crop. Men who went about the park, getting drunk and frightening decent females...

Although they hadn't thought she *was* decent, had they? They'd thought she was out there drumming up custom.

She shuddered.

And no wonder. She'd melted into *Ulysses*'s kiss like butter on to toasted bread. And then been so flustered she'd forgotten to conceal her legs when untangling them from her skirts, giving him a view of them right up to her knees, like as not.

Oh, but she wished she could hit something now. Though she was more to blame than anyone and she couldn't hit herself. Because it turned out that sometimes, just sometimes, Aunt Susan might just be right. Ladies *couldn't* go about on their own, in London. Because if they did, drunken idiots assumed they were fair game.

Why hadn't Aunt Susan explained that some of the rules were for her own good, though? If she'd only warned Harriet that men could behave that badly, when they were intoxicated, then...

Honesty compelled her to admit that she knew how idiotic men became when they drank too much. Didn't she see it every week back home in Donnywich? By the end of market day, men came rolling out of the tavern, wits so addled with drink they had to rely on their horses to find their way home.

And men were men, whether they lived in the country and wore smocks, or in Town and dressed in the height of fashion. So she should have known. Because the rules were made by men, for the convenience of men. So, rather than expect men to behave properly, at all times, women just had to stay out of their way, or go around with guards, just in case they felt like being beastly.

She slowed Shadow to a walk as she left the park via the Stanhope Gate, her heart sinking. She'd so enjoyed escaping to the park at first light. It had been the only thing making her stay in London bearable of late. But now, because men rolled home from their clubs in drunken packs and…and *pounced* on any female foolish enough to cross their path, she would never be able to do so again. She'd have to take a groom. Which would mean waiting until one was awake and willing to take her without first checking with Aunt Susan that she had permission.

And Aunt Susan wouldn't give it, like as not.

Oh, it was all so…vexing!

London was turning out to be such a disappointment that she was even starting to see the advantages of the kind of life she'd lived at home. At least nobody there had ever so much as raised an eyebrow if she'd gone out riding on her own. Not even when she'd worn some of her brothers' cast-offs, for comfort. Even the times she'd stayed out all day, nobody had ever appeared to notice. Mama was always too engrossed in some scientific tome or other to bother about what her only daughter was getting up to. And Papa had never once criticised her, no matter how bitterly Aunt Susan might complain she was turning into a hoyden.

Nobody who lived for miles around Stone Court would ever have dreamed of molesting her, either, since everyone knew she was Lord and Lady Balderstone's youngest child.

She sighed as Shadow picked her way daintily along Curzon Street. She'd been in the habit of feeling aggrieved when nobody commented on her absence, or even appeared to care if she missed meals. But the alternative, of having her aunt watching her like a hawk, practically every waking moment, was beginning to feel like being laced into someone else's corset, then shut in a room with no windows.

She reached the end of Curzon Street and crossed Charles Street, her heart sinking still further. The nearer she got to Tarbrook House, the more it felt as though she was putting her head under a velvet cushion and inviting her aunt and uncle to smother her with it.

If only she'd known what a London Season would be like, she would have thanked Aunt Susan politely for offering her the chance to make her debut alongside her younger cousin, Kitty, and made some excuse to stay away. She could easily have said that Papa relied on her to keep the household running smoothly, what with Mama being mostly too preoccupied to bother with anything so mundane as paying servants or ordering meals. Aunt Susan would have understood and accepted the excuse that *somebody* had to approve the menus and go over the household accounts on a regular basis. For it was one of the things that had always caused dissension between the sisters, whenever Aunt Susan had come on a visit. Mama had resented the notion that she ought to entertain visitors, saying that it interfered with her studies. Aunt Susan would retort that she ought to venture out of her workshop at least once a day, to enquire how her guests were faring, even if she didn't really care. The sniping would escalate until, in the end, everyone was very relieved when the family duty visit came to an end.

Except for Harriet. For it was only when Aunt

Susan was paying one of her annual visits, en route to her own country estate after yet another glittering London Season, that she felt as if anyone saw her. Really saw her. And had the temerity to raise concerns about the way her own mother and father neglected her.

But, oh, what Harriet wouldn't give for a little of that sort of neglect right now. For, from the moment she'd arrived, Aunt Susan hadn't ceased complaining about her behaviour, her posture, her hair, her clothes, and even the expression on her face from time to time. Even shopping for clothes, which Harriet had been looking forward to with such high hopes, had not lived up to her expectations. She didn't know why it was, but though she bought exactly the same sorts of things as Kitty, she never looked as good in them. To be honest, she suspected she looked a perfect fright in one or two of the fussier dresses, to judge from the way men eyed her up and down with looks verging from disbelief to amusement. She couldn't understand why Aunt Susan had let her out in public in one of them, when she'd gone home and looked at herself, with critical eyes, in the mirror. At her*self*, rather than the delicacy of the lace, or the sparkle of the spangled trimmings.

Worse, on the few occasions she'd attended

balls so far, Aunt Susan had not granted any of the men who'd asked her to dance the permission to do so. The first few refusals had stemmed from Aunt Susan's conviction that Harriet had not fully mastered the complexities of the steps. And after that, she simply found fault with the men who were then doing the asking. But what did it matter if her dance partners were not good *ton*? Surely it would be more fun to skip round the room with somebody, even if he was a desperate fortune-hunter, rather than sit wilting on the sidelines? Every blessed night.

Yes, she sighed, catching her first glimpse of Tarbrook House, the longer she stayed in Town, the more appealing Stone Court was beginning to look. At least at home she'd started to carve out a niche for herself. After being of no consequence for so many years, she'd found a great deal of consolation in taking over the duties her mother habitually neglected.

But in Town she was truly a fish out of water, she reflected glumly as Shadow trotted through the arch leading to the mews at the back of Tarbrook House. Instead of dancing every night at glittering balls, with a succession of handsome men, one of whom was going to fall madly in love with her and whisk her away to his estate where he'd treat her like a queen, she was actually turning out to be a social failure.

The only time she felt like herself recently had been on these secret forays into the park, before anyone else was awake. And now, because of those...*beasts*, she wasn't even going to be able to have that any longer.

She dismounted, and led Shadow to her stall, where a groom darted forward with a scowl on his face.

'I know,' she said. 'I should not have gone out riding on my own. But you need not report this to Lady Tarbrook. For I shall not be doing so again, you may be certain.'

The groom ran his eyes over her. His gaze paused once or twice. Over the grass stains on her riding habit, for example. At which his mouth twisted in derision.

He thought she'd taken a tumble and had now lost her nerve, the fool. She gripped her crop tightly as she warred with the urge to defend her skill as a horsewoman. But if she admitted she'd dismounted through choice, he'd wonder where the grass stains had come from. And since she was not in the habit of telling lies, she'd probably blush and stammer, and look so guilty that he'd go straight to Aunt Susan and tell her that her hoyden of a niece had been up to no good.

And Aunt Susan would extract the truth out of her in no time flat.

And she would die rather than have to confess she'd let a man kiss her. A strange man. A strange drunken man.

And worse, that she'd liked it. Because, for a few brief moments, he'd made her feel attractive. Interesting. When for most of her life—until she'd taken to giving the servants directions, that was—nobody had thought her of any value at all. She'd just been an afterthought. A girl, what was worse. A girl that nobody knew quite what to do with.

So she lifted her chin and simply stalked away, her reputation as a horsewoman ruined in the eyes of the head groom.

Jack Hesketh sat up slowly, his head spinning, and watched the virago galloping away.

'Do you know,' he mused, 'I think we may have just insulted a lady.'

Zeus snorted. 'If she were a lady, she would not have been out here unattended at this hour, flirting with a pack of drunken bucks.'

Jack shook his head. He couldn't believe Zeus—who'd pursued women with such fervour and conquered so many of them while he, and Archie, and Atlas had still been too pimply and awkward to do anything but stand back in awe—had become the kind of man who could now speak of such a lovely one with so much contempt.

If he were to meet Zeus now, for the first time, he didn't think he'd want to be his friend.

In fact, after the way he'd behaved tonight, he'd steer well clear of such a man. Zeus had always been a bit full of himself, which was only to be expected when he was of such high rank and swimming in lard to boot. But there had been a basic sort of decency about him, too. He'd had a sense of humour, anyway.

But now...it was as if a sort of malaise had infected him, rendering him incapable of seeing any good in anyone or anything.

And Archie—well, he'd turned into a sort of... tame hound, trotting along behind Zeus like a spaniel at his master's heels.

While Atlas...oh, dear God, Atlas. He winced as he turned his head rather too quickly, to peer into the gloom at the wreck of the man who'd been his boyhood idol.

Though, hadn't they all been his heroes, one way or another? Which was, perhaps, where he'd gone wrong. In keeping his schoolboy reverence for them firm in his heart during all his years of active service, like a talisman, he'd sort of pickled their images, like flies set in amber. That would certainly explain why it had come as such a shock to see how much they'd all changed.

Especially Atlas. Imprisonment at the hands of the French, and illness, had reduced him to an emaciated ruin of his former self. In fact, he looked such a wreck that Jack had been a bit surprised he'd managed to lift the virago on to her horse at all. Though at least it proved he was still the same man, inside, where it mattered. They hadn't given him the nickname of Atlas only because of his immense size and strength compared to the rest of them, but because of his habit of always trying to take everyone else's burdens on his own shoulders. Rescuing that girl from Zeus was exactly the kind of thing he'd always been doing. Atlas had always hated seeing anyone weak or vulnerable being tormented.

Which was what they'd been doing to that poor girl, Jack thought, his stomach turning over in shame. The four of them, making sport of her. No—make that three. Atlas had been the only one of them to behave like a perfect gentleman even though he was as drunk as the rest of them.

Or was he? He'd barely touched any of the drink Zeus had so lavishly supplied, at what was supposed to be a celebration of not only the

Peace, but also his return to England. Of the fact that for the first time in years, all four of them had the liberty to meet up. As though the poor fellow felt he couldn't trust himself to hold it down. Nobody had said anything, though. They'd all been too shocked at the sight of him to do more than squirm a bit as they drank his health. Health? Hah! The best that anyone could say of the gaunt and yellow-skinned Atlas was that he was alive.

'I tell you what, though,' he said aloud. 'You are still my hero, Atlas'

Atlas started, looking taken aback.

'No, really. After all this time, you are still the best of us. Always was.'

'You paid too much attention to the letters I wrote when I first went to sea,' he said, looking uncomfortable. 'I made it sound far more exciting than it was. Didn't want you all to…pity me, for having to leave. Didn't want to admit that I was seasick, and homesick and utterly wretched.'

'B-but,' said Archie, looking shocked, 'you *were* a hero. Read ab-bout your exp-ploits in the *Gazette.*'

Atlas made a dismissive motion with his hand, as though banishing the *Gazette* and all that was printed in it to perdition.

'Just did my duty. No choice, when you're in the thick of action. You either fight like a demon, or…well, you know how it is, Jack. Same in the army, I dare say.' He sent Jack a beseeching look, as though begging him to divert attention from him.

'Only too well,' he therefore said. 'Which is why your homecoming is worth celebrating. Glad you're alive. Glad I'm alive. Even glad Zeus is alive,' he said, shooting his godship a wry grin. 'Since he got us all together again, for the first time since…what year was it when you left school, Atlas?'

'You are foxed,' said Zeus with exasperation, before Atlas had a chance to make his response. 'If I'd realised quite how badly foxed, I would never have let you attempt to ride Lucifer.'

'Attempt? Pah! I *did* ride Lucifer.'

'Not very far.'

'Far enough to prove your boast about being the only man to be able to do it was patently false.' God, how he'd wanted to knock the sneering expression from Zeus's face when he'd made that claim. Which was why he'd declared there wasn't a horse he couldn't ride, drunk or sober.

Zeus shook his head this time as he stood over Jack where he lay sprawled.

But Jack didn't care. For a few minutes, directly after he'd made the wager, all four of them had shaken off the gloom that had been hanging over them like a pall. They'd even laughed and started calling each other by the silly names they'd given each other at school as they staggered round to the stables. They'd sobered slightly when Lucifer had rolled his eyes at them and snorted indignantly when they'd approached his stall. Archie had even suggested, albeit timidly, that he was sure nobody would mind if Jack withdrew his claim.

'Draw back from a bet? What kind of man do you think I am?' Jack had retorted. And Zeus had grabbed the stallion's halter and led the animal out into the streets before anyone could talk sense into either of them.

Good God. Zeus had been as intent on carrying through on the wager as Jack himself. Did that mean…?

Was there still something of the old Zeus left? Deep under all that sarcasm and sneering? He'd certainly been the one to arrange this reunion. And he'd also made sure they'd been given a chance to laugh at Jack's antics, the way they'd done so many times at school. They'd certainly all been roaring with laughter as Lucifer had shot off, with Jack clinging to his mane. And so sweet had been that sound that Jack hadn't cared that the beast had unseated him before he'd managed one circuit of the park.

'I still maintain that girl was not flirting with us,' he said defiantly. Was he imagining it, or was there an answering gleam in Zeus's eyes? As though he was relishing having someone refusing to lie down and roll over at his bidding.

Ah.

Was that why he'd become so jaded? Because nobody challenged him any more? It would explain why he'd jumped at the wager, ridiculous though it was. Why he'd whisked Lucifer out of his stall before the sleepy groom had a chance to fling a saddle on his back.

Perhaps, even, why he'd gathered them all together in the first place.

'She may not have been a lady, precisely,' Jack continued. 'But I stick to my guns about her not flirting with us. Else why would she have set about us with her riding crop?'

That had come as a shock, too, he had to admit. One moment she'd been melting into his arms, the next she was fighting him off. And she'd been kissing him so sweetly, after that initial hesitation, so shyly yet…hang on…shyly. With hesitation. As though she didn't know quite what to do, but couldn't help herself. As if she was catching fire, just as he'd been.

One moment she was with him, and then…
it was as if she'd come to her senses. As though
she realised it was a stranger with whom she was
rolling about on the grass.

'I would wager,' he said, a smile tugging at
his lips as he recalled and re-examined her every
reaction, 'that not only was she not flirting, but
that she was an innocent, to boot.'

That would explain it all. That gasp of shock
when he'd first started kissing her. Her inexpert,
almost clumsy, yet uninhibited response. Until
the very moment when she'd hauled up the draw-
bridge and slammed down the portcullis. The
moment when she remembered she was dabbling
in sin.

'And I don't care what you think, Zeus,' he
said with determination. 'We owe that girl an
apology. Well, I do, anyway. Shouldn't have
kissed her.'

'She shouldn't have put her face in the way of
your lips, then,' retorted Zeus.

'No, no, the girl was only trying to see if I was
injured.' Which had been remarkably brave of
her. Not many females would have come rush-
ing to the aid of a stranger like that. Nor would
they have been able to bring Zeus's bad-tempered
stallion under control, either.

'Which is more than any of you have done,' he finished pointedly.

'You are not injured,' said Zeus pithily. 'You are indestructible. And I have that on the best authority.'

'Must have been speaking to m'father.'

'Your brother,' Zeus corrected him.

'Oh? Which one?'

'I forget,' said Zeus with a wave of his hand. 'He did tell me he was Viscount Becconsall when he walked up to me in White's and presumed friendship with me because of my friendship with you.' His mouth twisted in distaste.

'Could have been either of them, then,' said Jack, who'd recently acquired the title himself. 'Poor sod,' he said, and not only because both his brothers were now dead, but because he could picture the reception such behaviour would have gained them. They hadn't started calling him Zeus without good reason. From the very first day he'd attended school, he'd looked down on all the other boys from a very lofty height. He didn't require an education, he'd informed anyone who would listen. He'd had perfectly good tutors at home. It was just that his father, who had suddenly developed radical tendencies, had decided the next Marquis of Rawcliffe ought to get to know how the lower orders lived.

Jack chuckled at the vision of his bumptious brother attempting to take such a liberty with Zeus. 'I can just see it. You gave him one of your freezing stares and raised your eyebrow at him.'

'Not only my eyebrow, but also my quizzing glass,' said Zeus, leaning down to offer him a hand, as though deciding Jack had been cluttering up the ground for long enough. 'It had no effect. The man kept wittering on about what a charmed life you led. How you came through the bloodiest battles unscathed. As though you had some kind of lucky charm keeping you safe, instead of being willing to acknowledge that you owed your successes on the battlefield to your skill as a strategist, as well as personal valour.'

Jack gasped as Zeus pulled him to his feet. That was the thing about him. He might be the most arrogant, conceited fellow he'd ever met, but he'd also been the first person to look beyond the way Jack clowned around to distract the bullies who'd been hounding Archie at school. The only person to take one look at him and see the intelligence he'd been at such pains to disguise.

To believe in him.

'Didn't come through this tussle unscathed,' he said, rubbing his posterior to explain his involuntary gasp. Zeus gave him one of his looks.

The kind that told Jack he knew he was avoiding an issue, but was magnanimous enough to permit him to do so.

'Which brings me back to the girl. Did you notice the way she spoke? And the horse? Expensive bit of blood and bone, that dappled grey.'

'Hmmph,' said Zeus. 'I grant you that she may have been gently reared, but just because she speaks well and rides an expensive horse does not mean she is an innocent now.'

'No, truly, I would stake my life on it.'

'Since n-none of us know who she is,' said Archie. 'There is n-no way for us to v-verify your conc-clusion.'

No, there wasn't.

Which was a horrible thought. In fact, the prospect of never seeing her again gave him a queer, almost painful feeling in his chest. And not only because she'd melted into his arms as if she belonged there. It was more than that. It was…it was…well, out of all the disappointments the night had brought, those few moments kissing her, holding her, and, yes, even fighting with her, had been…a breath of fresh air. No, he shook his head. More like a…well, the way the night had been going, he'd felt as if he was sinking deeper and deeper into a dark well of disappointment. And then, all of a sudden, she'd been in the centre of the one bright spot of the whole night. And that kiss…well, it had revived him, the way the sight of a lighthouse would revive a storm-tossed mariner, he suspected.

Hope, that was what she'd brought him. Somehow.

Was it a coincidence that right after meeting her, he'd seen that Atlas was still the same man, deep down, where it mattered? That there was even hope for Zeus, too?

Hope. That was the name he'd give her, then, while he searched for her. And why not? Why not remember the one bright spot of the evening as a glimmer of hope in what was, of late, a life that contained anything but?

And another thing. Hope was always worth pursuing.

'Right then,' said Jack, rubbing his hands together. 'We'll just have to search London until we find her.'

Zeus's eyes narrowed with interest. 'And then?'

'And then, we will know which one of us is right.'

'Another wager?' Atlas shook his head in mock reproof. Though nobody had said anything about a wager. 'At this rate, you will beggar me.'

'Not I,' said Jack, his heart lifting. Because Atlas was clearly doing his best to raise morale amongst his friends. He must have seen the effect the wager over Lucifer had on Zeus, the way Jack had. 'You and Archie will just act as witnesses,' he therefore informed Atlas. 'This wager, just like the one over Lucifer, is between me and Zeus.'

'And the stakes?' Zeus had gone all narrow-eyed and sneering again, as though he suspected Jack of trading on their long-ago connections to take advantage of him.

What the hell had happened to him, since school, to turn him into such a suspicious devil?

'Why, the usual, naturally,' said Jack. Which was almost as good as drawing his cork, since his head reared back in momentary surprise.

'The...the usual?'

'Yes. The usual between the four of us, that is.'

'You...' For a moment, Zeus looked as though he was about to express one of the softer emotions. But only for a moment.

'Which reminds me,' he drawled in that ghastly, affected way that set Jack's teeth on edge. 'You have already lost one wager.'

'Are you demanding payment?' Jack planted his fists on his hips and scowled. 'Are you accusing me of attempting to welch on the bet?'

'No,' he said softly. 'I was only going to suggest...double or quits?'

For a moment the four of them all stood in stunned silence.

And then Archie began to giggle. Atlas snorted. And soon, all four of them were laughing like the schoolboys they had once been.

Chapter Three

'Nobody is going to ask you to dance if you don't sit up straight and take that scowl off your face,' said Aunt Susan, sternly.

They might if Aunt Susan hadn't already repulsed the young men who'd shown an interest in her when she'd first come to Town, on the grounds that they were all fortune-hunters or scoundrels.

Nevertheless, Harriet obediently squared her shoulders and attempted the social smile her aunt had made her practise in the mirror every day for half an hour since she'd come to Town.

'That's better,' said Aunt Susan out of the corner of her mouth which was also pulled into a similarly insincere rictus. 'I know it must chafe that Kitty is having so much more success than you, but you must remember that you are no longer in the first flush of youth.'

Harriet only just managed to stop herself rolling her eyes. She was only twenty, for heaven's sake. But eligible gentlemen looking for brides, her aunt had informed her, with a rueful shake of her head, wanted much younger girls. 'It's perfectly natural,' she'd explained. 'Gels usually make their debut when they are seventeen, or eighteen, unless there's been a death in the family, or something of a similar nature. So everyone is bound to wonder why any girl who looks much older hasn't appeared in society before. And,' she'd added with a grimace of distaste, 'draw their own conclusions.'

'Please, dear,' she was saying now, 'do try to look as if you are enjoying yourself. Gentlemen are much more likely to ask you to dance if you appear to be good-natured.'

Harriet was beginning to suspect that actually she was not the slightest bit good-natured. She'd always thought of herself as being fairly placid before she'd come to Town. But ever since her aunt had descended on Stone Court like a fairy godmother to take her to the ball, she'd been see-sawing from one wild emotion to another. At first she'd been in a froth of excitement. But then had come the painful discovery that no amount of fine clothes could make her compare with her prettier, younger, more sociable cousin

Kitty. After that, in spite of her aunt's best efforts to bring her up to scratch in the short time they had, had come the discovery that actually, she didn't want to conform to society's notions of how a young lady should behave. And now she just felt as if she had a stone permanently lodged in her shoe.

'Now, *there* is a young man with whom you might safely dance,' said Lady Tarbrook, nudging Harriet in the ribs. And drawing her attention to the slender young man who'd just come into the ballroom. A man she'd been dreading coming across for the last two weeks. Ever since he'd fallen off his horse and tricked her into kissing him.

'Though I shouldn't like to raise your hopes too much. He hasn't asked any eligible female to dance since he came to Town. Not that he's actually attended many balls, to my knowledge. Well, not this sort of ball,' Lady Tarbrook was muttering darkly. 'Not his style. Not his style at all.'

No, his style was roistering all night with a pack of reprobates, then taking part in reckless wagers that ended up with him almost breaking his stupid neck. To say nothing of molesting people who went to help him.

And yet Aunt Susan was prepared to give her

permission to dance with him. In the unlikely event he were to ask her.

It beggared belief.

'Still, nothing ventured, nothing gained,' said Aunt Susan, fluttering her fan wildly and smiling for all she was worth in his direction.

While Harriet did her best to shrink into the meagre upholstery of the chair upon which she was sitting. Oh, where was a potted plant, or a fire screen, or…a hole in the ground when she needed one?

Ulysses—for that was the only name she knew him by—ran his eyes round the ballroom as though searching for someone before setting off in the direction of a group of military men gathered in the doorway to the refreshment room.

'Oh, I see,' said Lady Tarbrook with resignation. 'He must have wanted to speak to one of his…associates. I don't suppose he will stay long.' She folded her fan as though consigning him to history.

While Harriet fumed. The…the beast! He'd looked right through her, as though she wasn't there. Without the slightest sign he recognised her.

Well, he probably didn't. He probably kissed random women senseless every day of the week. The kiss that she'd spent so many nights recalling, in great detail, before she went to sleep, and at odd moments during the day as well, had obviously completely slipped his mind.

Because it had meant nothing to him.

Because *she* meant nothing to him.

Well—he meant nothing to her, either. And nor did that kiss. Just because it was her first and still had the power to make her toes curl if she dwelt on it for too long, did not mean that... that...

Oh, bother him for getting her thoughts into a tangle.

A loud burst of laughter gave her the excuse she needed to let her eyes stray to the doorway of the refreshment room and the group of men who'd opened up to admit him to their company.

She couldn't help noticing several other women turning their heads in his direction, too. And eyeing him with great interest. Which came as no surprise, seeing the way he moved. There was a vitality about him that naturally drew the eye, for it was so very different from the languid stroll affected by the other men present tonight. And in the candlelight his hair, which had just looked a sort of dull brown in the shade of that chestnut tree, gleamed with traces of gold.

She flicked her fan open and plied it vigorously before her face. Which she turned away from the part of the room in which he was standing. She would not stare at him. She would do nothing to attract his attention, either, in case he did have a dim recollection of her. You could sometimes get even quite stupid people to remember things if you constantly reminded them of it, or so Aunt Susan had told her, when she'd despaired of ever grasping the myriad rules of etiquette that seemed to come naturally to Kitty.

But then Kitty had been drilled into good behaviour from the moment she was born.

'I don't know what your mother was thinking, to leave you to run wild the way she has,' Aunt Susan had said upon discovering that Harriet had only the vaguest notion of how deeply to curtsy to people of various ranks.

'She didn't let me run wild, precisely,' Harriet had countered, because there had definitely been times when Mama had applied the birch. When she'd used phrases she'd picked up in the stables at the dinner table, for instance. 'It's just that she doesn't think things like teaching me to curtsy are terribly important.' Nor having a Season, come to that. In fact, she was beginning to think her mother might have a point. How on earth could anyone pick a life partner this way? Nobody really talked to anyone. Not about anything important. Everyone in Town seemed to

Harriet to behave like a swarm of giddy mayflies, flitting above the surface of a glittering pond.

'Clearly,' Aunt Susan had said frostily. 'But even if she couldn't prise herself away from her books and bottles to do it herself, she could have engaged a sensible woman to take over that side of your education. In fact,' she'd said, shifting in her seat as though she was itching to get up and stride about the room to make her point, 'for a woman who goes on so about how important the life of the mind is to her, you'd think she would have wanted you to have had the same education as her sons. Instead of no education at all. Why, if it hadn't been for me sending you that Person to teach you how to read and write you could have ended up as ignorant as a savage!'

Harriet had hung her head at that reminder of how much she owed to Aunt Susan, stifling the flare of resentment she'd been experiencing at being forced to curtsy over and over again until she got it right. Because the truth was that Mama *had* been too interested in her books and bottles, as Aunt Susan had so scathingly referred to Mama's laboratory, to concern herself with something as mundane as the education of her daughter. Papa had arranged for the education of his sons. But a girl's education, he'd said, was the province of her mother.

Between Papa's focus on his three fine sons and Mama's absorption with her hobbies, Harriet had been forgotten entirely.

And if her own parents could forget her existence for weeks at a time, it stood to reason that Ulysses would do the same.

Although perhaps it was just as well. Far better that, than that he should come over and start talking to her as if she was an old acquaintance, or something. Which would make Aunt Susan ask questions. All sorts of awkward questions.

At which point, naturally, he sauntered over to where they were sitting and bowed punctiliously to her aunt.

'Good evening, Lady Tarbrook,' he said in a voice that struck like a dart to her midriff.

'Lord Becconsall, how delightful to see you,' simpered her aunt.

Lord Becconsall?

Well, obviously, Ulysses couldn't be his real name, but she was still surprised he had a title.

Though perhaps she shouldn't have been. The kind of men who were out in the park after a long night of drinking could only be men who didn't have jobs to go to in the morning. She should have known he was titled, really, now she came to think of it.

And for all she knew, Ulysses *was* his real

name. She had an Uncle Agamemnon, after all. And a distant cousin by marriage by the name of Priam. The craze for all things classical seemed to have affected a lot of parents with the strangest urges to name their children after ancient Greeks lately.

She snapped back to attention when she heard her aunt say, 'And you must allow me to present my niece, Lady Harriet Inskip.'

'*Lady* Harriet?'

Though he bowed, he did so with the air of a man who wasn't sure he should be doing any such thing. How did he do that? Inject such... mockery into the mere act of bowing?

'Oh, you have not heard of her, I dare say, because she has lived such a secluded life, in the country. This is her first visit to London.'

Harriet gritted her teeth. For this was the excuse Aunt Susan was always trotting out, whenever some society matron quizzed her over some defect or other. Or a gentleman drew down his brows when she made an observation that ran counter to some opinion he'd just expressed. *'Oh, fresh up from the country, you know,'* her aunt would say airily. *'Quite unspoiled and natural in her manners.'* Which invariably alerted her to the fact she must have just committed a terrible faux pas for which she'd be reprimanded later, in private. Though the worst, the very worst fault she had, apparently, was speaking her mind. Young ladies did not do such things, Aunt Susan insisted. Which shouldn't have come as such a surprise, really. She should have known that females, and their opinions, were of less value than males. Hadn't that fact been demonstrated to her, in no uncertain terms, all her life?

Except when it came to Mama. Papa never found fault with anything she ever said, or did. Even when he didn't agree with it.

'That would account for it,' said Ulysses, with a knowing smile. And though Aunt Susan heard nothing amiss, Harriet could tell that he was remembering their last encounter. And decrying her behaviour. The way those society matrons had done. Though at least this time she knew exactly what she'd done to earn his scorn.

'You might know one of her older brothers,' Aunt Susan was persisting, valiantly. 'George Inskip? Major the Honourable George Inskip? He's a Light Dragoon.'

'Sadly, no,' said Ulysses, though he didn't look the least bit sad. 'The cavalry rarely fraternises with the infantry, you know. We are far, far, beneath their notice, as a rule.'

So he was in the army. No—had been in the army. He was not wearing uniform, whereas men who still held commissions, like the group still milling around in the doorway to the refreshment room, flaunted their scarlet jackets and gold braid at every opportunity.

So, that would account for the tanned face. And the lines fanning out from his eyes. And the energy he put into the mere act of walking across a room. And the hardness of his body. And the…

'Oh, I'm sure you are no such thing,' simpered Aunt Susan. Making Harriet's gorge rise. Why on earth was she gushing all over the very last man she wished to encourage, when so far she'd done her level best to repulse every other man who'd shown the slightest bit of interest in her?

'And probably too far beneath Lady Harriet to presume to request the pleasure of a dance,' he said. Placing a slight emphasis on the word beneath. Which sent her mind back to the moments he had been lying beneath her, his arms clamped round her body as he ravaged her mouth.

Which made her blush. To her absolute fury. Because Aunt Susan gave her a knowing look.

'But of course you may dance with Lady Harriet, Lord Becconsall,' trilled Aunt Susan, who clearly saw this as a coup. For a man notorious for not dancing with debutantes was asking her protégée to do just that. 'She would love to dance with you, would you not, my dear?'

Ulysses cocked his head to one side and observed her mutinous face with evident amusement. Just as she'd suspected. He was planning on having a great deal of fun at her expense.

'I do not think she wishes to dance with me at all,' he said ruefully. 'In fact, she looks as though she would rather lay about me with a riding crop to make me go away.'

Harriet was not normally given to temper. But right at this moment she could feel it coming to the fore. How she wished she were not in a ballroom, so that she could slap that mocking smile from his face.

'Oh, no, not at all! She is just a little…awkward, in her manners. Being brought up so…in such a very…that is, Harriet,' said Aunt Susan rather sharply, 'I know you are very shy, but you really must take that scowl off your face and tell Lord Becconsall that you would love above all things to dance with him.'

Ulysses schooled his features into the approximation of a man who had endless patience with awkward young females who needed coaxing out of their modest disinclination to so much as dance with a man to whom she had only just been introduced.

While the twinkle in his eyes told her that, inside, he was laughing at her. That he was enjoying taunting her with those oblique references to their previous meeting. And, she suspected, that he was going to enjoy holding that episode over her head every time they met from this time forth.

Oh, lord, what was she to do? What would happen if Aunt Susan found out she'd been caught, in the Park, by a group of drunken bucks and kissed breathless by this particular one? When she should have been in her room, in her bed, recovering from the exertions of the ball the night before?

Disgrace, that was what. Humiliation. All sorts of unpleasantness.

If she found out.

Therefore, Aunt Susan had better not find out. Had better not suspect anything was amiss. Or she would start digging.

That prospect was enough to make her draw on all those hours she'd spent in front of the mirror, perfecting that insincere smile. And plastering it on to her face.

'Lord Becconsall,' she said through gritted teeth. 'I would love above all things to dance with you.'

With a triumphant grin, he held out his hand, took hers and led her on to the dance floor.

Chapter Four

'*Lady* Harriet,' he said, raising one eyebrow.

'*Lord* Becconsall,' she replied tartly.

He grinned. Because addressing him by his title had not managed to convey the same degree of censure at all. But then, as she very well knew, lords could get away with staggering around the park, drunk. Or riding horses bareback for wagers.

Whereas ladies could not.

Not that she'd been doing either, but still.

'I suppose you expect me to feel flattered by your invitation to dance,' she said, 'when you are notorious for not doing so.'

'Flattered?' He raised one eyebrow. And then the corner of his mouth, as though he was biting back a laugh. 'No, I didn't expect that.'

'Do you want me to ask what you did expect?'

'Well, if we are about to delve into my motives

for asking you, then perhaps I should warn you that you might not like mine.'

'I'm quite sure I won't.'

'But would you like me to be completely honest?'

'Yes, why not,' she said with a defiant toss of her head. 'It will be a…a refreshing change.' At least, in comparison with all the other encounters she'd had in Town, where people only talked about trivialities, in what sounded, to her countrified ears, like a series of stock, accepted phrases they'd learned by rote.

'Well then, if you must know, I felt so sorry for you that I felt compelled to swoop in to your rescue.'

'My rescue?' That was the very last motive she would have attributed to him.

'Yes.' He looked at her with a perfectly straight face. 'You looked so miserable, sitting there all hunched up as though you were trying to shrink away from the silly clothes and hairstyle you are affecting tonight. And I recalled the impulsive way you dropped to your knees beside my prone body, to give what succour you could. And I thought that one good turn deserved another.'

Harriet sucked in a short, shocked breath. Though it was more in keeping with what she knew of him so far to fling insults at her, under cover of escorting her to the dance floor, than to *swoop in to her rescue.*

He would definitely never say anything so… rude to any other lady to whom he'd just been introduced. It just wasn't done. Even she knew that.

But then, since he held her reputation in the palm of his hand, he clearly felt he could get away with saying anything he liked.

'Well, if we are being *honest* with one another,' she said, since what was sauce for the goose was sauce for the gander, 'I have to say I agree with you.' There, that should take the wind from his sails.

'Surely not. Or—' A frown flitted across his face. 'Is your duenna compelling you to wear gowns of her choosing?'

'I wish I could say you were correct. But this display of poor taste is entirely my own doing,' she said.

'You are deliberately making yourself look ridiculous?'

Far from looking shocked, or disapproving, Lord Becconsall only appeared intrigued.

But the necessity of taking her place in line, and dipping a curtsy as the first strains of music blared, prevented either of them from saying anything further. Which made her grind her teeth. Because of course she had not been deliberately trying to make herself look ridiculous. She'd just never had the chance to spend whatever she wanted on clothes, that was all. And it was only with hindsight that she'd seen that modelling her wardrobe so slavishly on Kitty's, who had always looked so fashionable and pretty whenever she'd come to visit, had been a mistake.

But from now on, she was going to ask the modiste, and her aunt—and, yes, even Kitty— if the styles and fabrics she was choosing actually suited *her*.

For some time the intricacies of the dance meant that he could only take jabs at her during the few seconds during which they passed or circled each other. Jabs which she could deflect by looking blank, then twirling away as though she hadn't heard them.

'You are supposed to smile at your partner, just occasionally, you know,' he informed her at one point.

'I might do so were I dancing with someone I liked,' she snapped back.

'Tut, tut, Lady Harriet,' he said dolefully. 'You gave me to believe you wished above all things to dance with me.'

'You know very well I had to say that,' she hissed at him.

'Do I?' He looked thoughtful for a few measures. And then, with a devilish gleam in his eyes, asked her, 'Would you mind explaining why?'

'You know why.'

He widened his eyes in a look of puzzled innocence. 'But...how can you have changed your opinion of me so completely? Last time we met, you flung yourself into my arms—'

'I did no such thing,' she hissed at him. 'You... grabbed me—'

'You put up no resistance, however. And you appeared to be enjoying the interlude as much as I did.'

Well, what could she say to that? Though he was wicked to remind her that she'd behaved with dreadful impropriety, he'd also admitted to enjoying kissing her. Which went a good way to soothing the sting imparted by his taunts. As well as doing something to her insides.

The same sort of something his kiss had done to them, actually.

'No riposte?' He sighed, looking almost disappointed. 'I was so sure you would waste no opportunity to give me a tongue lashing.'

Since he looked at her mouth with a wistful expression as he said this, she couldn't help licking her lips. And recalling the way his own tongue had probed at them, seeking entrance.

Which made her unable to tear her eyes away from *his* mouth.

She cannoned into the lady to her right.

This was a disaster! Almost the first time she'd actually got on to a dance floor and he was ruining it by saying things that made her forget where she was, or which direction she was supposed to be hopping in.

'You are determined to humiliate me, aren't you?' she said, next time they drew close enough for him to hear her.

'I have no need.' He chuckled. 'You are doing an admirable job of it all on your own, what with the clothes and the scowls, and the growls and the missteps.' He shook his head. 'I cannot believe you are related to Major Inskip.'

Her head flew up. 'You know George? But you just said you didn't.'

He shrugged as he whirled away from her to promenade up the outside of the set. By the time she reached the head of it on the ladies' side, she was seething with impatience.

'Well?'

'I only said cavalry officers don't normally hobnob with the infantry. I didn't say I didn't know him. Though, to be precise, I only know him by sight.' He eyed her with amusement before adding, 'And what a sight he is to behold.'

She flushed angrily. George was, indeed, very often a sight to behold. For he had his uniforms made by a top tailor, out of the finest fabrics, and never looked better than when mounted on one of his extremely expensive horses. From which he did tend to look down his aristocratic nose at the rest of the world. Including her. And to her chagrin, although he'd always used to concede she was a bruising rider when they'd been much younger, the last few times he'd come home there had been a touch of disdain about his lips whenever his eyes had rested on her. Which had also, she now saw, influenced her decision to buy the most elaborate and costly gowns she could.

'What, no pithy retort?' Ulysses shook his head in mock reproof. 'I am disappointed.'

'Yes, well, that's the thing with swooping to someone's rescue, isn't it? They do tend to do things you didn't expect and make you wish you hadn't bothered.'

He threw back his head and laughed.

'Touché!'

She glowered at him. Far from showing the slightest sign of contrition, he was clearly thoroughly enjoying himself. At her expense.

'Come, come, don't look at me like that,' he said. 'I conceded the point. And far from being sorry I swooped, I have to admit I am glad I did so. No, truly,' he said, just as he whirled away from her.

'Well, I'm not,' she said as the interminable music finally gasped its last and everyone bowed or curtsied to everyone else in their set. 'I'm tired of being baited.' At least, she would very soon be if he kept this up for any length of time. It was just one more vexation she was going to have to endure. On top of everything else she was struggling with, it felt like the last straw. 'Why don't you just get it over with? Hmm? Go on. Tell Lady Tarbrook where you found me, two weeks ago, and what we were doing. And then...'

Her mind raced over Aunt Susan's inevitable disappointment and her tears, and the scolding and the punishment. Which might well, if Uncle Hugo had anything to do with it, involve being sent back to Stone Court.

Which would mean her ordeal by London society would come to an end.

Which would be a relief, in a way.

At first. But then she'd have to live, for the rest of her life, with the knowledge that she'd failed. Which she most emphatically did not wish to do.

She lifted her head to stare at Lord Becconsall who, though being thoroughly annoying, had at least made her see that she was nowhere near ready to throw in the towel.

He was shaking his head. 'I don't know what I have done to make you think I would behave in such a scaly fashion,' he said.

'What do you mean?'

'Only that I would never betray a lady's secrets.'

'Not if it didn't suit your schemes, no,' she said uncharitably.

Which made him look a bit cross.

'It wouldn't be in *either* of our interests for anyone else to hear about that kiss,' he snapped. And then went very still. And then he turned a devilish grin in her direction.

'I'm beginning to wonder,' he said, leaning close and lowering his voice to a murmur, 'if you aren't playing a similar kind of game to mine.'

'Game?'

'Oh, very nicely done. That touch of baffled innocence would have fooled most men. But I met you under, shall we say, very different circumstances. Revealing circumstances.'

'Revealing?' Her heart was hammering. What had she revealed? Apart from rather too much of her legs. And what game was it he suspected her of playing?

'Oh, yes. You are a rebel, aren't you?'

Well, that much was true. She had rebelled against Mama and Papa's wishes to come to London for this Season.

And since she'd been here, she'd been rebelling against all the strictures imposed upon her behaviour.

'Ha! I knew it. Your guilty expression has given it away. You are merely pretending to go along with all this...' He waved his hand to include not only the ballroom, but by extension, the whole society it represented. 'But the fact that you felt the need to go galloping round the park at dawn, unfettered by all the restrictions society would impose on you, coupled with the dreadful way you are dressed, hints at a cunning scheme to avoid falling into the trap of matrimony.'

'Absolutely not,' she retorted, stung by his continuing references to her poor choice of clothing. 'If you must know...' she drew herself to her full height, which meant she only had to tilt her head the slightest bit to look him straight in the eyes '... I dressed like this because...because...'

She paused, wondering why on earth Aunt Susan had permitted her to buy so many things that didn't suit her. When she was doing so much to make her a social success.

And it came to her in a flash.

'This is the first time I have ever been anywhere near a fashionable dressmaker and my aunt didn't want to ruin the pleasure of being able to feel satin against my skin, or picking out lace and ribbons and feathers by objecting to every single gaudy thing I set my heart upon.'

'But—'

'And I *do* want to get married. That is why I've come to London. To find somebody who will… value me and…admire me and talk to me as if what I have to say is…not a joke!'

He flinched.

'Oh, there is no need to worry that I will ever set my sights on you,' she said with a curl of her lip. And, as a fleeting look of relief flitted across his face, she had another flash of insight. 'That is what you meant, isn't it, about playing a game? You are avoiding matrimony. Like the plague.'

He started and the wary look that came across his face told her she'd hit the nail on the head.

And then, because he'd had so much fun baiting her, she couldn't resist taking the opportunity to turn the tables on him. It wouldn't take much. He'd practically handed her all the ammunition she needed.

'What devilish schemes,' he said in alarm, 'are running through that pretty head of yours?'

Pretty? She looked up at him sharply.

And met his eyes, squarely, for the first time that night.

And felt something arc between them, something that flared through all the places that he'd set ablaze when he'd crushed her to his chest and kissed her.

'You think I'm pretty?'

What a stupid thing to say. Of all the things she might have said, all the clever responses she could have flung at him, she'd had to focus on that.

Fortunately, it seemed to amuse him.

'In spite of those hideous clothes, and the ridiculous feathers in your hair, yes, Lady Harriet, you know full well you are vastly pretty.'

The words, and the way he said them, felt like being stroked all the way down her spine with a velvet glove. Even though they weren't true. She'd had no idea anyone might think she was pretty. Let alone vastly pretty.

Even so, she wasn't going to let him off the hook that easily.

'You are not going to turn me up sweet by saying things like that,' she said sternly. 'One word from me, just one, about that kiss in the park and my outraged family will be dragging you to the altar so fast it will make your head spin.'

'What? You wouldn't!'

'Oh, wouldn't I?'

'No, now look here, Lady Harriet—'

'Oh, don't worry. The ordeal of being shackled to you for the rest of my life does not appeal. In the *slightest*. I'm just reminding you that I have as much on you as you have on me.'

At that point, they reached the chair upon which Aunt Susan was sitting, beaming at them.

'Your niece, Lady Tarbrook,' said Lord Becconsall, letting go of her hand as though it was red hot and making his bow rather stiffly. He then gave her a look which seemed two parts frustration and one part irritation, before turning and marching away, his back ramrod stiff.

'Harriet, I despair of you,' said her aunt as Harriet sank to the chair at her side, her knees shaking, her palms sweating and her insides feeling as if they were performing acrobatics.

'There you had the chance of making a conquest of one of the most elusive bachelors in Town, and what must you do but frighten the poor man off. Whatever did you say to him on the dance floor to make him run away like that?'

She considered for a moment.

'Only that I had no wish to marry him, when he raised the subject,' she said daringly.

'What!' Aunt Susan looked aghast. 'You turned

down a proposal from Lord Becconsall? Not that I can believe he really did propose. Although,' she mused, fanning herself rapidly, 'he really is such a very harum-scarum young man it is probably exactly the sort of thing he would do. To fall in love at first sight and propose in the middle of Astley's Hornpipe.'

Of course he hadn't fallen in love at first sight. Nor had he proposed. But something inside her softened towards her aunt for believing he could easily have done both.

However, 'You cannot wish me to marry a... harum-scarum young man, can you?'

'What can that matter when it would be such a triumph for you? Oh, I know he is only a viscount and one would, in the normal way of things, hope for a much better match for a girl of your background, but the way your training has been neglected one cannot expect a man with very nice tastes to look twice at you.'

The soft feeling chilled into the more usual wedge of inferiority and loneliness with which Harriet was familiar.

'Not once he's seen your performance on the dance floor,' Aunt Susan continued. 'My dear, what were you thinking, to collide with Lady Vosborough in that clumsy way? Unless Lord Becconsall had just that moment proposed. Yes,

I suppose that would have shocked you enough to make a misstep completely understandable.'

'Well, yes, it would,' said Harriet, deciding that this had gone far enough. 'But—'

'If he proposes again, or if *any* gentleman proposes to you again,' continued Aunt Susan as though she hadn't spoken, 'you are not to turn him down out of hand. You are to tell him you will reflect upon the matter and come to me, and I will advise you. I know all there is to know about any gentleman who might propose, you may be sure.'

Although Harriet really had no intention of marrying Lord Becconsall, even if he ever did propose, which he'd just informed her he wouldn't, she couldn't help indulging her curiosity.

'What should I know about Lord Becconsall, then?' she said in as meek a tone as she could muster. Whilst looking down at her fingers as they played with the struts of her fan.

'Oh, so it is like that, is it?' Aunt Susan smiled. 'Well, in that case, we might still be able to repair the damage. I can drop a word in his ear,' she said, patting her hand.

'What? No! I mean, I'm sure that is very kind of you, Aunt, but—'

But Aunt Susan had got the bit between her teeth.

'Lord Becconsall has a very handsome fortune, my dear, and a couple of really lovely estates. All kept in immaculate condition by his family for generations. I admit, since he has come into the title, he has not behaved with— that is, he has gained a reputation for being something of a…wastrel, let us say, but then what can you expect? I mean, he never expected to inherit anything, I shouldn't think, what with having two such strapping older brothers.'

'Oh?' It felt strange to think he, like her, was the youngest out of a handful of brothers. 'What happened to them?'

'Oh, you need not worry about any sort of hereditary weakness that might carry him off the same way,' said Aunt Susan, completely missing the point. 'No, the eldest fell from his horse and broke his neck.'

Harriet winced.

'And the next in line contracted…well, a most unpleasant illness which was the scourge of the district at the time. Which came as a very great shock to everyone. Particularly him, I should think. Why, he probably assumed he would spend the rest of his life in the army. Where, I must say, he did at least acquit himself with honours. Though he only came out with the rank of major,' she mused. 'Although that was probably as much to do with finances as anything,' she added, brightening up. 'As the third son, I don't suppose he had much in the way of money to buy promotions. Oh. It has just occurred to me—yes, it probably went to his head, suddenly having so much money and the title as well. Is it any wonder he went just a little...wild? Just at first. I am sure he will settle down and do his duty to his family. Perhaps he is already starting to think along those lines. Yes,' she said, brightening up. 'Perhaps that is why he asked you to dance.'

Harriet swallowed, knowing it was no such thing.

But Aunt Susan was sitting there, plotting and planning ways and means of getting him to propose to her.

Because, deep down, she thought her niece only good enough to marry a...wastrel.

Worse, said wastrel had no intention of marrying her. Had indeed scuttled away with his tail between his legs at the merest threat he might have to do something so abhorrent should their kiss become common knowledge.

She was still seething by the time they called for their carriage. Which was an utterly stupid thing to do, since their own house was not two hundred yards away. They could have walked home far quicker. But, no, in London, ladies waited for the horses to be put to and the carriage to be brought round, rather than do anything as prosaic as walk home.

Oh, how she hated London tonight. Why had she listened to Aunt Susan's tales of balls and picnics and beaux? Why had she allowed herself to get swept along on the tide of Kitty's enthusiasm at the prospect of them making their come-out together?

Because, she answered herself as she clambered into the coach behind her two female relatives, Aunt Susan and Kitty had made her feel wanted, that was why. It would never have occurred to either of her parents that it was high time their only daughter made her social debut. And if it had, neither of them would have wanted to oversee it. Papa hated London and Mama considered it all a ridiculous waste of time and expense.

She sighed, and in the darkness of the coach, reached out and took Aunt Susan's gloved hand. It was not her fault Harriet had not, so far, found her feet in society. Her aunt had done all she could.

Nor could Harriet blame her for believing she was only fit to marry a wastrel. Not when she was so awkward, and…yes, rebellious, as Lord Becconsall had pointed out.

As the coach rumbled through the darkened streets, and Kitty prattled on about the many and various partners with whom she'd danced, Harriet wondered how she was going to break it to Aunt Susan that not even the wastrel looked on her as a potential bride.

Though time would probably take care of that. Since, after the way they'd just parted, he'd probably take good care not to come anywhere near her, ever again.

Chapter Five

Jack couldn't face returning to Becconsall House, the town house that now belonged to him. It was too full of ghosts.

Besides, he was still too unsettled after his encounter with Hope. Who'd turned out to be...of all things, the daughter of an earl. He certainly hadn't expected that. To think that the owner of those sparkling blue eyes, that tart tongue, and those lush lips, was not only a lady, but a *lady*.

He shook his head as he strolled aimlessly along the street. What had she been thinking, going out at that hour of the day without an escort? If she'd run into anyone but him, in the park, she would have ended up getting far more than just a kiss.

She was so...naive, that was the word. And she had no idea of the effect she had on men.

Although, to be frank, if he'd seen her for the

first time tonight, he wouldn't have looked at her twice. If he hadn't seen the other side of her, in the park, he would never have suspected she possessed anything to take a man's interest, except for her rank. The silly gown, and the even sillier hairstyle, completely distracted a man from noticing the subtle curve of her mouth, or the determined set of her chin, or the intelligence and wit lurking in the depths of her eyes. Not to mention the lush curves of her body.

Lush curves he'd held against his own body and would very much like to feel pressed closely to him again. The urge to do something about it had taken him by surprise, several times, while they'd been dancing. Even though she'd been doing nothing to attempt to interest him. On the contrary, she'd been all bristles and spikes.

Which had soon stopped him from feeling sorry for her. Nobody could possibly feel sorry for a girl with as much spirit as that, not for long.

A reminiscent smile played about his lips. He'd really enjoyed the thrust and parry of the verbal fencing match they'd fought as they'd danced round the events of their first meeting. Right up to the end, that was, he thought, his smile fading, when she'd lashed out rather too cruelly.

Not that he could blame her, he supposed.

He'd been unforgivably rude. Or so she must have thought. It was just that he'd thought he'd glimpsed the same sort of…hurt and rebellion, and desire to shock that he had lurking in his own heart, in her behaviour. Had thought he'd found a kindred soul. That she was doing what he was doing. Pretending to do as he'd been told, whilst making damn sure everyone thought he was completely ineligible.

He'd thought the way she dressed was due to a rebellion against what society expected of her. The way he'd rebelled when the lawyers had told him his best course of action would be to come to Town and find a respectable bride as quickly as he could, to ensure the succession. As if there was no worth in him apart from the blood which they wanted him to pass on to the next genera-tion.

Instead of which, she'd admitted she just had no clue about fashion. Or taste.

He groaned as he thought of the sheen of tears he'd told himself he'd imagined, at one point dur-ing the evening. She'd made a swift recovery, but there was no doubt in his mind now that he'd hurt her. Rather badly, to judge from the way she'd lashed out at him towards the end.

He couldn't blame her. Not when his own jibes must have seemed so cruel, to her.

Which left him no choice.

He was going to have to swallow his pride and tender an apology.

And so, the next day, he presented himself at Tarbrook House at the correct hour for paying visits, armed with a posy of spring flowers.

Though the room was full of visitors, Lady Harriet was sitting on her own, on a chair by the window, from which she was looking out on to whatever it was that was at the rear of the house. The other gentlemen who'd called were all clustering round another girl, who was wearing a gown almost identical to Lady Harriet's. Only wearing it rather better. And the aunt, Lady Tarbrook, was keeping her beady eye on her own daughter's visitors.

Lady Harriet gave a start when he stopped by her chair, so engrossed had she been by whatever she'd been watching through the window.

He craned his neck to follow her line of sight. But all he could see was a courtyard containing an ornamental fountain which sprayed water a few inches into the air.

So, she had been lost in thought, rather than admiring the view.

'A penny for them? Your thoughts?'

'They are not worth that much,' she replied tartly. 'And anyway—'

'You would rather walk barefoot along Piccadilly than share them with me,' he finished for her.

Her face turned a charming shade of pink.

Which was, to his way of thinking, the perfect moment to present her with the posy.

'Oh,' she said looking down at them with surprise. And then up at him with a touch of suspicion. And then, being the girl she was, she asked the question no other delicately nurtured female would ask.

'Why have you brought me these? Why have you come at all, for that matter?'

'Well,' he said, reaching for a nearby chair and placing it closer to hers, 'it is the done thing, you know, for a gentleman to pay a morning call upon a lady with whom he has danced the night before.'

'Yes, I know that,' she snapped.

'But you did not think that *I* would pay any attention to the conventions,' he said, flicking aside his coat tails as he sat down. 'I can see why you might think that, given the way we have…dealt with each other up to now. But the truth is…' He shifted, suddenly finding the chair rather hard and unforgiving.

'Oh, yes, by all means, let us always speak the truth to one another,' she said waspishly.

'The truth is,' he continued, leaning in closer, 'that I owe you an apology.'

She couldn't have looked more surprised if he'd leaned in and kissed her. Which he could easily do, since nobody was paying them any attention. The focus of the other visitors was all on the insipid, younger, paler copy of Lady Harriet.

'I was rude and hurtful to you last night, about your—' His eyes flicked to her gown. Back up to her hair.

'But truthful,' she said. 'And completely correct.'

'But it wasn't kind of me to say so—'

'No,' she said, holding up one hand to stop him. 'It made me see that I needed to do something, instead of wondering why Kitty always looks so much better than me. Your criticism made me go to my aunt and ask her, outright, what I was doing wrong. And why she hadn't stopped me before. And it was…' She paused and rolled her lips together as though trying hard to find the right words.

'Yes, I did wonder why your sponsor would let you go about looking so…' He trailed off. 'If she really cared about you, that is.'

'Oh, she does,' said Lady Harriet with some

vehemence. 'More than anybody else. But since she brought me to London she has had to be so strict with me about so many other things that she had not the heart, she told me, to ruin the one pleasure I had left. That is, shopping. And anyway, she said that since I have rank and fortune on my side she didn't think it would matter if I looked just a little eccentric in my own choice of clothes, just to start with. And besides...'

'Besides,' he urged her, when she appeared to realise that she ought not to be rattling on in such an indiscreet fashion with a man she hardly knew. 'Go on, you might as well tell me the besides, now that I know the rest.'

'I don't suppose there is any harm in it,' she admitted. 'Since it's only that my aunt was so touched that I was trying to model myself on Kitty, because I have always thought her so pretty and feminine, that she could never quite bring herself to stop me.'

'She is not that pretty,' he said, glancing just once at Lady Harriet's cousin.

'I thought you promised to be truthful,' said Lady Harriet with a frown.

'I am being truthful.'

'No, you are not. Because Kitty is pretty. Even Papa notices and tells her so whenever she visits. When he has never said—'

She broke off, and looked down at the posy she was clutching tightly in her lap.

'Well, he should have done,' he said irritably. 'Because you are *much* prettier than her.'

Her head flew up, her eyes widening in what might have been shock, which was swiftly changing to annoyance.

'No, truthfully,' he said, laying his hands just briefly over hers. 'She is just… Whereas you are…'

'Yes?' She tilted her head on one side, her eyes narrowing in challenge.

'That is, she looks to me the kind of girl who blushes and simpers and giggles when a man asks her to dance,' he said with derision. 'And you should not be trying to emulate either her looks, or her behaviour.'

'That is your opinion, is it?'

'Yes. You are…well, when I think of the way you looked in the park, bringing Lucifer under control, and then dashing to my side to see if I was hurt…that is how I wish you could look all the time. You ought to be wearing vibrant colours, to go with your vibrant character. And you should positively never crimp your lovely hair into silly curls that dangle round your face like this.' He reached out and flicked one ringlet.

'You are abominable.'

'To tell you how to make the most of yourself? When nobody else will?'

'I have already told you, Aunt Susan and I have had a little chat and, when next we go shopping, things are going to be different.'

'No more dresses that belong on a frippery little schoolgirl, I hope. No more of those silly frills and flounces.'

'For two pins,' she said, her eyes flashing fire, 'I would deck myself from head to toe in frills, just to annoy you.'

'If only you didn't have too much sense,' he reminded her.

'Well, yes, there is that. No sense in cutting off my nose to spite my face, is there?'

'None whatever. It is far too charming a nose. And anyway, I'm really not worth it.'

A frown flitted across her face.

'Oh, come now. Surely your aunt has already warned you not to set your sights on me.'

A rather mulish look came to her mouth.

'Actually, she thinks you might do very well for me. Seeing as how I'm not likely to attract a man with higher standards.'

'I thought you said she cared for you.'

'Oh, she does. But then…' She shrugged, as though the action was self-explanatory.

'And you said your own father never once told

you that you are pretty,' he growled. 'What is wrong with them all?'

Lady Harriet shrugged again. 'My parents were content with the three sons they already had, I suppose. They didn't really know what to do with a daughter.'

'That's family for you,' he said with feeling. 'My own father never had a good word to say about me, either.'

A stricken look came across her face. She reached out and touched his hand, just briefly, as though understanding, completely, what it felt like to be the runt of the litter.

For a moment, they sat there in silence. For some reason, he couldn't take his eyes from her hand, though she had withdrawn it and tucked it underneath the posy now, as though she couldn't believe she had lost control of it so far as to reach out and touch him.

He glanced up at her face.

'I suppose,' he said, 'I should take my leave, now. I have said what I came to say.'

'And a sight more.'

He grinned at her. 'Yes. You do seem to have the knack of provoking me into saying more than I should. More than I intended.'

'I do not! Provoke you, that is.'

'You do. You are the most provoking creature I have ever met.'

They smiled at each other, then. For a moment it felt as if they were in perfect accord.

He got to his feet. 'Time I was going.'

'Yes, indeed,' she said, getting to her feet as well. 'Are you going to Lady Wiscombe's ball tonight?'

'I had not intended to.'

Her face fell. Which gave him a peculiar feeling. But then nobody had ever appeared disappointed when he'd said he wasn't going to be somewhere. So it wasn't any wonder he was a touch surprised. Particularly since she did nothing but snipe at him.

'I suppose, I might be persuaded to attend…' he began slowly.

'Oh, no, really, it doesn't matter,' she said, blushing fiery red.

And the delight of teasing her took over his common sense.

'Well, do you know, I rather think it does.'

'No,' she said, her eyes narrowing in annoyance, 'it really, really doesn't.'

'Yes, it does. Because I rather think you ought to demonstrate that you have forgiven me for my appalling rudeness last night, by dancing with me again.'

'What?'

'Yes, and this time, I think you ought to try being polite.'

'You could try it yourself,' she snapped.

He laughed. 'Yes, I suppose I could, only,' he said, taking her hand to bow over it in farewell, 'where would be the fun in that?'

Though Harriet knew she ought not to keep on doing it, she couldn't help looking at the door. So that she'd know the moment he arrived.

She couldn't wait to see what he thought of the dress she was wearing tonight. The dressmaker had wrought a miracle with it, considering the short notice Aunt Susan had given her. It no longer had a single frill and only the one flounce was at the hem, and that only because Madame Grenoir had told them point blank they'd have to choose between removing the flounce or doing something about the sleeves and the neckline.

Harriet had chosen to do something about the sleeves and the neckline. To her way of thinking, that was two alterations, rather than just one. And it felt more important to remove the fuss from her upper half, than her lower, somehow.

She'd had her hair done differently, too. The man who'd come to do their hair for the ball was adamant about creating a row of tiny curls across her forehead, but he had agreed that she need not have bunches of ringlets hanging round her face as well. He'd pulled most of it up on to the crown of her head, leaving only a few curls trailing about her neck. Which tickled, a bit, but that was a price worth paying, when even Kitty had clapped her hands and said how much the new style suited her.

A group of men eyed her as they went past. And didn't give her that look she'd been getting from men so far. The one of mingled pity and amusement.

Not that she cared what they thought. It was Lord Becconsall's opinion that counted.

Oh, if only he weren't so abominably rude and so determined not to marry anyone, he would be perfect. He was so handsome and witty. And in spite of having a reputation for being a bit wild, he was eligible, just, in Aunt Susan's opinion. Even the way they had first met had been rather romantic, now she came to think of it. And as for the way he kissed…

Oh, well. At least he had said he would dance with her tonight. If he could be bothered to come to the ball at all.

And then, at last, there he was. Standing in the doorway glancing round at the assembled throng. Only this time, when his eyes finally quartered her corner of the room, they paused. And he smiled. And walked straight over.

'Good evening, Lady Tarbrook,' he said, bowing to Aunt Susan.

'Why, good evening, Lord Becconsall,' she gushed. 'So lovely to see you again. At a ball. Again.'

Lord Becconsall coloured, faintly, his lips compressing in what looked like irritation.

Oh, dear. She hoped Aunt Susan wasn't going to frighten him off by saying anything about him falling for her on the spot, or something equally embarrassing. And since the best way to prevent her from doing so would be to get Lord Becconsall out of her orbit, she got to her feet.

'Yes, thank you, I would love to dance,' she said.

Lord Becconsall raised one eyebrow.

'You really should wait to be asked.'

'But you asked me this afternoon.'

'Did I?' He feigned confusion.

'Well, you promised you would dance with me if you came tonight, which is the same thing. Practically the same thing.'

'Harriet, really,' protested Aunt Susan, in a scandalised voice. Fortunately. Because it gave Lord Becconsall the very prod he needed.

'Yes, and it has just occurred to me that as

soon as I get this dance with you out of the way, I shall be able to leave.'

Aunt Susan made a sort of strangled noise, as Harriet smiled and laid her hand upon Lord Becconsall's outstretched arm.

'Please, don't say anything about the way I look, until after we've danced,' said Harriet.

'Not even if it is flattering?'

'Oh.' She pretended to think about it. 'That might be agreeable, I suppose.' She darted a look at him from under her lashes.

'In that case, I shall say that you look fine as fivepence.'

'Do you mean that?' She ought not to let one throwaway comment, from a man she hardly knew matter so much. But she couldn't prevent her heart from giving a little skip.

'You know I never say anything I don't mean.'

'No. You are abominably rude,' she agreed cheerfully. 'Which is why it's so comfortable being with you, I suppose.'

'Really?'

'Yes. Because I don't have to mind my manners either, do I? And honestly, you cannot imagine what a relief it is to be able to speak my mind. Most men don't seem to like it.'

'I cannot think why,' he said gravely.

'No, nor can I. And the trouble is I have such

a struggle not to say exactly what I think. Even when it doesn't defer to the opinion of a man.'

'How shocking,' he said, with a twitch to his lips as though he was trying not to laugh.

'Well I did think it was, which was rather stupid of me.'

'Er, dare I enquire in what way?'

'In that I should have known that females, and their views, are of less value, in society, than men. Given the difference in the way my parents treated me and my brothers.'

'At least they had the excuse that you were a girl,' he said. And then grimaced. 'That is, my own father never had a good word to say about me. Whereas my brothers could apparently do no wrong.'

'How horrid for you. Why do you think that was?'

'It may have been,' he said drily, 'because they were big and strong and handsome, whereas I was small and sickly and bookish.'

'And yet,' she said, 'you are the only man I have ever met who has not been frightened when I speak my mind.'

'Frightened? Good God, no, why should I be frightened of a slip of a thing like you?' he said with amusement. 'I was a soldier for many years. I faced massed French troops. Not to mention the cut-throat band of ruffians I was supposed to be leading into battle myself.'

'Yes, and you were very brave on lots of occasions, weren't you?'

'What do you mean by that?'

'Oh, nothing much,' she said with a shrug, not liking to admit that she'd asked about his career in the army. 'It's just that I'm convinced that a few ideas, expressed by an impertinent female, are never going to make you quake in your boots, are they?'

He laughed outright at that. 'Never.'

Oh, what a pity it was that he was so set against marriage. He was exactly the sort of man she would love being married to. He wouldn't defer to her in everything, the way Papa deferred to Mama for being so clever. Nor would he lay down the law the way Uncle Hugo did, expecting unquestioning obedience from the females around him.

Lord Becconsall would be more like a partner. A friend with whom she could discuss anything she liked.

Ah well. Perhaps she would meet someone else just like him.

Except, she didn't think there *was* anyone else just like him.

'Your father must have been a very stupid

man,' she said, just as they took their place alongside the other two couples in their set.

'No, not all that stupid,' said Lord Becconsall. 'He just regarded me as the runt of the litter.'

After they'd performed the first change of place, he said, 'Did your brothers bully you?'

'No. They just ignored me, for the most part. Excluded me from their male pursuits. That sort of thing. Did yours…?' She didn't like to think of him being bullied. Nor did she want to say the word out loud, on a dance floor, even though the music would probably prevent her words from carrying very far and the other couples were concentrating on the intricacies of their steps.

Besides, he had the sort of look on his face that indicated he might be regretting speaking so frankly. Men didn't, as a rule, like to confess to any weakness whatever. At least, her brothers hadn't.

After that, he confined himself to the sort of commonplace remarks that everyone else was making as they danced.

Only when it was over did he draw close, his expression serious.

'Do you think you tried to become…less feminine in order to fit in? Is that why you had no idea of how to dress yourself to advantage, when you first came to Town?'

She thought it over. 'I don't think that was it. I just… Actually, Mama always said I should not be forced into some kind of mould, just because of my sex. That I should be free to act exactly as I wished.' It had never occurred to her before that Mama might have meant it. She'd always thought it was an excuse for not paying her any attention at all. But since she'd come to Town, and learned just how many rules there seemed to be that applied to girls, she was beginning to wonder if Mama might have a point.

'And anyway, didn't you accuse me of being a rebel? You will have to make up your mind,' she teased as he started leading her back to where Aunt Susan was sitting. 'Am I a rebel, or trying desperately to fit in?'

He gave her a thoughtful look. 'I think you are doing both. Trying to fit in, but not managing it because you cannot quite quench your rebellious tendencies.'

They were almost there. And once he'd thanked her for the dance, he would leave. And she couldn't face the thought she might never see him, or speak to him again.

'I don't suppose you have an invitation to Lady Lensborough's picnic outing tomorrow, do you?'

'As a matter of fact, I do. On account of the fact that her younger son is a friend of mine.'

'Oh,' she said, her heart lifting. 'Then I shall look forward to seeing you there.'

'What?' He gave her a strange look. 'No, I… I never said I was going.'

'But what possible excuse can you give for not going?'

Now the look was no longer indecipherable. It was plain irritation. 'I won't have to give an excuse. Nobody will expect me to go. And don't ask why they *did* send me an invitation. I get dozens of them. Mostly from matchmaking mothers attempting to foist their bran-faced daughters into my arms.'

She gasped, feeling as though he'd just slapped her. In fact, she did raise just one hand to her face, which had a smattering of the very freckles he'd just spoken of with such disdain.

'Lady Lensborough doesn't have a daughter,' she pointed out. 'Don't you think she might have invited you thinking you might actually enjoy yourself?'

'If she did, she must have windmills in her head,' he muttered grimly, before releasing her hand, giving Aunt Susan a brief bow and marching straight out of the ballroom.

Chapter Six

It was a lovely day. The sun was shining. A few white clouds were scudding across the sky on the wings of a light breeze. Perfect weather, in fact, for driving into the countryside for a picnic.

Good grief. He was actually considering going. Just for the pleasure of seeing her face light up at the sight of him, the way it had done last night.

And savouring the way she kept on looking at his mouth as though she was remembering their kiss. Fondly.

Oh, the way she talked. The way she danced. The way she smiled. The way that tendril of hair caressed her neck, the way he'd like to caress it with his tongue.

Oh, hell! He whisked his hat from his head and rammed it on to the peg on the wall. If he was not careful he was going to fall for Lady Harriet. And would start trying to become the kind of man she wanted him to be. Some kind of… Prince Charming to her Cinderella.

And he wasn't that man. He'd told her to her face he wasn't that man. Warned her that nobody thought him worth a rap.

But she hadn't cared. That was what got to him. That was what was tempting him to go on a stupid picnic, where he'd have to sit on damp grass and consume soggy sandwiches and drink flat champagne. Because she actually seemed to enjoy being with him. No matter how…frank he was. Because it meant she could be frank, too.

A chill trickled down his spine. How had it got this far? How had he reached the stage where they were being *frank* with one another? As though they were *intimate*?

And why the hell hadn't he gone straight to Zeus, and Atlas, and Archie, the moment he'd found her, so that he could claim his winnings, come to that? Why was he prolonging this period of…getting to know her?

When it couldn't lead anywhere.

Because he was damned if he was going to marry anyone this Season.

Not even her.

He slammed into his study and spent several hours excluding her from his thoughts by concentrating on the mountain of paperwork that he'd inherited along with the title.

When the light started to fade, he stalked round to Zeus's club. To do what he should have done straight away. Tell him he'd found...damn it, if he thought of her as Hope, he'd weaken and keep her to himself.

Gritting his teeth, he mounted the steps. It would be better for his peace of mind to stay away from her altogether. But he would have to see her at least once more. To settle the wager. They all had to see her and agree she was indeed the girl who'd set about them with her riding crop and concede that he'd been the one to track her down. Or Zeus would think he'd won. Which was unthinkable.

Yes, at least he was going to enjoy the look on the know-it-all's face when Zeus learned that all his assumptions about Lady Harriet were completely wrong.

What was more, the next time he saw her, with the others at his back and his attitude fixed on the wager, she wouldn't have the same effect upon him. She couldn't have.

Taking comfort from those two things, he tossed his hat and gloves to the doorman.

'Lord Rawcliffe in?'

'Yes, my lord. He and his guests have just dined and are taking coffee in the lounge.'

Jack could hazard a guess at the identity of Rawcliffe's guests. And was proved correct when he entered the lounge a few moments later to see Archie and Atlas flanking the Marquis of Rawcliffe, Atlas with a despondent air and Archie with an abstracted one.

'You really know how to entertain your guests, eh, Zeus,' said Jack, approaching the gloomy trio. 'Anyone would think someone had died.'

'My g-grandmother d-did,' said Archie.

'Oh? Well, in that case, I beg pardon. When did that happen?'

'Six months ago,' said Zeus laconically.

'Six months?' Archie looked puzzled. 'As long ago as that?'

Zeus met Jack's gaze and rolled his eyes.

'Dare say you have had other things on your mind,' said Jack soothingly. 'Nevertheless, my condolences.'

'Yes, it was all very unpleasant,' said Archie. 'Things c-came out about her that none of my family ever suspected.'

Jack pulled up a fourth chair, summoned a waiter and ordered a drink.

'That's the thing with family,' he said affably. 'Always doing the damnedest things and leaving you totally spifflicated. But that's not what I came here to discuss,' he said, as he sat down.

'Oh?' Zeus raised one eyebrow. 'You have come here to have a discussion, have you?'

Jack grinned. 'Not that either. Astute of you to guess.'

'It was not a guess. In all the years that I have known you, you have never once shown any interest in starting a discussion for its own sake.'

'I think I detect a slur upon my character in there somewhere. But I shall let it pass. Because I've come to tell you that I have won the wager.'

'You've found the girl?' Atlas sat up a bit straighter.

'Yes. And you'll never guess who she is.'

'No, I won't,' said Zeus. 'You will spare me the effort of doing anything so tedious by informing me instead.'

'Her name is Lady Harriet Inskip. She's the daughter of the Earl and Countess of Balderstone.'

'Is that so?' Zeus didn't look convinced. 'I was not aware they had a daughter. Three sons, yes, but...' He spread his hands wide.

'She's never been up to Town, according to her aunt. Kept in seclusion in the countryside, apparently.'

'That accounts for the rustic manners, then.'

Not for the first time in recent weeks, Jack felt a very strong urge to knock a couple of Zeus's teeth down his throat. Even though he'd teased her along the same lines himself, it was vastly different hearing the words come from Zeus's mouth, larded as they were with a hefty dose of contempt.

'How ever d-did you manage it?' Archie was looking at him, for once, in something like the way he inevitably looked at Zeus. As though he had some kind of divine wisdom.

'I did not give him the nickname Ulysses for nothing,' Zeus drawled. 'He does have a cunning, low-down sort of intelligence.'

Jack grinned at him. 'That's me,' he said, promptly forgiving Zeus for his apparent ill humour.

He leaned back in his chair, crossing his legs. That was the thing about Zeus. Deep down, beneath the camouflage of unpleasant manners and cutting barbs, Zeus actually rated him fairly highly. Or at least, as highly as he rated any other mortal who crossed his orbit.

And not many men did.

'And for another thing,' said Zeus as though Jack had not spoken, '*he* was actually looking.'

'Meaning you were not?'

'I confess,' said Zeus with a shrug, 'that I did

not have as much interest as you. Besides—' He
pulled up short, with what might, in any other
man, have passed for an apologetic shrug.

'What you mean is that you have more important things to do than run round Town hunting
down mystery females, I take it?'

Zeus managed to look down his thin, aristocratic nose at Jack, even though they were sitting on a level. 'I could point out that you also
have more important things to do than run round
Town hunting down mystery females. Or making wagers which are likely to end up with you
breaking your neck, come to that.'

'You could, but you would not do so, lest I
take it as an insult and decide to draw your cork.'

'I am surprised you do not simply do it, since
you are clearly spoiling for a fight and have been
doing so ever since you sold out.'

At some time during this interchange, Jack
had actually clenched his fists. Though he only
realised he'd done so when the waiter came over
with his brandy, obliging him to unclench them.

Zeus watched him pour and down his drink,
with what looked to Jack like a trace of disappointment. Almost as though he was spoiling for
a fight, too. Though he couldn't imagine why.
There were no estate managers telling *him* he
didn't know what he was talking about and had

better leave matters to the men his father and older brothers had trusted. *He* hadn't rushed home from a life that had suited him down to the ground, hoping for a deathbed reconciliation with his dying father, only to have the man weep at the cruelty of a fate which had seen his two splendidly brawny sons precede him to the grave, leaving everything in the hands of what he termed the runt of the litter.

Atlas cleared his throat. 'Gentlemen, don't you think there is enough fighting in this world without friends turning upon one another over the question of a wager? Or a woman?' He frowned. 'Or whatever this is about.'

Both Jack and Zeus turned to glare at him.

'What will you do, knock our heads together? The way you used to do at school?'

'I'd like to see him try,' said Zeus scornfully. 'In his present state, I think even Archie could overpower him.'

'What?' Archie blinked in a bewildered fashion at the other three, having clearly drifted off again and missed the swirling undercurrents that had brought them close to the brink of quarrelling.

'I was just saying,' said Zeus, 'that you could overpower Atlas these days, if you put your mind to it.'

'Yes, of c-course I c-could,' said Archie. 'Under the right c-conditions. Or if I had a weapon that meant I would not have to c-come within reach of his fists. Though why should I wish to? Atlas is my friend.'

'We are all your friends, Archie,' said Jack. Though he wondered how long their friendships with each other would last, now they were grown men who had little in common beyond their shared past.

'Just because Zeus is the only one who has been in a position to do anything for you,' put in Atlas bitterly, 'that does not mean that we wouldn't have done so. Wouldn't do anything in our power to help you, that is, should you need it.'

'Well, I know that…' said Archie, looking baffled. 'I really d-don't know why—'

'Enough!' Zeus bit out the one word with savagery. 'It is clear that we all have…difficulties in our lives, which are making us resent what we see as the good fortune of the others. Let us…cease dwelling on them. For tonight, at least. And…'

This time, when he ran out of words, it was Jack who felt obliged to come to the rescue.

'And tomorrow night, let us all meet again at Miss Roke's come-out ball. I am sure you have an invitation, Zeus?'

'I have no idea. My secretary deals with the flood of invitations I get to those kinds of events at this time of year. I generally avoid them wherever possible.'

'Yes, but tomorrow night, you will delight Miss Roke by making an appearance. And bring these two along with you,' he finished, waving in the direction of Archie and Atlas.

'And why, pray,' said Zeus, pokering up the way he invariably did when anyone else had the temerity to attempt to take the initiative when he was in the room, 'should I do any such thing?'

'Why, because that is where Lady Harriet will be.' At least, he was fairly sure that was where she would be. It was the most exclusive of the balls being held, that he knew of. The kind where all the better-born debutantes would be doing their utmost to attract a husband from the highest echelons of society. 'And you all need to see her. To verify my claim that she is the same woman who came galloping to my rescue, then thought better of it and let us all feel the force of her displeasure. With her riding crop.'

'And then this thing between the pair of you will be settled,' said Atlas hopefully.

Jack very much doubted it. It had been a long time, a very long time, since he'd hung on Zeus's every word. He'd become an officer. Grown accustomed to command. Had led men into battle. And could no longer go back to the attitude of hero-worship which Zeus still seemed to feel was his due.

'The *wager* will be settled,' said Zeus, confirming Jack's suspicions. 'But what ails Ulysses, I fear, will not be remedied until he returns home and deals with the usurpers attempting to keep him from his kingdom.'

Jack sucked in a sharp breath as the dart went home.

Damned if Zeus wasn't right.

As always.

Chapter Seven

On the face of it, the picnic had been a success. It hadn't rained, the food had been delicious and only one person had been stung by a bee.

And yet it would have been so much more enjoyable if Lord Becconsall had been there.

In the coach, on the way home, Aunt Susan took her to task for looking bored.

'I should not need to remind you that a lady must always be charming in public. She must never let anyone suspect she is not perfectly content with things as they are.'

At which point Kitty giggled.

'Yes, well, dear,' said Aunt Susan, pursing her lips, 'you did behave much better than some of the girls present, I have to admit. So we will say no more.'

And she hadn't. They'd all travelled home in perfect amity, Harriet with the sensation of having been given a great accolade. She'd behaved *much better* than some of the other girls at the picnic. Girls who'd had years and years of coaching in correct behaviour. And who should have known better.

She was smiling to herself as their coach pulled up outside the imposing mansion in Berkeley Square known to all and sundry as Tarbrook House. And kept on smiling as they gathered their shawls, reticules and skirts in preparation for alighting.

The footman let down the steps, Keeble, the butler, pulled the front door wide and stood to one side.

To reveal Lord Tarbrook, standing with his fists on his hips, glaring out at them.

Oh, dear. What had she done now? She racked her brains, but could come up with nothing.

'You,' he snarled, pointing not at Harriet, but at Aunt Susan. 'My study. Now.'

Though Aunt Susan looked puzzled, she only hesitated for a moment before doing as she'd been told, following her husband along the corridor and through the door which he was holding open.

Before it had even shut on the pair of them, he started bellowing. Harriet was too shocked to register the exact words, but between his hectoring tone and Aunt Susan's protestations, it was clear he was accusing her of something which she was strenuously denying.

And before she could start to strain her ears, Kitty took her arm and propelled her at breakneck speed to the staircase.

'It's best to steer well clear of Papa when he's, um, in a bit of a taking,' she explained apologetically, thrusting Harriet into her room and scurrying off in the direction of her own.

A bit of a taking?

If ever she did get married, she vowed as she closed the bedroom door, it would be to a man of an even temperament. Not one who flew up into the boughs over every little thing.

Someone more like Papa, who was contented pottering about in his stables, and kennels, and seeing to estate business. Who was happy to let his wife spend all her time on what he considered her hobbies. Who didn't demand anything...

Well, except heirs, naturally. And he'd always told Mama, and anyone else who cared to listen, how very grateful he'd been to her for presenting him with three such strapping sons in rapid succession in the early days of their marriage.

He'd never said what he thought of the way she'd inexplicably given birth to Harriet—after such a lengthy gap she looked like an afterthought—or if he had, she'd never heard about it.

She supposed that was one point in Uncle Hugo's favour. He really did seem to dote on Kitty. Even though she was merely a girl.

She shook off the contrary thought and applied herself to the task of making herself presentable for the evening's outing. It was another ball. This one to celebrate the betrothal of a pretty young heiress to an elderly earl. At last she had a truly lovely gown to wear, of white satin with a white crape overdress which made it look deliciously filmy. Best of all, though, the bodice was of rich green satin, decorated only with touches of silver at the waist and neckline. No more pure white for her, Aunt Susan had agreed. With a bandeau of pearls twisted into her upswept hair, and pearls at her throat, Harriet felt as pretty as she was ever likely to look.

When it was time to go out, Aunt Susan gave a splendid demonstration of her earlier advice about how a lady ought to behave. From her calm demeanour nobody would ever guess she'd just spent a couple of hours being scolded. Nor did Kitty betray any curiosity about the way her parents had been arguing.

Though Harriet tried to emulate them, she couldn't help glancing at the doorway rather more often than she ought. But she also kept a smile pasted to her face, even when Kitty's admirers made the most fatuous comments, and pretended to be interested in what they had to say. And to her surprise, she reaped the rewards at once. One of Kitty's more bashful admirers, a Mr Swaffham, who'd been thrust to the back of the queue by his rivals, gave Harriet a rueful smile when Kitty informed him that she regretted being unable to dance with him and asked if she wouldn't mind standing up with him instead.

Mr Swaffham did not give any sign that she was a less acceptable partner than Kitty. Even though he would much rather have been dancing with her cousin. He was unfailingly polite. And yet by the end of the dance, she couldn't say she'd enjoyed it half so much as she had done when Lord Becconsall had been so rude he'd goaded her into colliding with another lady in her set.

Not that she gave Mr Swaffham the slightest hint how she felt. This time she could see the point in disguising her true feelings. After all, Mr Swaffham had concealed his, so that he wouldn't hurt her. The least she could do would be to return the favour.

She must have done so convincingly, because later on another of Kitty's admirers, a Lord Frensham, also asked her to dance and appeared to be perfectly content with the arrangement until the very moment he returned her to Aunt Susan's side and abandoned Harriet to return to the pursuit of her cousin.

On their return home, Aunt Susan gave Harriet the first completely unqualified compliment she'd received since the Season had begun.

'You are finding your feet in society at last,' she said, with a satisfied smile. 'I am proud of you.'

Harriet basked in that compliment all the way home.

But all her pleasure evaporated the moment they set foot in Tarbrook House, to find Uncle Hugo once again pacing the hallway, waiting for them to come back.

'Hugo, surely, not now,' Aunt Susan protested, indicating the girls.

'Right now, madam,' he replied.

'But, I've already told you—'

'My study,' he said implacably.

And far from voicing any more objections, Aunt Susan trudged wearily in his wake. And Kitty hustled Harriet up the stairs.

Poor Aunt Susan must have been exhausted already, after a full day out in the countryside, then a good hour's scolding before hastily preparing for a ball where she'd sat watching over both her young charges all night.

Yet Uncle Hugo had no pity.

In fact, she could still hear him shouting at her the next morning, the moment she emerged from her bedroom. The only difference was that now his angry voice was filtering through Aunt Susan's bedroom door, rather than through the one to his study.

Good grief, had he been shouting at her all night? No, surely not. Even Uncle Hugo would have needed to sleep at some point.

Though Harriet could just imagine him leaving his study and marching Aunt Susan up the stairs so that he could continue accusing her of whatever it was she was still insisting she hadn't done, in more comfort.

She was just passing Aunt Susan's closed bedroom door, on her way to the staircase, when something shattered against its other side. She flinched, before scurrying along the corridor to the head of the stairs, out of range. If Uncle Hugo had opened the door at the moment Aunt Susan had thrown whatever it was at his head, she might have been struck by a flying porcelain shepherdess.

That was another thing to be said for her own

parents. They might not have what she would describe as an ideal marriage, she reflected as she reached the stairs, down which she needed to go to arrive at the breakfast parlour, but each was content to let the other go their own way. There were never any scenes such as the one Uncle Hugo had enacted last night and Harriet had certainly never felt the need to run and hide from Papa at any time, the way Kitty had advised her to do from Uncle Hugo.

Nor did Mama ever reach the stage where she felt her only recourse was to throw breakables about.

But then…oh, good heavens! Harriet came to a standstill in the doorway to the breakfast parlour, wondering if it was possible to conjure someone up just by thinking about them. For there sat her mother, scattering toast crumbs in all directions from behind the pages of whatever obscure publication she'd brought to the breakfast table with her.

'Good Lor… I mean, good heavens, Mama? When did you arrive? I had no idea you were coming to stay.'

'Hmm?' Mama peered up at her with a distracted air, as though she couldn't quite recall who she was.

'She got here late last night,' said Kitty, who

was standing by the sideboard, where a gargantuan breakfast lay spread out.

Since Mama was engrossed in her paper once more, Harriet went over to her cousin.

'Was that,' whispered Harriet, since Peter, the second footman, was standing close to the sideboard, in case anyone had need of him, 'what started the…um… *discussion*? Between your father and mother?' What a silly question. Harriet felt like kicking herself the moment she'd asked it. Kitty couldn't possibly have heard what the argument had been about. But instead of pointing that out, Kitty shook her head, and leaned close, lowering her voice.

'Not directly. Though Papa did say something about it being the last straw. Though I have to say your mother was absolutely splendid in the face of his accusations,' she said, darting her mother a glowing look.

'Mama was?'

'Oh, yes, she said that if it was a question of him being in the basket,' said Kitty, clattering the dome over a dish of eggs, in order, Harriet supposed, to prevent the nearby footman from overhearing, 'he ought to send all the bills for our come-out to your father, who was ready to stand the nonsense. Which practically sent him off into an apoplexy on the spot.'

Golly. It sounded as though, having advised Harriet to steer well clear of Lord Tarbrook, Kitty had crept back downstairs and put her ear to the keyhole.

'I cannot quite see why,' Harriet began. 'I mean, if your father is having money troubles, why on earth did your mother insist on sponsoring me for a Season?'

'Because he isn't having money troubles at all,' hissed Kitty indignantly. 'It is just that Mama,' she breathed, her eyes suddenly lighting up with excitement, 'seems to have pawned off a lot of jewellery and had it copied. Papa found out when he took an old family heirloom to the jewellers to be re-set for my engagement ball.'

'Your engagement ball? I didn't even know you had received a proposal. When did that happen?'

'It hasn't happened yet, silly,' said Kitty with a giggle. 'But when it does, I was dreading being weighted down by the hideous parure that has been worn by all the Tarbrook daughters for the past two centuries. And Papa knows how much I detest it. So he sent it off to be put into new settings. As a surprise for me when I do finally choose a husband.'

'My…my goodness,' said Harriet, absentmindedly scooping a spoonful of scrambled eggs on to the plate Kitty had just pressed into her hand.

'Yes, and now everyone is whispering about Mama,' said Kitty, glaring round the room at the wooden-faced servants. 'They must have all heard Papa shouting at her last night.'

'And this morning,' said Harriet. 'I heard him myself as I was coming down.'

'What, still?'

Apparently not. For at that moment, the door opened and Aunt Susan herself came in, red-eyed but straight-backed as she swished to her place at the foot of the table. Even before she sat down the butler snapped his fingers and Fred, the first footman, brought her tea and a plate of toast cut into fingers, the breakfast which she habitually consumed every morning.

Harriet's mother peered at her sister over the top of her paper, frowned and laid it aside.

'Never say the brute is still refusing to listen to sense?'

Aunt Susan stuck out her chin, her cheeks quivering as though with the effort of not bursting into tears again.

'I cannot comprehend why he should think you would rob your own daughter,' said Mama with exasperation. 'You have no need of the money, after all. He gives you a very generous allowance, doesn't he?'

'He won't believe a word I say,' said Aunt Susan indignantly. 'Not one word. After all these years.'

Well, that explained the sound of shattering crockery. Or at least, it was probably one of those funny little statue things that Lady Tarbrook kept handy on every available surface. If someone had accused *her* of theft, Harriet thought she might very well be inclined to throw something at her accuser's fat head.

'It would serve him right if you did start going to gaming hells and taking heavy losses,' said Mama, startling Harriet so much she put her thumb in her eggs. 'In fact, if it was me in your shoes, that is exactly what I'd do.'

'Not all husbands are as easy to tame as yours,' said Aunt Susan bitterly, as Peter deftly took Harriet's plate from her, walked to the table, set it at her place and pulled out her chair.

'To think of all the years I have been the perfect wife…'

Harriet and Kitty crept to the table while Aunt Susan began enumerating the dozens of ways in which she'd borne with her husband's odd tempers over the years. The servants all adopted carefully bland expressions as they went about their work, though some of the tales about Uncle Hugo's doings were so risqué they made Harriet's cheeks burn. It wasn't long before she started to wonder whether she ought to send the servants from the room. But then she remembered what Kitty had said and reasoned that not only was it too late to prevent them learning more than they should, but also that it wasn't her place.

'And now,' Aunt Susan was complaining, 'the first time something inexplicable occurs, instead of trusting me, he accuses me of…of…' Her lower lip wobbled. She raised her napkin to her eyes and hid her face for a moment.

By the time she lowered it, Mama was looking thoroughly annoyed.

'Do you know what you should do?'

'I feel sure…' Aunt Susan sighed '…you are about to tell me.'

'Well, in your place, I think I might get some Bow Street Runners on the case. To see if they can find out what happened to the rubies.'

Aunt Susan froze, a finger of toast halfway to her mouth. But then she shook her head and sighed.

'I would not know how to go about hiring them. Do you?'

Harriet's mother shook her head. 'It is a great pity James did not wish to come to Town with me. He may be a bit of a dunderhead, but it is the sort of thing even he would know, I dare say. Or if he didn't, he could find out.'

Harriet grabbed a piece of toast and slapped it on to her plate. Then hacked off a slice of butter to spread on it, wishing Mama would not speak of Papa in such a derogatory fashion all the time. Why couldn't she appreciate what an absolute lamb he was? In comparison with the tyrannical Uncle Hugo, particularly?

'I don't think Hugo would like that,' said Aunt Susan, confirming Harriet's opinion of him. 'He might regard it as interference in his private business.'

Harriet's mother curled her lip in scorn at what Aunt Susan believed her husband might think.

'If anyone could find out how to hire such a person,' said Aunt Susan, reaching across and patting her sister's hand, 'I feel sure it is *you*, Mary.'

'Me? Oh, but I only came to Town to—'

'Attend some important lecture and speak to some genius who has written some paper that has a bearing on what you yourself are looking into at the moment, I know, dear, you told me all that last night. But don't you think you might find the time to…'

Mama withdrew her hand swiftly. 'You know

I won't. I told you, that is why I didn't even have Stone House opened up. I don't have time for distractions of that sort. My work is important,' she said firmly. 'Not that I expect you to understand…'

'Oh, I understand perfectly,' snapped Aunt Susan, the brief moment of harmony between the sisters shattering. 'If your work is more important to you than your own daughter's future, not to say well-being, then naturally the troubles of a mere sister must fade into insignificance.'

'There is no need to take that attitude—'

'You were always a selfish little girl,' said Aunt Susan, her blood clearly up. 'But after I've gone to all the effort of making up for your neglect, teaching your daughter all the things you should have done, dressing her, taking her about and all the rest of it, and you will not even—'

'Well, nobody asked you to do any of those things,' replied Mama, unperturbed. 'She—' she glanced across the table at Harriet, who promptly buried her face in the cup of tea which had been sitting beside her place '—was perfectly content living quietly in the country.'

'And what would have happened to her when Charles took a bride and brought her home? What would she do then with another woman taking the reins of Stone Court? Where would her place have been then?'

It felt as if someone had just jabbed a knife into Harriet's gut. She'd never looked that far into her future. She'd never wondered what her role would be, once a woman came to live at Stone Court who would be entitled to take on the duties her mother shirked.

But Aunt Susan had.

Harriet lowered her half-empty cup to its saucer with a snap. Once again, Aunt Susan was the only person who'd considered Harriet's welfare.

The scraping of the chair next to her alerted her to the fact that Kitty was getting to her feet.

'If you will excuse us, Mama, Aunt Mary,' she said, dropping a curtsy as both women's heads whipped round and treated her to almost identical glares. 'But we need to attend to some, um, mending.'

Harriet gave her half-eaten plate of eggs and toast just one rueful glance before getting to her feet as well. Because she would rather go without breakfast than be a witness to any more quarrelling. Let alone revelations about what went on within such a stormy marriage as her aunt and uncle were conducting. It had been the most uncomfortable mealtime she'd ever endured. No wonder Kitty had suggested a way of escape.

Aunt Susan gave a wave of her hand, dismissing them, and the girls scuttled out of the room, their breakfast abandoned.

Fred darted before them to open the door, and, as they heard their respective mothers take up the cudgels once again, followed them out into the hall.

'Shall I send some fresh tea and toast to the drawing room, Miss Kitty?'

'Yes, thank you, Fred,' said Kitty as though it was the most natural thing in the world to resume breakfast in another location. Which, in this house, it probably was, Harriet reflected as Kitty took her by the elbow and steered her across to the stairs.

'Your poor mother,' said Harriet as they started up the stairs. So far, though she'd been grateful for all the things Aunt Susan had tried to do for her, she rather thought she'd taken her for granted. To start with she'd seen her, she realised, in the light of a fairy godmother creature, who existed only to grant her wishes. But since coming to London she was coming to know her as a real woman, who, though having plenty of troubles of her own, had a heart big enough to constantly look out for her lonely, socially awkward niece. And take practical steps to ensure she had a comfortable future.

Aunt Susan had never once counted the cost. Neither financially nor in terms of the potential for embarrassment.

Whereas Mama had done nothing to prepare her for life outside Stone Court. Which she *would* have to leave when Charles found a bride. At least, once Papa left the place to Charles, that was. Which would hopefully be a long way off. But...ugh. The thought of lingering in the place, with no real function, once Charles brought a wife in to run the place the way she saw fit. It was bad enough as it was, feeling as though she had to earn her place to win anyone's notice by running the household, rather than just taking it for granted, the way Kitty did. But once they no longer needed her to stand in for Mama, she would be nothing. Worse than nothing—an encumbrance, that's what she'd be. Hanging about the place with no real purpose and no value.

It would be unbearable.

'Come on, Harriet, this way,' said Kitty, making her realise she'd come to a standstill at the head of the stairs.

'Beg pardon,' she said, setting off again along the landing in the direction of the drawing room. She only wished she could beg Aunt Susan's pardon so easily. For all the times she'd let her down. For rebelling against the strictures, even if she'd only done it inwardly. For wasting the chance Aunt Susan was giving her by comparing perfectly eligible men to Lord Becconsall, who'd told her outright he didn't want to get married at all.

Well, no longer. From now on she would stop mooning about, wishing for Lord Becconsall, or some other man, to come into her life and turn it into something that only existed in the pages of a storybook. She would focus on the things that mattered. On making it up to Aunt Susan, somehow, for what she was going through. Because it was terribly unfair that all she was getting, in return for her generosity, was half-hearted compliance from her niece, and indifference from her sister, whilst enduring such persecution from her husband.

'Kitty, we have to do something,' she said, penitence for being so self-centred in the face of her aunt's unhappiness making her stomach squirm.

'Yes. I know. I only said that about sewing to get us out of the breakfast parlour because I couldn't think of anything better. What would you like to do?'

'No.' Harriet felt like stamping her foot. 'I mean, to help your mama.'

Kitty frowned. 'Like…rubbing her temples with lavender water, do you mean?'

'No. Though I suppose we could. Would she like that? But, no, actually, what I meant was finding out what really happened to those rubies and clearing her name.'

'Oh, but we can't possibly! I mean…' she dropped on to the nearest chair '…how?'

'Well, we can start by talking to the servants about it.'

'The servants?' Kitty clapped her hand to her breast in shock. 'But, one should never discuss family matters with them.'

Harriet pursed her lips. 'Look, Kitty, the way my mother and yours were arguing at the breakfast table, the servants already know all about it.'

'That's different.'

'I don't see how.'

Kitty sighed and rolled her eyes. 'That's the thing about you, Harriet. You just do not grasp the subtler points of governing a household such as this.'

No. And she didn't want to, either. It all seemed to consist of one set of people pretending they didn't know what they knew, while the other set expected them to keep their mouths shut about it. Instead of everyone just being open and honest.

'Well, since I am so…lacking in subtlety, nobody will be surprised when I start blundering about asking awkward questions then, will they? Besides which,' she put in hastily when Kitty opened her mouth to make another objection, 'as you pointed out, the servants overhear everything. If anything suspicious has happened inside your household, ten to one, most of the servants will know all about it.'

'Well, then, why didn't one of them come forward?'

Harriet felt like running her fingers through her hair. Except that would dislodge the pins which were holding it in place and ruin the style which had taken longer to create than the so-called *fussy* ringlets to which Lord Becconsall had objected.

'Because,' she said slowly, 'they aren't in the habit of speaking to the family openly, are they? And anyway, all this about the jewels has only just come to light, from what I can gather?'

Kitty nodded.

'Well then, let's give them a bit of time to talk about it and start to speculate about what must have really happened to the parure. And then I shall start asking them if they can recall… I don't know…the last time anyone saw them before your father took them to the jewellers. I take it they don't get an airing very often, if they're so hideous?'

Kitty shook her head. 'As I said, it is tradition for the ladies of the family to wear them for their betrothal ball and new brides usually wear them when they have their portrait painted, but other than that, they tend to stay locked away.'

'So they might have been copied years ago?'

Kitty nodded, slowly. 'Yes, I suppose so. But then…if that is the case, who is likely to remember anything helpful?'

'I don't know. But one thing I do know,' she said with resolution, 'I am not going to rest until I have cleared your mother's name.'

Chapter Eight

'Papa!' Kitty could not conceal her surprise when, that night, Lord Tarbrook climbed into the carriage which was taking them to Miss Roke's come-out ball. He'd never bothered to attend any of the events of the Season thus far, claiming they were insipid affairs which bored him to death.

'Clearly, your mother is not to be trusted to put your welfare first,' he grumbled as he took the seat beside his wife, 'so what choice do I have but to keep a closer watch on her doings?'

Aunt Susan gasped as though he had slapped her. Harriet did not know where to look. It was hard to avoid catching anyone's eye in the confines of a small carriage, but by putting her mind to it, she managed to do so all the way to the ball.

'It is of no use putting on that martyred air,' snapped Uncle Hugo as they drew up outside the

brightly lit house, causing everyone to start guiltily and look up. He was glaring at his wife, which
relieved Harriet and probably Kitty, too, by the
look of it. 'What can you expect,' he snarled,
'after letting your daughter down so badly?'

Aunt Susan gave his back, as he pushed open
the carriage door rather than wait for one of their
footmen to perform the task, a wounded look.
Though she replaced it with an emotionless mask
almost instantly.

Harriet couldn't help admiring the way Aunt
Susan wrapped her dignity round her like a man-
tle as she climbed out of the carriage. And the
way she held up her head as she placed her hand
on her toad of a husband's sleeve as they mounted
the steps was nothing short of regal. This was exactly the way she was always encouraging Harriet to behave. And if Aunt Susan could do it,
under the strain of such unfair accusations, then
so could she.

Harriet took a deep breath, mentally renewing
her vow to do all in her power to show support
for her poor beleaguered aunt. She had not made
much progress with questioning the servants so
far. But anyway, what Aunt Susan seemed to
want most, from Harriet, was to see her married
off to someone *suitable*.

With that in mind, Harriet vowed that for tonight at least, she would behave impeccably. She could certainly *try* to recall all the advice Aunt Susan had given her and apply it diligently. She would not slouch in her chair, or pick at her gloves, or sigh, or fidget, or any of the things she was not supposed to do. And when some man did happen to ask her to dance, she would act as though she was thrilled, no matter who he was, if her aunt appeared to approve of him. What was more, she would treat him as though she thought he was amazingly handsome and witty, for the entire duration of the dance, no matter how dull and stupid he was. She would bite her tongue, if necessary, to prevent herself from speaking her mind.

And even if she didn't get asked to dance, at least Aunt Susan would see she was doing her best, for once. It was not much to do for her, but at least Aunt Susan would feel she'd made a success out of transforming Harriet from a country bumpkin to a society miss.

The moment they entered the ballroom Kitty's usual crowd of admirers began to gather round, asking for various dances throughout the evening. And since Kitty couldn't possibly dance with all of them at once, Harriet managed to snare one or two of her leftovers, by the simple ruse of smiling hopefully up at them.

* * *

Mr Swaffham was the first to lead her on to the dance floor. This time, instead of merely concentrating on getting through the steps without mishap, she put herself out to make sure he enjoyed himself, paying rapt attention to everything he said and smiling at him frequently. She felt drained by the time he returned her to Aunt Susan's side at the end of the dance, but at least he didn't look as though dancing with her was a poor substitute for standing up with the girl he really admired.

On any other night, Aunt Susan would probably have congratulated her for making so much effort. But tonight, it was Aunt Susan who was fidgeting, and sighing, and generally looking thoroughly miserable. It was probably due to the fact that Uncle Hugo was nowhere in sight. The moment both she and Kitty had secured partners, he'd taken himself off in the direction of the refreshment room. Taking all Aunt Susan's self-esteem with him, by the looks of things.

What her aunt needed was something to put the heart back in her. Though Harriet could not think what.

But then she spotted the perfect opportunity, in the person of Lord Becconsall.

'Oh, look,' she said, in a desperate attempt to

dispel the cloud of despondency hanging over her aunt like a greasy grey cloud. 'It is Lord Becconsall, just come in.'

'Hmm?' Lady Tarbrook brought her attention back to the ballroom with a visible effort. 'Oh, yes. That handsome young wastrel who has been showing an interest in you.'

'The one who spoke of matrimony the first time we danced,' Harriet reminded her shamelessly. 'The one you said has not danced with anyone else this Season.'

'The one,' said Aunt Susan drily, 'for whom you have been looking everywhere we've been these past few days. Unless I am very much mistaken.'

'Um, yes.' Well, there was no point in denying it. Even though it would probably mean a lecture for wearing her heart too much on her sleeve.

'Is your heart fixed on him, then?'

What sort of a question was that? Usually, Aunt Susan's first concern was with a gentleman's pedigree and fortune. Whether Harriet liked him or not was an irrelevancy when it came to his matrimonial worth.

'I...well, that is...' No, she couldn't admit that she still tingled all over whenever she dwelled on his kiss. Even the thought of it was making her go hot.

'Your blush is answer enough. Attract him, if you wish, then,' said Aunt Susan gloomily. 'Better a husband who makes your heart flutter to start with, than one who is chosen for you by your parents, who you have done your best to like, and to please, for years, and for what? To discover he never trusted you!'

Harriet winced. She had no idea how to cope with moods of this sort. Nobody ever had them at Stone Court. They just…got on with life. Even when she'd been a very little girl, nobody had ever bothered to cajole her into a good mood if she was ill or out of sorts, so she had absolutely no idea how to do the same for someone else. Why, even when her pony had put its foot down a rabbit hole, tossing her over his head with such force she'd broken her arm, nobody had done more than chuck her under the chin and say they were proud of her for not making a fuss when the groom who was with her set the bone.

She twisted her fan between her fingers, wishing she could say, or do, something to cheer her aunt up. And found herself looking, beseechingly, in the direction of Lord Becconsall.

As if in answer to her silent plea for help, he made his way across the increasingly crowded ballroom to where they were sitting.

'Good evening, Lady Tarbrook, Lady Harriet,' said Lord Becconsall, bowing from the waist.

Instead of simpering and gushing, Aunt Susan looked him up and down, as though she wasn't sure what to make of him.

'Have I,' he said, looking a touch uncomfortable, 'offended you in some way?'

'Oh, not at all, my lord,' said Harriet. And then almost shuddered. Because, to her utter disgust, what had just emerged from her lips could only be described as a simper. 'Whatever gave you that idea?' And with the feeling of in for a penny, in for a pound, she lowered her head and darted a look up at him from beneath her eyelashes, in the prescribed manner to indicate modesty, yet interest, at the same time.

He blinked.

'Ah, um. What was I about to say?'

'That you feared you had offended me in some way and was about to explain what gave you that idea,' she said. And then, from nowhere but her own desperation, she hit upon what could be the very thing.

'Though, of course, I was terribly disappointed you did not come on the picnic.'

And then she blushed. Because that sounded rather too desperate and she didn't want to scare him off.

'I fear the prospect of sitting on damp ground and eating stale sandwiches did not appeal,' he said.

'Oh, but the sandwiches were not stale. All the food was positively delicious,' she gushed. Oh, lord, she was sounding like a complete ninny. Fortunately, her attempts to behave exactly the way a debutante should appeared to amuse Lord Becconsall. At least, his eyes were twinkling now and his lips relaxing from the rather grim line in which he'd been holding them when he first approached.

'I hope you are not about to reprimand me for dereliction of duty,' he said playfully.

Which was a sort of quip. She was supposed to laugh at a man's attempts at humour, no matter how feeble.

And so she did. At least, she tittered. To her shame. The sound emerging from her mouth was such an artificial, brittle sound she was sure even Aunt Susan would say she'd gone too far. But, having darted a look at her from the corner of her eye, it was to see her aunt was gazing into space, her mouth pinched up in very obvious bitterness.

Harriet gave up.

'The truth is we are all a bit out of sorts this evening. We have had a…that is…' She racked her brains for a plausible excuse to give him which would account for Aunt Susan's mood, without giving away any family secrets.

'We had an unexpected visitor,' she said, finally hitting on an excuse that was near enough to the truth to be useful. 'It set us all at sixes and sevens.'

'A visitor?'

'Yes. My mother.'

He cocked his head to one side, eyeing her as though he wasn't sure what to expect from her next. 'I beg your pardon, but I fail to see...'

'Oh, for heaven's sake,' she said crossly. 'Are you going to ask me to dance, or not?'

On any other night, such a comment would have shocked Aunt Susan to the core. Tonight she didn't even seem to notice.

But Lord Becconsall did. His eyes flicked from her, to her aunt, and back again, thoughtfully.

'I think I should ask you to dance.'

'Thank you,' she said, leaping to her feet and placing her hand on his forearm, before he'd even had the chance to extend it in her direction.

'I sense a mystery,' he said softly as they made their way to the dance floor.

'Oh, very observant of you,' she said sarcastically. And then mentally kicked herself. Hadn't she vowed she would be all sweetness and light tonight? To prove that Aunt Susan's lessons in how to behave around eligible men were bearing fruit?

'I mean, yes, how observant of you,' she said, shooting him what she hoped was a worshipful smile.

'Oho! Now my curiosity is really roused. What on earth can have happened to dull the edge of that sharp tongue of yours? And were you actually attempting to flirt with me just now?'

Attempting? She *had* flirted. She'd given him the benefit of a coy look, and a simper, and a titter, and had rounded it all off by fluttering her eyelashes.

'Absolutely not,' she snapped back. 'I never flirt. And if I was to start, you may be sure I would not waste my time flirting with *you*.'

'That's better,' he said affably. 'I was beginning to worry that the strain of being polite to me might give you the headache.'

The beast! He'd deliberately goaded her into losing her temper.

Making sport of her, to be precise. If only it wouldn't cause a scene, she'd march right back to her chair and leave him standing on the dance floor alone.

But it would. And her aunt had enough on her plate without that. So she had to satisfy herself with shooting him a daggers look as they took their places in the set forming.

The only effect it had on him was to make his grin a touch triumphant.

But at least during the dance she didn't have to speak to him again. And as she concentrated on performing her steps correctly, she also, almost, regained control over her annoyance.

When the dance ended, instead of leading her directly back to where Aunt Susan was sitting, Lord Becconsall steered her in the opposite direction.

'Um, what are you doing?'

'I thought you would benefit from a short turn on the terrace,' he replied.

'What?' She whipped her hand from his sleeve as though it had burned her.

Far from looking offended, he looked at her with respect.

'You have learned your lesson, I see, since the last time I got you alone.'

'Yes, and—'

'But if you come out on to the terrace with me, we shall not be alone. I have already observed several other couples going out to take the air.'

'Oh.' What game was he playing now? She'd assumed he'd been sending her a message by not attending the picnic. Which she'd interpreted as a declaration that she must not look upon him as a prospective suitor. But now he was behaving just like a man who was determined to fix his interest with her.

'Look, there is even a maid, waiting to hand out shawls to protect the shoulders of young ladies from the night air. I wouldn't be surprised to find a footman out there, serving refreshments,' he said as a final inducement.

Why he wanted to take her outside was a mystery, but if she were truly serious about wanting to discover whether or not she could consider marrying him, then she'd leap at the chance to spend a little time in relative privacy. And it would be just what Aunt Susan would expect.

'Oh, very well,' she said, far from graciously. 'But don't…try anything.'

'Try anything?' He looked at her in mock surprise. With just a dash of innocence thrown in for good measure. 'Whatever do you mean?'

She heard a noise well up in her throat which was rather like a growl. Which appeared to amuse him immensely. Because he was chuckling as he took the proffered shawl from the maid stationed by the double doors, and draped it round her shoulders himself.

'There,' he said with what sounded like satisfaction. And took his time removing his hands from her person.

And just like that, she was reliving the moment they'd been lying together on the grass. He with his arms wrapped tightly round her, and she…melting into him.

She sucked in a short, shocked breath and inhaled the scent of him, since he was standing so close to her. And it was just like smelling the kiss. Or The Kiss, as she was coming to think of it.

Until this moment, she hadn't known that she'd remembered what The Kiss had smelled like. Or that a kiss could even be said to have a smell. Only now, breathing in the scent of his clothes, and his…well, she supposed it was his body, too…did her nostrils detect the absence of crushed grass, and horse, and even the brandy fumes that had sweetened his breath.

He frowned at her. 'What is it? What is troubling you?'

'Wh-what?' She had to give herself a mental shake. Now was not the time to wish she was in the park, or in a stable, or some other location suitable for snatched kisses.

He took her by the arm and steered her away from the door.

'I can see you are deeply troubled, Lady Harriet,' he said, setting up a pace that anyone watching them would describe as a casual stroll. 'About your aunt, at a guess.'

'What makes you think that?'

He chuckled. 'Lady Harriet, you are practically doing cartwheels in the attempt to restore her to her normal frame of mind.'

'I don't know what you mean.'

'Yes, you do. Nothing but the direst need would have induced you to come outside with me like this. Not after the…er…lesson you received in the park that morning.'

She glowered up at him as he described what she was starting to regard as one of the most pleasant experiences of her life as a lesson.

'But we are not alone. As you pointed out, there are several other couples taking the air. As well as a brace of single gentlemen poisoning their lungs with cigar smoke.'

He drew her to a halt and turned her to face him.

'If you don't want to tell me, I can understand that. But don't take me for a fool, Lady Harriet.'

She didn't. Lord Becconsall, for all his playfulness, was nobody's fool. He was the only man tonight who had noticed that anything was amiss with her aunt. The only man who'd bothered to enquire about it. The only one to seem to care.

Oh, how she wished she could tell him all about it. That they could revert to the easy way they'd got into, albeit briefly, of talking about all sorts of personal things. Like his odious brothers and her inability to choose clothes wisely. But she couldn't. He'd made a strategic withdrawal when she'd asked him if he was going on that picnic. She'd seen it in his eyes. She supposed she should be glad he was doing what he could not to raise false hope in her heart. It was honourable of him. If he were a different sort of man he could very well use the easy way they'd got into of speaking to each other to take advantage. Right now he could be luring her into a darkened corner and kissing her again. She wouldn't resist. And he knew it.

She whirled away from him, clasping her hands to her breast.

He followed, her, laid his hands on her shoulders, and turned her round, a questioning expression in his eyes.

'Lady Harriet?'

'I… I cannot!' She gulped. 'Ask me about something else, instead. Or let me tell you all about the picnic.'

'The picnic?'

'Yes. You would have enjoyed it immensely, you know. Some of the girls there behaved really badly. First of all Miss Angstrom got stung by a bee and let loose a screech that set all the dogs for miles around howling. And then, when Miss Jeavons saw that it made certain gentlemen take notice, she pretended to faint.'

For a moment, it looked as if he was going to object to her conversational choice. But then he half-shrugged, as though giving in.

'How do you know she was only pretending?'

'Because she sort of slid all the way down Lord Lensborough's front, then landed in a graceful pose right at his feet.'

'Did she?' He almost smiled at that.

'Yes, and then his younger brother, Captain Challinor, dashed a cup of water in her face. Which brought her round in a twinkling.'

'Water has a tendency to do that. I wonder you didn't try that remedy on me when you found me in a similar condition.'

'Oh, well, there wasn't a river nearby to fetch it from. Or any empty glasses to hand.'

He gave her a look.

'I know what you are doing, Lady Harriet,' he said.

'Isn't it for the best?'

He turned away from her and leant his hands on the balustrade bordering the terrace. 'Yes,' he said grimly. Causing something inside her to curl up and whimper.

Until that moment, she hadn't realised just how lonely she was. Only now that he was agreeing with her, that it was best they maintain a distance from each other, did she understand just how badly she wanted to confide in him. To unburden herself. Even ask him for help.

'It…it really isn't my secret to tell.'

'I understand,' he said, turning to look at her over his shoulder. 'And I commend your loyalty.'

'You…you do?'

'Yes, and, Lady Harriet, should there be any way in which I may be of service…'

'There isn't,' she said more sharply than she'd intended. 'And don't ask about it any more.'

He raised his hands as if in surrender. 'I wouldn't dream of it.'

And now she was angry with him for giving in so easily.

'You had better take me back to my aunt now.'

'Very well,' he said, without even making a token protest.

Well, naturally not. Because he didn't really care. This was all some kind of game to him. He'd told her so. She wasn't sure yet what part he wanted her to play in his game, but the one thing she did know was that she couldn't rely on him.

No matter how much she wished she could.

Oh, how she wished she'd never come out

here. Well, that was one thing that was easily remedied. All she had to do was go back inside.

And so, giving him one last look which she hoped revealed how disappointed in him she was, she whirled away from him and marched across the terrace with her fists clenched.

Chapter Nine

'Lady Harriet, wait!'

Lord Becconsall grabbed her hand before she'd gone more than a couple of paces from him and placed it on his sleeve, matching his own pace to her stride.

'It needs to look as if I am leading you,' he warned her out of the corner of his mouth. Which brought her to a standstill. It was things like this that made her like him so much. Oh, how could he do this to her?

Injecting every ounce of disdain she could muster into her movement, she removed her hand from his arm.

'Don't think you can bully me,' she hissed.

'What? I say, that's a bit extreme, even for you. Especially when I was only trying to observe the conventions which—'

'Stuff conventions!'

To her irritation, he grinned. 'Well, most of the time I'd agree with you, but if I just let you flounce back into the ballroom with your fists clenched, after everyone saw us going outside together, it would create the kind of speculation that your aunt wouldn't like, even if you don't care what anyone thinks of you.'

Having delivered that little homily, he extended his arm to her in the correct manner.

Giving her the choice whether to lay her hand on it and behave correctly, or resume her headlong flight from the terrace.

She didn't have to think it over for long. She'd come here tonight vowing to support her aunt by behaving impeccably. Creating gossip by making it look as though Lord Becconsall had insulted her in some way, after she'd strayed out of sight of her chaperon, was the exact opposite. And it was a good job Lord Becconsall had reminded her in time.

'I apologise for implying that you are a bully,' she said grudgingly as she laid her hand on his sleeve.

'Was that what you did? I assumed,' he said as they stepped back into the ballroom, 'that it was the equivalent of kicking the cat.'

'Cat? What cat?'

'The metaphorical one that takes the brunt of

your anger when whatever it is that has made you angry isn't in reach.'

'Oh, that cat.' Goodness, but he was perceptive. It was Uncle Hugo with whom she was really angry. Lord Becconsall was...she darted him a glance...incredibly endearing, actually. Even though he'd teased her rather a lot, there had never been any malicious intent to it. He'd warned her how he felt about marriage and stayed away rather than raise false hope in her breast. He'd even taken steps to prevent her from creating a scene—though he had been the one to goad her into losing her temper in the first place.

She was just starting to wish she hadn't been quite so sharp with him when she noticed that Lady Tarbrook was no longer sitting by herself. Lord Becconsall's three friends, from the park, were standing all round her.

She felt his arm tense beneath her hand and darted him a look. Hadn't he known they were going to be here? Was he as embarrassed to see them, with her clinging to his arm, as she was going to be, to have to acknowledge them in front of Aunt Susan? Unwittingly, her fingers gripped Lord Becconsall's sleeve rather tightly, which was excessively stupid, since he was at the root of her potential humiliation.

But, as if sensing she needed reassurance, he

patted her hand and kept his own resting over hers when they drew to a halt before her aunt's chair.

'Lady Harriet,' he said, 'permit me to introduce you to my friends. Lord Rawcliffe…' he indicated the one they'd called Zeus in the park '…Captain Bretherton of his Majesty's navy…' who was the skeletal giant '…and Mr Thomas Kellett.'

She let out a relieved breath as she curtsied to them all in turn. For he'd made it sound as though they had only just met for the first time tonight.

They all bowed in their turn and muttered suitable responses. Though each of them stared at her rather harder than absolutely necessary. And in the case of the one they called Zeus, with so much contempt in his eyes that he made her feel like some kind of…insect that he dearly wished to flick from his friend's sleeve and crush under his heel.

'Lady Tarbrook,' said Lord Becconsall, 'I can see they have already made themselves known to you.'

'Oh, I have known this scamp ever since he was in short coats,' she said, reducing Zeus from god to toddler with one offhand remark and a dismissive motion with her fan. The look on his face was priceless. Oh, how she admired her aunt.

'He has introduced me to his two friends,' said Aunt Susan. 'And yours, I now learn, Lord Becconsall.'

'Yes. We were all at school together.'

'Oh, that accounts for it,' said Lady Tarbrook, casting Mr Kellett a rather scathing look. As though he had no business hobnobbing with titled gentlemen. Or captains in his Majesty's navy.

Harriet felt indignant on his behalf. She hated to see anyone dismissed as being of no account, knowing exactly how it felt. For she'd been of no account pretty much all her life.

'I have heard of you, I think,' she said to the man she could have sworn they'd called Archie.

'Have you?' He peered at her through the fringe flopping into his puzzled brown eyes, putting her in mind of a shortsighted spaniel. 'C-can't think why you should have.'

'Lady Harriet is, perchance, a follower of all the latest scientific investigations,' said Lord Rawcliffe sarcastically, 'and has been impressed by the brilliance of your latest publication regarding your theories concerning the properties of dephlogisticated air.'

If there was one thing Harriet knew about, thanks to her mother's obsession with all things scientific, it was the vast range of theories currently being hotly debated regarding various gases.

'Not at all,' she said, flinging up her chin mutinously. 'There is nothing the least bit impressive about suffocating mice under glass domes.'

All three men changed the way they were looking at her.

Aunt Susan sighed. As if to say, *that is the end of that*. For she firmly believed that if there was one thing more detrimental to a girl's chances of success in the matrimonial stakes than being too old, it was being too clever.

But Lord Becconsall chuckled.

'You have underestimated her, Rawcliffe,' he said. 'She clearly knows all about the experiments to determine what it is in the air that sustains life.'

Something flashed between the two men. Something that looked suspiciously like rivalry. And for some reason she didn't understand, she felt like confirming the confidence Lord Becconsall had shown in her, whilst taking the odiously cynical Rawcliffe down a peg or two at the same time. She reached into the deepest recesses of her memory for anything her mother might have said, which she could fling at him.

'Well, who could fail to be interested by the experiments of the British Pneumatic Institution to attempt to treat disease by the inhalation of various gases,' she said, hoping she'd recalled the name of the society correctly.

'Science being put to a practical use, rather than merely for its own sake,' said Lord Becconsall at once, approvingly.

'Exactly,' she said without a qualm. Although she had no idea what gases were inhaled, or for what purpose, she didn't think she'd been too far from saying something vaguely intelligent, because Mr Kellett was nodding eagerly.

'It is a great p-pity Mr Davy d-did not pursue his initial experiments with factitious airs,' he said. 'I think he might have b-been on to something there. My own work—'

'For the lord's sake, do not start boring the present assembly with an exposition of your current experiments,' said Rawcliffe scathingly.

To her fury, Mr Kellett subsided at once, with the air of a spaniel who'd just been kicked by its master.

The naval officer patted Kellett's drooping shoulders in a sympathetic manner, which made her rather like him. He'd been the one to put a stop to the teasing in the park, too, now she came to think of it. That he'd done it by flinging her up into the saddle had infuriated her at the time, but at least he had enabled her to escape a situation that had been becoming down-right unnerving.

'That's the trouble with being a genius, Ar-chie,' said Lord Becconsall. 'You leave the rest of us floundering in the wake of your brilliance. We wouldn't understand the half of what you are saying.'

'Yes,' said Mr Kellett. 'Not the t-topic for a b-ballroom.' He shot Rawcliffe an abject look. 'Forgot.'

'No matter,' said Rawcliffe, his expression mellowing a touch. 'That is what you employ me for, is it not?'

'Employ you?' Aunt Susan's eyes rounded. 'But—you are one of the wealthiest men in Eng-land.'

So why wasn't she attempting to get him to notice Harriet? she wondered. Or, more to the point, Kitty? It could only mean there was something seriously wrong with him as a pro-spective husband. She'd have to ask her what it was later.

'It was my little joke, my lady,' said Rawcliffe with a sardonic smile. 'For, although my friend is, nominally, employed by me in the capacity of, ah, chaplain, is it not—' he gave Kellett a wry look '—I have long since learned that, when in pursuit of some new theory, he will give me orders for raw materials and equipment as though I am merely his assistant, whilst shamelessly poaching my staff to act in various menial capacities.'

Mr Kellett hung his head. 'Forget, sometimes. Sorry.'

'No need. When you make the discovery that will rock the scientific world, my name, too, will go down in history. As your sponsor and benefactor.'

'And indeed, I am sure it is very generous of you,' said Aunt Susan. Although she didn't look the slightest bit impressed. 'But, look, Harriet my dear. Here is Mr Swaffham come to claim his dance. If you will excuse her, my lords, Captain, Mr Kellett?'

Harriet had never been so glad to see someone coming over with the intention of asking her to dance. There was something about Lord Becconsall and his three friends that made her extremely uncomfortable. And it wasn't just the way she reacted, physically, to him. It was…the way they spoke as if each word had a hidden meaning, known only to the four of them. As if there were undercurrents beneath their behaviour that only they understood. Which effectively shut out the rest of the world.

And she'd had quite enough of being made

to feel like an outsider by her own family. She had no desire to suffer the same kind of exclusion from people who were practically strangers.

Chapter Ten

Poor Mr Swaffham did not receive anything like the attention she'd bestowed upon him during their previous dances together. Because Harriet couldn't stop watching Lord Becconsall and his three friends, in spite of having told herself she wanted nothing to do with a group of men who'd first witnessed her behaving badly, then given her a bit of a scare and finally just made her feel excluded.

She watched them making their excuses to Aunt Susan and leaving her side almost as soon as Harriet had taken her place in the set. She watched them strolling round the room, greeting acquaintances or, in the case of the odious Lord Rawcliffe, cutting people he clearly regarded as impertinent for daring to accost him. And she watched them making their way, inexorably, in the direction of the exit.

She was glad they were leaving. She had no wish to speak to Lord Becconsall again. Or, heaven forbid, dance with him. No, twice in one night was entirely too much. People would start to link her name with his if she danced with him twice.

Oh. Would they do that with Mr Swaffham? She shot him a speculative glance as the dance came to an end. Thankfully, he was looking rather disgruntled, which meant that any speculation in that quarter was likely to be short-lived.

She smiled at him apologetically as he extended his arm to lead her back to her aunt. But from the cool way he took his leave of her it was highly unlikely he would be asking her to dance with him any time soon.

Oh, dear. Aunt Susan would be so disappointed.

In an effort to mitigate her offence Harriet sat up straight and drew her shoulders back. Not that Aunt Susan had admonished her for slouching. In fact, she wasn't watching Harriet at all. She was simply staring off into space and fanning herself rapidly. And, Harriet noticed with alarm, looking a most unhealthy colour.

'Aunt Susan, are you feeling quite well?'

Her aunt turned her head very slowly. And gulped.

It was all the answer Harriet needed.

'Come along, Aunt Susan,' she said, taking her by the elbow to encourage her to her feet. 'We'll go in search of fresh air, shall we?'

'Fresh air,' her aunt repeated in a weak voice.

'Yes, just the thing. It is very hot in here.' From the way the older woman was leaning on her, and the slight trembling she could feel through her limbs, Harriet thought her aunt might be perilously close to a faint. A *real* faint.

She glanced to right and left, desperately trying to recall the layout of the house. She'd been to the ladies' retiring room when she came in, of course, to leave her cloak and change into her dancing shoes. She was pretty certain that once they left the ballroom, they had to turn right and it would be down the stairs and just along the corridor.

She found a room exactly where she thought the retiring room should be, but the moment they went in, she realised her mistake.

'Oh, dear, I am so sorry,' she said, gazing round the empty room in consternation. 'I have lost my way.'

'It doesn't matter,' said Aunt Susan wearily. 'In fact, I would as soon sit in here quietly for a few minutes as have some gossipy maid fussing round me in the retiring room.' She tottered to the solitary sofa positioned before an empty hearth and sank on to it. 'It is cooler in here, anyway, which is the main thing.'

'Is there something I can get for you? A glass of water?' There would have been all that sort of thing if only she'd got her aunt to the correct place. And although she'd said she didn't want a maid fussing, at least there would have been one who knew the layout of the house and who could fetch…she didn't know…a vinaigrette, or something.

'A glass of water?' Aunt Susan looked at her sharply. And then closed her eyes. 'That is it. That is why I came over all peculiar. With all the…fuss…today, I quite forgot to eat. I am feeling faint, that is what it is.'

'Well, then, shall I go and fetch you something to eat?'

Aunt Susan lay her head against the back of the sofa. 'Yes, please, if you wouldn't mind, dear. Just something light.'

Harriet backed out of the room, concern for her aunt chasing every other concern from her mind. But…where was the refreshment room? Back through the ballroom, unfortunately. She didn't want to go there, get a plate of food and a glass of water, and carry it back through the ballroom to her aunt. That would be such unusual behaviour it was bound to attract exactly the kind of attention her aunt wanted least. She racked her brains. Oh, if only Lord Becconsall *were* a proper suitor, she could go to him and ask him for help. As it was, she'd just have to find a footman to do the fetching and carrying for her.

She retraced her steps to the ballroom, aided by the sound of music, hoping there would be a servant free to see to her needs. And who could be persuaded to employ discretion.

The doors to the ballroom opened outwards and had been left open so that people could come and go with ease. But they had not been pushed quite flat to the wall. There was a slight gap behind which she could easily squeeze and from that vantage point she could peep in through the crack between the hinges and the wall, and locate a servant without anyone seeing her searching.

She was really glad she'd ducked behind the door out of sight of the other guests when not two seconds after she'd put her eye to the crack, Lord Becconsall and his three friends came strolling in her direction.

It was the shock of seeing them when she'd thought them long gone that made her watch them, rather than begin to search for a footman, she told herself the moment she realised what she was doing. It *wasn't* because there was something about Lord Becconsall that drew her gaze like iron filings to a magnet.

Although she couldn't deny he was a feast for the eyes. It was something about the way he carried himself. With that brisk, upright bearing that was in such stark contrast to the languid slouch of men who'd never done anything with their lives but drink and gamble and amuse themselves. The neat way his clothes moulded his muscular frame, without the slightest hint of flamboyance about his attire was pleasing, too. As was the way he looked as though he was never far from laughing.

Though the laughter was very often at her expense, the beast.

By the time she'd reached this stage in her cogitation, the four of them had drawn close enough to her hiding place for her to hear snatches of their conversation over the background noise of a ball in full progress.

'So, you agree then,' Lord Becconsall was saying. 'Lady Harriet and the girl in the park are one and the same person?'

She froze. Well, she'd been standing still anyway, but the mention of her name on his lips, in that context, made even the blood stop swirling through her veins.

'If you insist,' Zeus said, in a bored tone.

'No, come on, old chap, that is no way to treat such an important subject,' said Lord Becconsall, though he was grinning.

'The wager was only important to you,' said Zeus. 'I have genuinely important things on my mind.'

Wager? Lord Becconsall had made her the topic of a wager?

Harriet flattened herself against the wall as they passed on the other side of the door.

Lord Becconsall was laughing. 'You mean, that is what you are going to claim as the excuse for not finding her first,' he said. Quite clearly. 'That you were too busy to bother. And then say, when you pay up, that if you had more time, you would have beaten me...'

She didn't hear any more. They'd strolled past her and were heading for the stairs. Besides, there was a roaring sound in her ears that was drowning out everything else.

She'd thought...no, she'd hoped he'd been... fascinated by her. That he'd sought her out in the ballroom and brought her flowers because he... liked her. That he'd taken her out on to the terrace because he was concerned about her. That he'd prevented her from causing a scene because he felt protective of her. Even if he didn't want to actually marry her, she'd thought he *liked* her.

Oh, what an idiot she was! She was nothing more to him than the object of a bet. By the sound of it, whoever discovered her true identity first, out of the four of them, would win a tidy sum of money.

He'd probably kept her out on the terrace until he could see that his friends were all gathered round Aunt Susan's chair. Aunt Susan, who had, she now saw, confirmed her identity for them.

She clenched her fists against the pain that was tearing at her insides. The rage that felt as if it was clawing its way out of the same spot.

She would never speak to him again.

And as for pressing one of the flowers he'd given her as a keepsake, that felt like the height of absurdity now.

To think she'd actually…

There was the sound of someone clearing his throat.

'Excuse me, miss, may I be of assistance?'

She whirled round to see a wigged and powdered footman eyeing her as though she was some kind of lunatic.

She supposed she must look like one, leaning against the wall behind the door, with her fists clenched and her mouth twitching with suppressed rage.

She uncurled her fists, lifted her chin and looked the footman in the eye.

'Yes, you may. My aunt, Lady Tarbrook, has been taken unwell.'

The moment she claimed Lady Tarbrook as a relative, the footman's demeanour became far more respectful.

'Do you wish me to call for your carriage?'

'No, thank you. She does not want to…to leave early, or…do anything to spoil the evening for my cousin. Her daughter.' Well, it must certainly be true, even though Aunt Susan had not said so. 'I have taken her to a little room downstairs, where it is cool and quiet. The one with the mirrors in the alcoves just outside?'

The footman nodded to indicate he knew exactly which room she meant.

'But…could you possibly bring us some refreshments? A glass of water. And some sandwiches and cake, too…' She bit down on her lower lip for a second, as it struck her that her aunt would not want even a servant to know she'd turned faint from forgetting to eat.

'I am going to sit with her, you see, which means we might well miss supper,' she said, hoping the explanation would throw him off the scent. She blushed though, not being used to telling fibs.

'Dancing does have a powerful effect on the appetite, doesn't it, miss,' said the footman, with a wink.

Well, it did, so she could nod, bashfully, and hope it made her look exactly like a maiden who was embarrassed to own up to having a healthy appetite. In public, gently reared girls were only supposed to pick at their food, as though they were merely being polite to their hostess. That was one of the tests she'd passed at the picnic, actually—refraining from showing too great an appreciation of all the dainties on offer, when she could easily have wolfed down three times the amount.

Once the smirking footman had gone about his business, she hurried back down the stairs, heading for the little room where she'd left her aunt, her mind whirling.

She should have known a handsome, experienced man like Lord Becconsall would not find her as interesting as she found him. She might have known there would be an ulterior motive behind the attention he'd paid her. After all, the only other men who'd sought her out had only done so because of her rank and fortune, or because Kitty hadn't time for them. But…to make her the subject of a wager!

She paused at the foot of the stairs as she

caught sight of her reflection in both the mirrors hanging on either side of the door to her aunt's sanctuary. She'd always known she was nothing much to look at. She had a square face and nondescript brown hair. Ordinary eyes and a squashed-up-looking nose. Why on earth had she suddenly forgotten how very plain and ordinary she was? How completely lacking in personality, too. She'd never mastered the art of sparkling repartee. Well, nobody had taught her how to sparkle. Actually, nobody had taught her anything very much at all. If it hadn't been for the governess Aunt Susan had sent, cajoling her to run her fingers along the words as she'd read to her from all those books of fairy stories, she might never have learned to so much as read and write. And it had only been because the housekeeper had reached her wits' end over Mama's lack of interest in running Stone Court, and had started training Harriet to do what was necessary, that she knew the first thing about domestic economy, either.

The images in the mirrors blurred at the reminder of the haphazard way she'd been educated, if you could call it an education. She'd been of so little account that neither of her parents had even bothered to hire another governess for her, once the one Aunt Susan had sent had left to go and care for an elderly relative, let alone think of sending her to school. Most people in London already made her feel like a complete country bumpkin. But, actually, she was little better than a savage.

No wonder Lord Becconsall and his friends had no compunction about wagering on her the way they'd wager on a horse, or a dog.

She blinked rapidly to clear her vision. She'd been of no account to anyone, all her life. So why should it hurt so much to find she was still of no account, now she'd come to London? She had never expected anything else, had she?

But, oh, once Lord Becconsall had kissed her, and then turned up at a ball and asked her to dance, she'd…

She'd started to fall for him, that's what she'd done. In her head, she'd turned him into something like one of those handsome princes from the fairy tales she'd loved so much as a little girl. Because he was the first handsome, eligible man to speak to her as though she had something about her to interest him.

But it had all been a hum.

Of course it had.

The only person to ever really look out for her, and consider her future, and do something about it, was Aunt Susan.

Poor Aunt Susan, who was sitting alone, in a dark little room, waiting for her glass of water and cake. Because she'd been too upset by her husband's refusal to believe in her innocence to eat today, when normally it was one of her greatest pleasures in life.

Casting her unimpressive reflections one last glance of loathing, Harriet headed for the room where she'd left her aunt.

Since Aunt Susan was the only person who'd ever put herself out for her, the least Harriet could do was find out what had really happened to the rubies she'd been falsely accused of pawning.

She'd spend the rest of this evening taking the very best care of the only person in the whole world who'd ever put themselves out for her, and then, first thing tomorrow, she'd resume investigations with a vengeance.

Chapter Eleven

It was all very well deciding she was never going to speak to Lord Beconsall again. But she soon discovered that it was not so simple putting that decision into practice.

Her first attempt to administer a resounding snub ran aground the moment she asked the butler not to admit him to the house.

Keeble raised his left eyebrow an infinitesimal fraction and gave her the kind of look she wished she could perfect herself so that she could use it on Lord Becconsall.

'You are passing on a message from Lady Tarbrook,' he suggested.

'Well, no.'

The eyebrow went up a further fraction.

'I just don't want to bother her with my, um, that is, she has troubles enough at the moment without…' She dried up, then, as Keeble's expression turned positively arctic.

'I could not possibly take it upon myself to deny admittance to a gentleman of Lord Becconsall's rank,' he said repressively, 'without direct orders from either his lordship or her ladyship.'

Harriet had found herself wrapping her arms about her waist. 'Oh, oh, well then, never mind,' she'd said lamely. And decided she would just have to give him the cold shoulder when he came to call. Which he was bound to do. Even if he had only danced with her for low, nefarious reasons he would still observe the proprieties the day after. All gentlemen did so. Even Mr Swaffham, who'd only asked her to dance because Kitty hadn't had time for him, had paid his duty call the day after. True, he'd spent the entire half-hour gazing across the room at Kitty rather than attempting to make conversation with her, but he'd come.

And today was no different. Mr Swaffham made his bow, sat next to Harriet on the sofa which Aunt Susan had decreed she occupy and accepted his cup of tea politely. But then his glances across the room to where Kitty was sitting, accepting compliments, very prettily, from a bevy of gentlemen who *had* managed to secure her hand for dances the previous night increased in frequency until they merged into one continuous stare.

He started as badly as Harriet when Keeble announced the arrival of Lord Becconsall and got to his feet at once.

Which left the spot on the sofa beside her perilously vacant.

When Lord Becconsall sat down she didn't know where to look. Or what to say. She knew what she wanted to say, of course, but she didn't have the courage to spit it out. Not in Aunt Susan's drawing room. Not after vowing she was going to do all in her power to defend and support her.

'This is pleasant,' said Lord Becconsall, glancing with amusement at the two gentlemen currently attempting to outshine each other with the wittiness and gallantry of their compliments to Kitty. 'I do so enjoy watching other men making complete cakes of themselves.'

Harriet grappled with the urge to ignore him. But then, she suspected that if she did so, he would carry on goading her and goading her until she…flew at him and slapped his impudent face.

So she schooled her features into what she hoped looked more like mild disdain than what she was really feeling and put on a voice that was frigidly polite.

'Are you implying that Mr Congleton and

Lord Frensham are fools for paying court to Kitty in particular, or for taking any woman at all seriously?'

He leaned back and ran his eyes over her, one of his most annoyingly amused grins playing about his lips.

'Got out of bed the wrong side, did you? Or,' he said, leaning closer and lowering his voice, 'are you just jealous that she is having so much more success than you?'

She turned to face him, her blood boiling. Oh, how she wanted to slap him. Or…pull his nose, or tweak his ears or…simply poke him in the eye. Anything to wipe that horrid smirk from his face.

But if she did any of those things, it would create a scene. Which would wound Aunt Susan far more than it would hurt Lord Becconsall. In fact, he would probably find the whole thing vastly amusing.

He would be impervious to anything she could do.

Because he thought she was a joke. A huge joke.

Just then, the door to the drawing room opened again. But instead of Keeble announcing another visitor, it was her uncle standing in the doorway. Which caused all conversation in the room to falter, for he so very rarely strayed into this room when it was full of callers.

'Lady Harriet,' he said, beckoning to her in a peremptory manner. 'A word, if you please.'

It felt like a reprieve. If she'd stayed sitting next to Lord Becconsall one second longer, who knew what she might have done next?

She got to her feet at once. Dropped Lord Becconsall a perfunctory curtsy, since that was what Aunt Susan would expect of her, and hurried over to her uncle.

He stepped out into the hall, inviting her to follow. As soon as he'd closed the door on the drawing room, her anger with Lord Becconsall faded to the back of her mind. What on earth could have induced her uncle to summon her this way? Surely, only some dire emergency would have him obliging her to leave the room like this, in front of everyone. Could there be bad news from home?

Papa? Oh, no. Her heart began to pound sickly in her chest as she followed her uncle down the stairs and along the hall to his study, which lay towards the back of the house. She'd only ever been in here once before, on the first night she'd arrived. She'd thought what a lovely room it was then and had spent most of the time he'd been telling her what he expected of her while she was staying in his house admiring the view out of the window, which overlooked a pleasant courtyard with an ornamental fountain.

Today, however, she couldn't drag her eyes from her uncle as, having indicated with a brusque gesture that she should sit in the chair before his desk, he went round it to sit down himself.

He huffed. Frowned. Leaned back, making the chair creak. Leaned forward, folding his hands on the desk.

Harriet swallowed.

'I have had…something in the nature of a complaint,' he finally said. 'About your behaviour.'

'Oh?' Not Papa, then. Thank heaven. But… had somebody told him about her tussle on the grass with Lord Becconsall? How typical that would be, to be found out now she'd vowed never to speak to him again. Knowing her uncle, he'd insist it was grounds for marriage. And the only person who would be more appalled at the prospect would be Lord Becconsall himself.

It wouldn't surprise her if he was so appalled that he sought out a regiment that was serving overseas and joined up at once.

But what if he was wounded? Killed? Her stomach turned over.

'It pains me to have to be the one to say this,' said Uncle Hugo, breaking through the chaos raging inside her head. 'But as things stand, I cannot trust Lady Tarbrook to set you to rights.' He scowled.

She said nothing. What was there to say? That she'd already learned her lesson, in the worst way possible? To confess that at some time just after dawn, having been unable to sleep, she'd seen that most people would say she'd probably deserved for Lord Becconsall to treat her as a joke, because of the way she'd behaved. That she shouldn't have been out in the park, unattended. And that, therefore, whatever had happened since was entirely her own fault.

That on the whole, she could see their point.

'It is one thing ordering my staff to refuse admittance to my house to certain gentlemen,' he began. 'Though really, if you find some suitor unacceptable, you should have spoken to your aunt and explained why, and then she would have taken care of it.'

She hung her head to conceal any expression of relief that might have flitted across her face. It didn't sound as if he'd found out about her escapade in the park. Or he would have opened with that. Besides which she was a bit ashamed of having tried to go round the problem of Lord

Becconsall instead of facing it head on. She knew
it wasn't her place to give such orders to Lord
and Lady Tarbrook's staff, but if she'd gone to
her aunt in the regular way, she'd have wanted to
know what her objection was to Lord Becconsall.
And she simply couldn't face telling her.

'But as for questioning them about the fate of
the Tarbrook parure...' he breathed very loudly
through his nostrils, which were pinched and
white, she noticed as she raised her head in surprise '...that, I have to tell you, young lady, is
going beyond what is acceptable. My staff,' he
said, getting to his feet, 'have been for the most
part with me since I was a boy. I trust them all
implicitly. And to have them all upset by accusations of...theft, is something I will not have.
Do you understand me?'

By the time he spoke the last words he was
standing right over her, his brows drawn down.
If he hadn't been, she might have blurted out that
it was a great pity he didn't feel the same about
upsetting his wife with similar accusations.

'I... I didn't accuse anyone of anything,' she
said mulishly. 'I only asked if anyone had any suspicions. The servants are, after all, the best people to know what goes on in a big household—'

She flinched as Uncle Hugo slammed his fist
down on his desk.

'Enough! I will not have you answer me back in that insolent fashion. A mere chit of a girl like you. It would serve you right if I packed you back off to the country, where you clearly belong if you are so ungrateful for this chance my wife has seen fit to give you, that you go round upsetting the household by making the servants fear they are about to be accused of something that is a hanging offence!'

Only a few days ago, she'd thought the threat of being sent back to the country might have come as a relief. Because it was where she belonged. London, and London society, was like a foreign country to her. She scarcely spoke the same language as the natives. And their customs and habits made very little sense to her.

But at that time she hadn't fully appreciated just how much she owed Aunt Susan. To abandon her, now, would be an appalling act of self-ishness. Even if it would be a means of escaping Lord Becconsall.

So she hung her head and attempted to look repentant.

Actually, she *was* a bit repentant now that Uncle Hugo had told her how she'd made the staff feel. She hadn't considered the fact that theft of such precious items was a hanging offence.

'I never meant to frighten anyone,' she said

with genuine remorse. She lifted her head to look her uncle straight in the eye, to show him that she was being completely honest. 'I just thought that one of the staff might have seen something suspicious. Or at least been able to say exactly when the last time the genuine stones had been seen...'

'You are not to plague any of my staff with any more of your impertinent questions about this matter, do you hear me?'

She nodded. For just about everyone in the house must have heard. When Uncle Hugo got angry, his voice carried.

'Because if you do, I shall most certainly send you back where you came from. And that will be the end of any chance some decent man might marry you. Though why on earth any man of sense would wish to...' He looked at her as though she was a worm. 'I believe there is a certain type who would overlook your lack of address because of your fortune, but what man could stomach a woman who...meddles in things that don't concern her? That answers back?'

'I...' She bit down on the retort that she hadn't answered back, since that would have been answering back.

'Go to your room and stay there,' he bellowed. 'And think about the consequences of your actions this day.'

She didn't hesitate. She got out of her chair and scurried to the door. Oh, not because her uncle frightened her. Although it was a bit disconcerting to have a grown man standing over her, shouting right into her face. It was Harriet's guilty conscience that was making her so uncomfortable. Because it really was unforgivable to upset the servants so badly. Badly enough for them to break with all the etiquette that appeared to govern them and make a complaint about her.

As if that weren't bad enough, worse was to come. Just as she reached the foot of the stairs, who should she see descending them but Lord Becconsall.

He was frowning. And his eyes were flicking from where she was standing clutching at the newel post for support to the door of her uncle's study.

He must have seen her coming out. He'd probably heard her uncle shouting. And he'd definitely seen her being hauled unceremoniously out of the drawing room.

Not that he cared. Not about her. That frown, that expression of concern, couldn't possibly be concern on her behalf. For a man like that cared only about himself. And his stupid friends. And their stupid wagers.

So he was probably wondering if somehow,

someone had told her uncle what she'd been up to in the park. Or, more likely, told tales about her going out on to the terrace with him last night.

Yes, he was probably scared that her warning about him having to marry her if anyone should find out he'd kissed her was about to come true.

Well, he need not be. She would rather spend the rest of her days…well…*anywhere* than married to him when it was clearly the last thing he wanted. In the hopes of conveying her determination to do anything rather than be dragged down the aisle to marry him, she lifted her chin, prised her fingers from the newel post, urged her feet into motion and began to mount the stairs.

'Lady Harriet…' he began in an urgent undertone as she drew level with him.

She shot him a scathing glance, tossing her head for good measure, and kept right on climbing the stairs.

And then she strode along the corridor to her room with her head held high. Without looking back to see his reaction to her snub.

Not even once.

Chapter Twelve

She didn't slam the door to her room behind her. But she did attempt to relieve her feelings by marching across to the dressing table and kicking the stool. Which hurt like blazes.

Cursing under her breath, she hopped over to her bed and sat down quickly. As she sat there cradling her foot, wondering if she'd broken a bone, she listened to callers leaving and callers arriving. Eventually the hour for paying such calls came to an end and the house fell quiet. Relatively quiet. She heard Kitty's footsteps hurry past her room and then the sound of her bedroom door open and close. Her little bedroom clock struck the hour twice, but it wasn't until she heard the family making their way to the dining room that she began to wonder if she was not only confined to her room, but also going to be deprived of food and drink.

Which made her get up and start pacing the room angrily. That she was able to do so came as some relief in regard to her toe. At least she had only bruised, rather than broken, it.

Nevertheless, she didn't kick any other item of furniture, even when she heard evidence that the family had not only dined without her, but were also getting ready to go out, without a single one of them deigning to see if there was anything she might need.

She'd just flung herself on to her bed, with her poor injured foot at the head so that she could treat it to the softness of half-a-dozen pillows, when the door opened to reveal her aunt, all dressed up ready to go out, but looking far from well enough to do so.

'Aunt Susan, I am so sorry,' said Harriet, instantly struck with remorse for having spent the day thinking of nobody but herself. Uncle Hugo had probably used her behaviour as yet another stick to beat Aunt Susan with. Metaphorically, that was.

'I didn't mean to cause you any trouble,' she said, scrambling to sit up. 'Or upset the servants. I just couldn't bear to think of you bearing the blame any longer. I hoped to find out…'

'Oh, my dear,' said Aunt Susan, glancing over her shoulder guiltily before coming in and shutting the door behind her. 'It is better, really, that the world should believe that I sold the jewels to pay gambling debts and had the stones copied, than that a serious enquiry should be made.'

'What? No! Surely—'

'Hush.' She came across the room and sat down on the bed, next to Harriet. 'Let me explain something to you,' she said, taking hold of her hands. 'It will help you to understand your uncle's attitude over this. I know you think he is being harsh and unforgiving, but it is not the case. You see,' she went on hurriedly when Harriet took a breath to protest that it *was* the case and she would *never* forgive him. 'When he was a boy, his mother…lost a string of pearls. She accused a servant, who hadn't been with the family for very long, of stealing them. The maid swore she was innocent, but his mother insisted it must have been her, since nobody else had access to them. She was found guilty and hanged. And then…the pearls turned up.'

'What? How dreadful!'

'Yes. His mother never forgave herself. She'd sent an innocent woman to the gallows. You can imagine the effect it must have had upon him. Which is why, though it has upset me, I… I can forgive Lord Tarbrook for being so insistent on blaming me, when he must know…' Her lower lip trembled.

'Well, anyway, enough of that. You are not to be permitted to come out with us tonight. Though, I take it, that will not concern you too much?' She tilted her head and looked Harriet in the eye. 'Since you seem determined to avoid a certain…gentleman?'

'Oh, dear. Yes, that is something else I need to apologise for. Uncle Hugo told me I had no right to have your butler refuse admittance to any of his guests. It was just that—'

'You have taken him in strong aversion.'

'Yes.' She found she couldn't look her aunt in the eye. Instead she gazed down at where her own hands were being held between her aunt's bejewelled fingers as she braced herself to face some awkward questions.

But her aunt only sighed.

'Well, no matter. He is not exactly a splendid catch. Although he comes from a good family and has a comfortable income, his reputation is that he is not all that…steady. Had I been think-ing more clearly I might have given him a hint he was wasting his time in the first place. How-ever, you appeared to like him, so…'

'Yes, I did, at first. It is just that…' She swal-lowed, wondering how to continue that sentence without owning up to what she'd done, or what he'd done, or what she'd subsequently overheard.

'First impressions can be deceptive. And I don't forget that he was the first man of any real consequence to pay you attention. However, I am sure he won't be the last, so we will say no more.'

She was sure he wouldn't be the last? Harriet lifted her head to stare in astonishment at her aunt. That definitely wasn't what Uncle Hugo thought. He'd told her she was so worthless and unattractive that only a desperate fortune-hunter would be prepared to overlook her faults. He'd been so cutting and cruel that if she'd been a sensitive sort of girl she would have been devastated. Fortunately, he'd already revealed his true colours by the way he'd treated his own wife. Her lovely, lovely Aunt Susan, who was trying to make her feel better instead of crushing her when she was already down.

'I shall tell your uncle that I have found you suitably penitent,' said Aunt Susan. 'And not mention your obvious relief that you don't have to face the ordeal of yet another ball. It would quite spoil his conviction that he is being extremely strict with you,' she said, much to Harriet's amazement. In the space of three minutes, Aunt Susan had not only expressed an opinion which was the very opposite of the man she normally deferred to on all matters, but now she was proposing to actually hoodwink him!

'I shall have Maud bring you up some supper the moment we have gone out. You can manage until then? You are not too hungry?'

'No, thank you Aunt Susan,' she said, wishing there was some way to express the sudden surge of affection she felt for her brave, kindly and compassionate aunt. Who was always trying to see the good in people, even when experience must have taught her that there wasn't all that much, all that often.

'I will also select a few journals and books for you to read. I see no reason why you should be deprived of all forms of entertainment, just because you are not allowed to leave your room. Especially since...' She trailed off, looking guilty. Leaving Harriet wondering what she'd been about to say. She hoped that Aunt Susan might have thought about saying she was touched by Harriet's belief in her innocence. Or that she didn't think the things she'd done warranted confinement in her room. But to do either would have meant openly declaring that she no longer believed her husband was infallible. And she clearly wasn't yet ready to commit such open sacrilege.

It wasn't long after Aunt Susan left her room that Harriet heard everyone going downstairs. She went to the window to watch the family get into the coach and go out. She folded her arms as the coach merged with the traffic going around the square and shook her head over the tale Aunt Susan had told her, about the innocent servant going to the gallows. She'd done it to try to make her believe that Uncle Hugo wasn't a complete ogre, of course. But, well, it had given her food for thought.

For one thing, she could see that Uncle Hugo did have a good reason for behaving the way he'd done. For another, if she'd known about the awful fate of that poor servant girl in his childhood, she would never have asked the servants so many questions about Aunt Susan's rubies. They must all be terrified the same kind of thing might be going to happen all over again.

Which made it impossible to ask them anything else.

Which meant poor Aunt Susan was just going to have to bear the blame.

Which wasn't fair! She couldn't have had the jewels copied. She just wouldn't do such a thing.

She leaned her head against the cool panes of glass. And it was just as if some of its clarity seeped right into her head. Because she could suddenly see that although the horrid fate of that serving girl had come as a complete surprise to her, there must be plenty of other people who knew all about it. A story that shocking was bound to have been broadcast far and wide at the time. You couldn't keep a story like that hushed up, no matter how hard a family tried to do so.

She straightened up. Anyone who knew about it would also know how reluctant Uncle Hugo would be to question his servants very closely. That he'd be much more likely to pretend nothing had happened rather than risk sending another innocent to the gallows.

And if they knew the family well enough to have heard about that old scandal, then they'd probably also know how infrequently Aunt Susan got the rubies out of the…well, wherever it was she kept them.

Oh, how she wished she hadn't promised she wouldn't ask the servants any more questions. Because now Aunt Susan had told her all about those pearls, it had shone light on the mystery of the fake rubies in a whole new way. She no longer needed to look for the kind of thief who'd climb in through a window. Someone like…a close friend of the family would have had far more opportunity to effect the swap. Someone who could walk into the house as though they had every right to be there.

She'd just reached that conclusion when someone scratched at the door, then came straight in. It was Maud, with her supper, and Peter with a bundle of magazines and a couple of novels.

Neither of them looked at her, but simply set their burdens down on the nearest surface.

'Please,' said Harriet, darting forward, her hand outstretched. 'Would you be so kind as to convey my heartfelt apologies to all the staff? I never meant to frighten anyone. I never imagined I *could* frighten anyone. It is just that my aunt has been so good to me and, seeing her so upset over being accused of something I just know she couldn't have done, well, I wanted to clear her name. It never occurred to me that clearing her name might mean casting suspicion on any of you. I am sure none of you would do anything so disloyal. I just thought you might have some suspicion of…well, how an intruder might have got in. Or something,' she finished, her heart sinking as both maid and footman regarded her with identically stony faces.

'Will that be all?'

'Yes,' said Harriet, on a sigh. She'd done what she could. It was up to them whether they chose to forgive her or not.

* * *

The next morning, when Maud came in to open her curtains and set out her wash water, Harriet could barely resist the temptation to pull her quilt up over her ears and pretend she was still asleep. *Still* asleep? She didn't feel as if she'd slept for more than brief snatches all night. If it wasn't her guilt over the mess she'd made of trying to question the servants that had kept sleep at bay, it was cringing reminders of the way she'd started to feel about Lord Becconsall. In spite of him warning her not to.

Whenever she did drop off to sleep, the dreams that plagued her were so uncomfortable she jerked out of them as soon as she could. Either Lord Becconsall and his friends were lurking behind some bushes, all pointing and laughing at her. Or he was holding her in his arms and kissing her breathless. And in the dreams where he was kissing her, he sometimes had the rubies held behind his back. Whenever she woke up she puzzled over that, because she didn't really believe he had anything to do with the theft. Eventually she worked out that it was just her mind jumbling up the one fraud—the switch of the jewels for fakes—with his deceptive appearance of friendship. Or whatever it was that she'd thought had been growing between them.

In any case, all the dreams told her the same thing. She was a fool. A gullible, clumsy, ridiculous fool. And now it was morning and her eyes were gritty and her head felt as if it was full of sponge. Sponge that had soaked up too much unpleasantness and was consequently pressing at the inside of her skull.

But Maud, once she'd seen to her chores, seemed to be in no hurry to leave her in peace to mope. In fact, she stood at the foot of the bed, her hands clasped at her waist, and cleared her throat.

Repressing a moan, Harriet sat up, hugged her knees to her chest and looked the maid in the eye.

'Yes?'

Maud cleared her throat again. 'Well, Miss Harriet, it's like this. We, all of us, want to say that we're that sorry about the way Lord Tarbrook has taken our complaint. We never dreamed he'd haul you out of the drawing room like that, not when it was chock full of visitors. Especially not when that nice Lord Becconsall what is just starting to show an interest in you was there.'

Harriet made a dismissive wave of her hand at the mention of Lord Becconsall.

'We just wanted you to stop asking so many questions,' persisted Maud. 'For the older ones, see, it brought back so many bad memories.'

'I know,' said Harriet. 'That is, Lady Tarbrook explained it to me last night. It must have been dreadful.'

'Oh, yes it was, miss. I mean, my lady,' Maud corrected herself, dropping a curtsy.

'And as I said last night, I wasn't trying to point the finger of blame at any of you. I just thought that someone might have come into the house while you were all away. Or out for the evening, or something of the sort.'

'What, and broke in again another time to put the fakes back in place?' Maud shook her head. 'Couldn't have been done.'

'No, I quite see that,' said Harriet, her breath quickening a bit. Because she was technically breaking her word about not talking to the servants about the rubies.

Or was she? After all, it had been Maud who'd brought the subject up.

'Couldn't have been done when we were all away at a house party, neither,' Maud continued of her own volition. 'Her ladyship takes all her gewgaws along with her, rather than leave them behind in an empty house. Even the ones she has no intention of wearing.' Maud frowned as if in confusion.

And Harriet racked her brains to remember the exact wording of what she'd promised her uncle. She was pretty sure she'd only promised not to ask the servants any more questions. Not to refrain from speaking about the topic at all. Especially not if they were the ones who brought it up.

Having squared it with her conscience, Harriet made a statement that could in no way be interpreted as a question.

'It's…it's a puzzle, isn't it?'

'That it is. But we none of us can believe her ladyship done it. What his lordship suggested. Only if she didn't, then it must have been one of us, that's what they'd say.'

By the sound of it, overnight the servants had been discussing not only whether to accept Harriet's apology, but also the mystery of the fake rubies as well.

If she subtly dropped her own ideas into the conversation, they might go away and discuss it some more. That wasn't actually asking them questions, was it?

'I was thinking,' she said tentatively, 'that if it wasn't any of you, and it wasn't my aunt, and it wasn't a burglar who broke in, then that only leaves…'

'Yes?' Maud leaned forward, clearly eager to hear Harriet's theory.

'Well, a close family friend. Or at least, someone who could come and go without rousing suspicion.'

'Yes, but I still don't see how they *could* have done it. Her ladyship would know straight off if those rubies had been missing long enough to have them copied.'

'Oh.' Harriet sank back on to her pillows. 'Well, I suppose that's that then. Lord Tarbrook,' she said airily, 'will no doubt hold this over my aunt's head for the rest of their married lives.'

Maud's face fell. She clearly didn't like that outcome any more than Harriet did.

'Will that be all, my lady?'

'Yes, thank you, Maud,' said Harriet. 'And thank everyone below stairs, won't you, for understanding why I was so…well, tactless.'

'Oh, we understand that right enough,' said Maud, with a shy smile. 'You didn't mean no harm. Not one of us has ever thought that.'

'Thank you,' said Harriet, blushing.

Maud curtsied, turned away and had just reached the door when she suddenly paused. And stiffened.

'What is it?' Harriet sat bolt upright again. 'You have thought of something, haven't you?'

'Well, it's probably nothing,' said Maud, turning slowly. 'It's just, now I'm not so angry about you accusing us, and thinking about it a bit more clear, like, about what you said about some outsider coming in…' She shook her head again. 'No, I still don't see how…'

'What? Please tell me. After all,' she said with a hollow laugh, 'it isn't as if I can do anything, can I?'

The maid shook her head again. 'Even if you could, I'm not the sort to go casting blame on those who can't defend themselves. But, well, I think I shall just ask Mr Keeble what he thinks.'

And having delivered that tantalising hint that she did, finally, have a suspect in mind, she whisked out of the room, closing the door firmly behind her.

Harriet flung herself back on to the bed with a shriek of frustration. The maid knew something. Or suspected something. But she didn't trust Harriet enough to confide in her.

Still, at least the servants were all talking about it. Which was all she'd wanted them to do. If anyone could work out what had really happened to those rubies, it was bound to be one of them.

So all she had to do now was wait until they'd done so. And hope that they had the courage to confront Uncle Hugo with their conclusions.

And in the meantime, she might as well get

up and get washed and dressed. It would give her *something* constructive to do. Because she could see that it was going to be a long, long day.

Chapter Thirteen

$\sim\!\!\sim\!\!\sim\!\!\sim\!\!\sim$

Once Harriet was dressed there didn't seem to be anything to do but go and lay back down on the bed again. Where she stared up at the ruched canopy. For about five minutes. It was just too hard to stay here, with nothing to do, when she so badly ached to *do* something.

She strode to the window and imagined going out there and…

Doing what?

She whirled away in frustration. She had no idea where to start, that was the trouble. Because she was so ignorant.

An ignorant, naive country miss, that was all she was. A girl who was no good for anything in London but to serve as the butt of jokes made by sophisticated, heartless males with nothing better to do with themselves than make sport of ignorant, country…

She was going round in circles. On the carpet as well as in her head.

Though at least she hadn't yet yielded to the temptation to kick anything. She'd learned her lesson on the dressing-table stool.

See? She wasn't a *complete* idiot. She could learn some things. When it came to the hardness of dressing-table stools or men's hearts, that was.

From then on, her day followed pretty much the same pattern. For hour after hour, it seemed to Harriet, she either lay on the bed staring at the ruched canopy, or paced up and down, glaring at the carpet. She had just reached the stage where she was cursing the canopy for its inability to inspire her with a clever plan of campaign and the carpet for being entirely too frivolous with its stupid swirly patterns that only encouraged her mind to go round and round in circles, when the door flew open.

'I cannot believe Hugo could be such a tyrant,' said her mother, stalking across to the bed on which Harriet was currently lying. 'Besides which he has no right to confine you to your room. He is not your father.'

Goodness. Harriet sat up, slowly, stunned to see her mother so worked up on her behalf.

'Get up and get your hat on. You are coming out with me.'

'With you?' Golly. Mama had never invited her to go anywhere with her before. Not even to church. Although that was because Mama frequently forgot what day it was when she was deep in some piece of experimentation and so rarely attended Saint Martin's herself.

As her mother disappeared into the dressing room, Harriet swung her legs to the floor.

'The things he said,' Harriet heard her mother exclaim, although in a rather muffled voice since she'd just opened the door to the armoire and stuck her head inside. 'As if it was my fault you have an enquiring mind and have been asking awkward questions.'

Ah. That explained Mama's sudden interest in her daughter. Uncle Hugo must have declared his conviction that Harriet took after her and said it as though it was an insult, and Mama had obviously taken it personally.

'This will do,' she said, thrusting a relatively plain bonnet at her. 'I am not off to some foolish *ton*nish event, so there is no need to make any work for one of Hugo's precious servants, since he appears to hold them in higher regard than his own family.'

Oh, dear. Uncle Hugo must have told Mama exactly why Harriet had been confined to her room.

'And the dress you are wearing,' she said,

flicking her eyes over Harriet's crumpled gown, 'is perfectly acceptable for a lecture at the Royal Institution. Besides which you will put on a coat to cover it up,' she declared, turning to rummage in the armoire again.

'The Royal Institution?' Harriet gulped. 'You are actually taking *me* to a public lecture? With you?'

'Why should I not? It will be an educational experience for you. Mr Babbage, who is giving the lecture today, is one of the greatest minds of our age.'

Wonderful. Harriet pictured an elderly man with unkempt hair and less than pristine clothing droning on about some subject she knew absolutely nothing about. Possibly in Latin.

'And there is no need to look like that. It will be most interesting, I promise you.'

That wasn't likely. But it was certainly better than staying here staring at either the canopy or the carpet.

And going out would feel as though she was thumbing her nose at Uncle Hugo, a prospect that cheered her up to no end.

Besides which, this was the first time her mother had taken up the cudgels on her behalf about anything. And though it had more to do with her long-standing feud with Uncle Hugo

than genuine affection for her daughter, it was
still a sort of milestone in their relationship. And
deserved acknowledging.

'Thank you, Mama,' she therefore said meekly,
setting the bonnet on her head and tying the ribbons under her chin.

Mama nodded and set off at a brisk pace along
the landing, obliging Harriet to trot to keep up
with her. She then sailed down the stairs and
across the hall with her nose in the air. Harriet
wasn't at all sure the footman on duty would have
opened the door and let them out, when he'd seen
her trailing behind her mother, but fortunately
for all concerned, just as they reached the door,
somebody knocked on it. So when Peter opened
it to admit an afternoon caller, he could not be
blamed when the two houseguests made use of
the fact to escape.

'Ah, good afternoon, Lady Balderstone,' said
the plump matron panting her way up the front
steps as they were descending.

'Is it?' said Mama frostily, carrying on her
way without so much as a pause to nod a greeting.

Harriet eyed her mother with grudging admiration. Wouldn't it be wonderful to be able
to get away with ignoring people to whom one
didn't wish to talk? Especially women who were

only trying to push their noses into your private business.

'We can catch a hackney cab at the corner,' said Mama, setting off in that direction, 'if memory serves me correctly.'

Harriet scurried off after her. 'Shouldn't we have,' she began hesitantly, 'a footman to procure one for us?' Or a maid to go with them.

Mama made a noise Harriet was sure no lady ought to make, being something less than a snort, but very much more than a sniff. 'If you think I am going to send Hugo's servants on errands, when he has made it quite clear he thinks their sensibilities are of more importance than the welfare of any member of the Inskip family, then he is very much mistaken.'

'It isn't that,' panted Harriet. 'It is just that Aunt Susan said I was not to go anywhere in Town without a maid or a footman.' She didn't mind flouting Uncle Hugo's edicts, but it was a different matter to appear to disregard everything her aunt had been trying to teach her.

'As your mother I am a perfectly adequate chaperon, *wherever* I choose to take you,' she said, waving her umbrella in a militant fashion at the first cab she saw.

'Yes, of course you are, Mama, I didn't mean—'

'Although I must say that the rules that apply

to girls are completely unfair. They are designed to restrict the freedoms of an entire sex,' she said, causing the jarvey to stare and fumble the reins, just as they were attempting to climb into his vehicle, 'whilst bolstering the mastery of the other. The world would be a better place,' she said, taking her seat, 'if such rules did not exist and mankind lived in a state of intellectual, spiritual and legal harmony.'

Goodness. She'd never expected to hear her own views pouring from the lips of her own mother. But then, when had Mama ever bothered to sit down and have a conversation with her?

'Why are you pulling that face,' said Mama peering at her across the narrow space between the seats. 'I sincerely hope that my sister and her tyrannical husband have not managed to indoctrinate you with their views, in so short a space of time.'

'Goodness, no, Mama,' said Harriet. 'On the contrary, I was just thinking that I am more like you than I ever suspected.'

'Oh?' Now it was Mama's turn to look surprised. 'Are you become interested in the natural sciences, then?'

How was that likely to have happened, when Harriet had never had the kind of education that would have made it possible?

'No,' she said coldly. 'I was referring to my temperament.'

'Oh, that, yes. Tarbrook did mention something about the apple not falling far from the tree. He has never liked me,' she finished with a curl of her lip, indicating the feeling was mutual. 'He prefers his women meek and submissive. I sometimes wonder if he does not have a great deal of confidence in himself, that he has to browbeat all those around him to such a degree.'

Harriet tried to imagine her uncle feeling insecure about himself and failed. If anything, she suspected the opposite of what her mother had suggested. That he believed in himself so completely that he couldn't understand why anyone could possibly have an opinion that ran counter to his own.

Much like Mama.

No wonder they clashed.

'Ah, here we are,' said Mama unnecessarily as the cab jerked to a halt. It had taken such a short time to reach Albemarle Street that, once again, Harriet wondered why they had taken a cab at all. Why was it such a crime to use one's own legs to get wherever you wanted to go in Town?

Mama clambered out first and, while she was paying the driver, Harriet studied the large colonnaded building in which she was about to endure several hours of boredom. She was rather surprised by the number of other carriages drawing up along the street and the many people heading their way. She would never have guessed, from the way Aunt Susan behaved, that so many people of the *ton* would willingly spend an afternoon attending something educational. But there was no disputing the quality of many of the carriages coming and going, or the stylish clothing of their occupants.

Inside the lecture hall the benches were arranged in a vast semi-circle that reminded her of a Roman amphitheatre and looked as though they could seat several hundred people. Most people who were already there had taken seats at the front, near a central sort of pit in which stood a table loaded with books. Those who hadn't, nodded greetings to Mama as she stalked past them, though she didn't pause to make any introductions.

She learned why as they took their seats.

'Only just made it in time,' said Mama. 'I should have been most displeased if my detour to fetch you had caused me to miss the opening statements.'

Having neatly put Harriet in her place, Mama then gave her full attention to the talk that followed.

To Harriet's surprise, it was not about gases—which she'd thought was Mama's latest field of enquiry—but stars. And she could actually understand some of it.

Still, it wasn't long before her attention began to stray. There was only so much science a girl could stomach. Which made her wonder why there were so many females present. And some of them dressed, contrary to what Mama had said, with what could only be described as flamboyance.

She was just wondering what on earth had prompted an extremely thin young lady to wear a turban with feathers in, unless it was to annoy the gentlemen seated behind her, when she noticed that the gentleman in question was Lord Becconsall. And far from seeming annoyed by the feathers, he had his eyes closed. And his arms folded across his chest. As though he was taking a nap.

Which was just typical. While everyone else was hanging on every word uttered by Mr…she frowned as she tried to recall the name and only came up with Cabbage, though she wasn't convinced that was correct… Ulysses—that was, Lord Becconsall—was gently snoring.

She sniffed and turned her head away. What kind of man attended a lecture only to fall asleep during its course? A man who would…make a girl think he found her attractive, intriguing, only to…dash her hopes by…well, to be honest he had no idea he'd dashed any hopes. Because he didn't know she'd discovered he was only interested in her as the subject of a wager.

But if he thought she was going to dance with him again, let alone speak to him, then he'd very soon discover his mistake.

For the next few minutes Harriet amused herself by constructing several speeches in her head, all of them designed to annihilate his considerable self-esteem with the eloquence of her witheringly crushing wit. And was therefore rather surprised when suddenly everyone around her began to applaud. And the man at the central desk bowed. Then people began to get to their feet.

'Well,' said Mama. 'What did you think of that?'

'Um…' said Harriet, desperately trying to think of a polite response.

Mama sighed. 'If I had brought William *he* would have found it most instructive.'

Harriet flinched at the mention of Mama's favourite child and, since her head was already full of pithy rejoinders, she found herself uttering one.

'Well, since William is several thousand miles away, hunting for plants, you could not very well have done so, could you, Mama?'

Instead of slapping her down for her impertinence, though, Mama just shook her head. 'The only one of you to take after me,' she said morosely. 'Or so I have always believed.' She looked at Harriet. Really looked at her, instead of through her. 'But there is more of my temper about you than I had thought. Perhaps,' she said, gathering her reticule as though in preparation for standing up, 'though you do not show any signs of great intellect, it might be worth my while spending more time with you.'

What? All it had taken for Mama to wish to spend more time with her was for her to be rude? She wished she'd known that years ago.

Or perhaps not. Spending time with Mama would mean sitting through more lectures like this one, only to be told at the end that she was a disappointment for not having much in the way of intellect. She preferred going round the shops with her aunt. At least at the end of what Mama would condemn as an afternoon frittered away, she had some new clothes to show for the experience. Which had been purchased from motives of generosity, even if they hadn't, so far, been exactly a success.

'Good afternoon, Lady Harriet,' said a voice close to her ear. The voice of Lord Becconsall.

For a moment she contemplated cutting him. But before she could sniff, or turn her head away, or anything like that, he'd turned his attention to her mother.

'And you must be Lady Balderstone.' He bowed over Mama's hand.

'Indeed,' said Mama. 'A friend of Harriet's, are you?'

'I like to think so,' said Lord Becconsall provocatively. To Harriet's mind. Since he was nothing of the kind. And then he stepped slightly to one side to reveal Archie. 'Allow me to introduce my friend, Mr Kellett,' he said to Mama.

'Kellett?' Mama practically thrust Harriet aside to seize the young man's hand. 'Not Thomas Kellett? *The* Thomas Kellett?'

'Ah,' said Archie, going rather red in the face.

'The Thomas Kellett who has been doing such splendid work with the isolation of the essential elements?'

'Ah, well, you know,' he said, his face lighting up, 'nothing like the strides being made by Nicholson and Carlisle with natronium and kallium, but I am hoping, now that I have constructed my own voltaic pile…'

Harriet stifled a sigh. Once people began to

pepper their sentences with words ending in -*ium* there would be no understanding the half of it.

'So now I know where you have acquired your knowledge of all things scientific,' said Lord Becconsall, with a mocking smile. Which set her teeth on edge all the way down her spine. 'Your mother is, according to Archie, something of a phenomenon.'

'And I suppose he wouldn't let you rest until he had been introduced,' she said acidly.

'Correct,' said Lord Becconsall, oblivious to her dig about him sleeping through the lecture. Clearly she was going to have to speak more bluntly if she was going to succeed in insulting him.

'You managed to get quite a bit of sleep, none the less, though, didn't you?'

'Lady Harriet,' said Lord Becconsall with a mocking smile. 'Never say you were watching me, rather than attending to the lecture?' He laid his hand upon his heart. 'I am touched. Deeply touched.'

'I was not watching you rather than attending—'

'No? Then, you will be able to fill me in on the salient points. Archie is bound to want to talk about them on the way home and I should not wish to disappoint him by being unable to contribute to the conversation.'

'First of all, I very much doubt that. I think you are far more likely to tell him, to his face, without the slightest hint of shame, that you slept through pretty much the whole lecture. And second…'

'Second?' His smile twisted into a grin. 'Let me guess. Knowing you, I suspect you were about to admit that your mind wandered far too often for you to be able to so much as tell anyone even one thing Mr Babbage said.'

Babbage, that was it, not Cabbage.

'But you do not know me,' she retorted, despite the fact that he'd just described *exactly* what she'd been doing.

'Then I shall look forward to that particular pleasure,' he said, leaning close and lowering his voice. Which sent a velvet caress all the way down to the places he'd previously set on edge with his mockery.

'You will do no such thing,' she replied.

'Oh, but I shall. Bound to, during the course of the Season, since we will be going to the same balls and lectures…and parks.'

The way he said that, all low, and sort of meaningfully, turned the velvet molten. How did he do that? Make her remember the kiss, that was? And the feel of his body, pressed up against hers? Just by saying the word *parks*, with a slightly different tone to his voice and a certain sort of glint in his eye?

'We will not!' She was never going to go to the park again. Not on her own anyway. Not when it was such a dangerous thing to do.

'One outing to the Royal Institution enough for you, was it?' He chuckled. 'Cannot say I blame you. All I have gained from coming here is a crick in my neck.'

'I was not referring to this lecture hall.'

'No?' He shook his head. 'Well, since it cannot be the balls I was mentioning, you must mean…'

'That is just where you are wrong. I did mean the balls.'

'Oh? You are giving up dancing then, are you?'

'With you, yes.'

'Come, come, just because we got off on the wrong foot…'

'It has nothing to do with our feet,' she said, stupidly. But then that was what happened when she got cross. Her words came out half-wrong. 'I mean, it wasn't to do with the way we met. It is what I have learned about you since.'

The laughter died from his eyes.

'Oh? And what, pray have you learned?'

'You know very well what it is,' she said, although she knew he probably didn't. 'So don't bother asking me to dance. And don't come calling again. I shall not receive you.'

'Is that so?' His face had set into an expression that looked as though she'd just handed him a challenge. 'We'll see,' he said softly.

And with just a hint of menace.

Chapter Fourteen

It stung.

He didn't know why it should, but when she'd flung her chin up like that and told him she would never dance with him again, nor admit him to her home, it had most definitely stung.

'I s-say,' Archie suddenly panted, from somewhere behind him. 'C-could you slow d-down a t-touch?'

'What? Oh, sorry, old friend, I was miles away.' And had started walking much faster as irritation had gone fizzing through his veins.

'Alm-most literally,' said Archie with a smile. 'Civilians like me aren't used to c-covering the miles on f-foot like you military men.'

And that was when it struck him. He'd felt the same, when she'd rebuffed him just now, as he'd felt every time he'd been passed over for promotion. When the credit had gone to someone who didn't *play the fool*. In other words, to some stiff and starchy booby who had no imagination and stuck to the rules like glue.

Was that what she wanted, then? Some stickler for propriety, with no sense of humour, who probably voted Tory and sent tenants to the gallows when they had the temerity to poach from his land instead of meekly lying down and starving?

He hadn't thought so. He'd thought she was…

He couldn't put it into words. It was just as though he'd recognised her, somehow. The way she struggled to fit in. The way she…

Hang it. What did it matter anyway? It wasn't as if he was in love with her.

He clapped Archie on the back and smiled. The devil-may-care smile that was his armour against all of life's setbacks.

'Enjoy the lecture, did you?'

'Very much. Although the highlight of this afternoon had to be meeting Lady Balderstone. Never usually stirs from her estate, you know, and one c-can't simply ride out there and visit.'

Something stirred in the labyrinths of Jack's mind. Something mischievous.

'You…ah…keen to see her again, then, are you, old man?'

Archie nodded, his eyes gleaming through the

hair that Jack itched to set about with a pair of scissors.

'Then we must definitely call upon her.'

'We?'

'Yes.' Archie had just handed him the perfect way to exact revenge on Lady Harriet. Because he would not be calling upon *her* again. Oh, no. He would be calling upon the fascinating Lady Balderstone instead, in the company of one of her most fervent admirers.

He might even set up a flirtation with her, while he was at it. See how Lady Harriet liked *that*.

'B-but you must have b-better things to do,' said Archie.

'Well, that's just it, I haven't.' The old army cronies with whom he'd spent the first few weeks in Town, drinking and going over old battles, only reminded him of what he'd lost. Oh, he wouldn't have had a brilliant career in the army, he was too apt to ignore orders from superiors when they were stupid, or worse, downright dangerous. But he'd been good at what he did. And he knew it. And his men had known it. Even some of his brother officers had admitted they wished they had his knack of getting their men to follow them the way his men followed him.

But being Lord Becconsall—that was something he had no idea how to do. And nobody on his estates expected him to make so much as even a token effort to be him, either.

All they'd asked of him was to do the Season and go back with a wife.

Set up his nursery.

Ensure the succession.

Which was another reason why he'd been at such pains to avoid society events. He might have come to Town, but that didn't mean he was going to meekly obey orders to find a wife.

On the contrary.

Which was why the moment his fascination with Lady Harriet had begun to alarm him, he'd gone into full retreat. She was only supposed to have been a minor and pleasant diversion. Once he'd satisfied his curiosity about her, he was supposed to have reported straight back to Zeus and consigned her to his past. Instead of which he hadn't told any of them anything about her. And he'd been drawn to any event where she might be, like iron filings to a magnet.

Even now, when she'd given him the perfect excuse to walk away and forget about her, he just couldn't do it.

Not at *her* bidding, anyway.

No, because she had no right to forbid him to

do anything or go anywhere. She was going to find that wherever she went, he would be there.

Flirting with every other woman in the place. Showing her that she meant *nothing* to him.

'I really think,' said Archie plaintively, 'that I c-could manage to get myself to a house in Gros-venor Square on my own without…g-getting lost, or c-committing some social solecism.'

'I'm sure you could.'

'Then, you don't need to come with me, do you?'

'What's this, Archie? Want the lady scientist all to yourself, do you? Afraid I'll queer your pitch?'

'No.' Archie went a bit pink in the face. 'It's just that…well, I don't see why you all spend so much time p-pretending an interest in the things I am interested in, when—'

'You aren't going to upbraid me for catching forty winks during that lecture, are you?' Jack cut in before Archie could really get going.

'N-no, but see—'

'Look, if you must know, I wasn't asleep at all. I was just pretending.'

'P-pretending? Why?'

'Because I'd seen Lady Harriet come in, with her mother and…' He'd been afraid he wouldn't be able to keep his eyes off her. That she'd catch him staring at her, and think…well, he hadn't been prepared to let her start thinking anything. 'She was too distracting, if you must know,' he admitted. Which was true. He'd hoped that once he'd told his friends who she was, that her identity was out in the open, she'd lose some of the fascination she held for him. It hadn't worked. When her uncle had hauled her out of the drawing room, in a way that presaged trouble for her, he'd scarcely managed to stop himself from going with her. Because he wanted to defend her from whatever was about to happen. And when he'd seen her face, after the thundering scold she'd received for who knew what crime, he'd wanted to gather her into his arms and comfort her.

And to crown it all, when he'd seen her earlier, all he'd wanted to do was drink in the sight of her like some…brainless, infatuated sapskull.

Of course he'd shut his eyes and pretended she wasn't there. What other defence did a man have?

'Thank you for t-telling me. I wouldn't have thought…' He trailed off, his face flushing slightly.

'What?'

'Oh, nothing. A…thought I had. That's all. A stupid thought, I c-can see. B-but then…truth is, I've b-been a b-bit b-blue-devilled of late.'

Jack darted him a glance. Why hadn't he noticed the way his friend had been walking, with his head bowed as though weighted down with invisible burdens?

'Want to tell me what ails you? I know I ain't as clever as you, but you didn't all start calling me Ulysses for nothing.'

Archie glanced up, and smiled sadly. 'You are out, there, I'm afraid.'

'In what way?'

'In the way of thinking you are not as c-clever as I am. You are a master tactician. Couldn't have led so many men into battle, and lost so few of them without having k-kind of mind that c-can implement c-complex strategies. And what you have done actually matters. To the outcome of the c-campaign as well as the men you k-kept alive. Whereas I…' He sighed again. 'Lady B-Balderstone reminded me of it, inadvertently of course, when she spoke of the discoveries being made of late in the field of isolating the elements. It feels as if every time I get to the point of a b-breakthrough, someone else b-beats me to it.' He sighed again. 'I am starting to feel like an imp-postor. That I ought to stop leeching off Zeus and go to t-teach in a school or something.'

'I say, that's a bit drastic, isn't it?' Schoolboys would eat Archie alive.

'P-possibly, but at least I would feel as if I

was earning my living. Instead of sponging off Zeus.'

'You aren't sponging off him. He employs you as his chaplain, doesn't he?'

Archie made an impatient movement with his hand. 'It's a n-nominal appointment. Designed to give me p-pin money. I have never p-presided over a single service whilst living in K-Kelsham Park.'

'Well, I don't think you need to let that side of things bother you. Zeus didn't employ you to say prayers for him. He ain't the slightest bit bothered about his soul. Since he thinks he's God already.'

Archie let out a surprised bark of laughter.

'D-don't be impious, Ulysses,' he said. 'Else he'll strike you down with a b-bolt of lightning.'

'I'd dodge it,' said Jack, relieved to see that Archie's mood was lifting. 'That's why he named me Ulysses. I'm adept at wriggling my way out of what look like impossible situations, by dint of my low cunning.' He waggled his eyebrows theatrically.

Archie smiled again. Briefly. 'Seriously, though, I do wonder how much longer he will tolerate my c-constant stream of failures to discover anything that will make him famous as a sponsor of the sciences. The way he has b-been looking at me, of late...'

Ah. 'Well, you know what, Archie? If he does turn you out of your comfortable quarters, you can come to me. Now that I'm a lord, I am swimming in lard and have all sorts of gifts and benefits at my disposal. And if,' he said quickly, when it looked as if Archie was going to voice an objection, 'you don't want to carry on researching any longer, why don't you just come for a prolonged stay? Spend some time thinking about what you really do want to do with your life?'

'Th-that's good of you, but…'

'Just think about it, that's all. Take some time.'

'Yes, that is just what Zeus said when I raised my c-concerns with him.'

'What? You've already told Zeus how you feel?'

Archie nodded. 'That is why we c-came up to London, when we heard that Atlas was ashore again.'

'Not because I'd sold out and was kicking my heels in Town?' Which was *his* problem in a nutshell. His friends were prepared to disrupt their routines and travel up to Town to celebrate the fact that Atlas had returned safe from the wars. But not him.

Archie shrugged. 'There is no telling why he chooses to do anything. That is the one way in which he does resemble G-God, actually.' He shot Jack a challenging look.

'Ah, yes,' said Jack, remembering. 'Because he moves in mysterious ways.'

'And so do you,' said Archie, his brows drawing down. 'I thought you only ran the g-girl from the p-park to earth out of some sort of...'

'Well, so did I, at first,' said Jack. 'But the thing is...' He trailed off as they finally reached the front door of their club, where they'd arranged to meet Zeus himself. 'To be honest, I'm dashed if I know what the thing is,' he said, with what he hoped was a disarming smile.

'But you hope that you might find out, if you c-call on her again?'

'Indeed I do,' he said and jogged up the steps before Archie could ask any more questions about his intentions with regard to Lady Harriet, which might mean not being completely straight with the fellow. Because he had no wish to embroil Archie in his schemes, which were not the slightest bit honourable. Especially not when it sounded as if Archie had enough troubles as it was.

Besides which, he couldn't trust Archie not to blurt out the truth, if he learned it. Because, clever though Archie was, when it came to subterfuge and cunning, he was the veriest babe.

Chapter Fifteen

The moment Keeble opened the front door of Tarbrook House, Harriet could tell there was going to be trouble.

'His lordship has requested that you attend him in his study, as soon as you return,' he said sternly.

'Does he?' said Mama, undoing the strings of her bonnet and handing it to him, neatly reminding him of his place. 'I shall bear that in mind,' she said, turning in the direction of the staircase and making as if to ascend.

She had not climbed up more than two steps before the door to Uncle Hugo's study burst open and the man himself erupted.

'I might have known you would ignore a civil request,' he said, striding across the hall. How on earth he'd known that Mama was not heading in the direction of his study, Harriet had no idea.

Unless he had some sort of telescopic contraption mounted in there somewhere, through which he could observe the comings and goings that went on in his hallway. Which wouldn't surprise her, now she came to think of it.

'So why,' said Mama, turning to look down at him over her shoulder, 'did you bother to make it?'

'It is all of a piece with the rest of your behaviour,' he said from the foot of the staircase. 'You undermine me at every turn.'

'If you did not make so many foolish decisions, there would be no need to flout them.'

Mama's statement was like a red rag to a bull.

'May I remind you,' seethed Uncle Hugo through his nostrils 'that the reason I confined your daughter,' he said, pointing an accusing finger in her direction as she attempted to sidle up the stairs past Mama, 'to her room is that she turned my household...' he slapped his hand to his chest to emphasise exactly whose house it was '...upside down with her outrageous accusations of theft and skulduggery. She needed to learn a lesson. And you took her out of her room, nay, out of the very house,' he cried, pointing to the front door, 'against my express orders.'

Mama, from her vantage point on the stairs, looked down on him with disdain and clucked her tongue. 'It has come to a pretty pass if a woman cannot take her own daughter out whenever she pleases.'

'Well, that is it, in a nutshell, is it not? You only think of her when it pleases you to use her to make a point. May I remind you that it has been *my* wife who has gone to all the trouble of launching that graceless daughter of *yours* into society. And what thanks do we get? From either of you?'

The sound of a muffled sob, emanating from the half-open door to the drawing room, drew Harriet's attention to her aunt, whom she could just see, sitting on a sofa with her head bowed. And a handkerchief to her face.

'Nobody asked Susan to bring Harriet up to Town,' said Mama, oblivious to everything but her quarrel with Uncle Hugo. 'She knew exactly what my objections were and chose to override them.'

'That was because they were foolhardy.'

'No, they were not. Do you think I had any wish to see my own flesh and blood laced into the constraints that made me so unhappy as a girl and paraded about Town like some brood mare for idiot men to appraise? I brought her up to be completely free of all restraints normally imposed on the behaviour of females so she wouldn't be stunted and Susan planned to undo it all in the space of two short months!'

Goodness. Harriet would never have guessed that Mama's treatment of her stemmed from anything more than indifference. But now it sounded as though, all along, Mama had been following some radical approach to rearing her, so that she wouldn't end up…well, as unhappy she'd been as a girl, by the sound of it.

'She was perfectly happy at Stone Court,' Mama was continuing, a touch inaccurately. 'Bringing her to Town has been like shutting a wild bird into a tiny gilded cage.'

'Then you will have no objection to taking her back there, then, will you, when you leave.'

'None whatever,' said Mama cheerfully.

'Which you will be doing this very night,' he finished.

'Tonight? Oh, no. I have no intention of leaving Town just yet. I have not finished—'

'Whatever it is you have not finished, madam, I give leave to inform you, you will not be doing from under my roof. To be blunt, you are no longer welcome to stay here. And neither is your daughter.'

'That's not fair, Hugo! Your quarrel is with me. Banish me if you like, but don't vent your spleen on Harriet.'

Good grief. Now Mama was actually trying to defend her.

'I thought you said she was like a wild bird in a gilded cage. Should I not, then, free her?'

'Oh, don't throw that in my face. You know as well as I do that she doesn't see it like that. She *wanted* to come to Town, or nothing Susan said would ever have convinced me to give in.'

'Nevertheless,' he said, his face turning an interesting shade of puce, 'you will both leave. As soon as I can have the carriage brought round.'

'Don't bother,' Mama hissed, whilst moving between Uncle Hugo and Harriet as though to put up a shield between her daughter and this man's anger. 'We are perfectly capable of hiring a hack—'

'If you think I am about to permit you to remove from my house in a hired hack and cause every Tom, Dick and Harry to speculate about what might have prompted such unprecedented behaviour,' he bellowed, 'you are very much mistaken.'

'Still more concerned about appearances,' Mama sneered, 'than the welfare of your family.' Having rendered him speechless with rage, Mama stuck her nose in the air and stalked up the stairs.

There was nothing Harriet could do but trot

obediently up the stairs behind her mother. Though, when they reached the landing, she did not make for her own room, but followed Mama to hers.

'Mama…'

'Not one word, Harriet. If you think I will stay one moment longer in the house of a man who can lock girls in their rooms simply for asking a few innocent questions, then—'

'Yes, Mama, I quite see that you have no choice, but to leave here…' Indeed, Uncle Hugo had given them none. 'It is just that I was wondering where we are to go. Isn't it a bit late in the day to be thinking of returning to Stone Court? Even if Uncle Hugo is lending us his carriage for the journey?'

'Did you not hear? I have no intention of leaving Town until I am good and ready. We shall only be going as far as St James's Square.' Which was where their London residence was situated.

'But we haven't written to have Stone House opened up. Everything will be under holland covers.'

Mama waved a hand, airily. 'Then the staff will just have to remove them.'

'What staff?'

Mama's brow wrinkled. 'There are some people there whose job it is to keep an eye on the place and forward any mail, aren't there?'

'Yes, but I think you will find there are only two of them. And they are quite elderly.'

'Really, Harriet, I don't see why you are throwing so many obstacles in the way. Unless it is that you wish to stay here. Is that it? Well,' she continued before Harriet had a chance to answer, 'I am afraid that is out of the question. You heard your uncle.'

Yes. And she was fairly sure everyone in the house had heard him as well. 'I do not wish to stay here, no,' she said, suddenly realising that it was the truth. She was sorry to be causing her aunt even more distress by the manner of her leaving, but there would be certain compensations. Mama would soon be so wrapped up in whatever she was doing that she would not care what Harriet did as long as the household ran smoothly. In fact, to judge from that impassioned speech earlier, Mama would positively encourage Harriet to do exactly as she pleased. At any rate, Mama would most certainly not expect her to attend any more balls where she would be ignored by decent men, hounded by fortune-hunters and made a game of by scoundrels like Lord Becconsall.

She would, in short, have far more freedom

than she ever would have in a more convention-
ally run household. And she could use that freedom to investigate what had happened to Aunt
Susan's rubies. Which would be a far better way
of showing her gratitude than simpering at so-
called eligible men and learning to do embroidery.

'I am just thinking of the practical details, that
is all,' said Harriet. 'Like getting meals on the
table and freshly laundered sheets on the beds.
That sort of thing.'

'You were born to be a housewife,' said Mama,
scornfully. 'Whereas I, if I found the place not
to be habitable, would merely remove to a hotel
until—'

'Until I have managed to engage enough staff
to make our lives comfortable at Stone House'
said Harriet with an acid smile. She might have
misjudged Mama's motives for treating her the
way she had done so far, but she hadn't suddenly
turned into someone else.

'Precisely,' said Mama, the insult gliding right
off her impenetrable self-consequence. Leaving
Harriet understanding exactly why Uncle Hugo
found Mama so infuriating.

She whirled away before she said something
she might later regret and went to her own room
to pack.

She hadn't been in there for long before some-one scratched at the door and came in. She looked over her shoulder to see Maud.

'I'm come to help you pack, miss,' she said, looking apologetic. 'Leastways, that's what Mrs Trimble said I was to say.'

'Are you not, then, going to help me to pack?' Harriet looked in frustration at the armoire stuffed with ball gowns, walking dresses, carriage dresses, pelisses and spencers, and shook her head. 'It will take me a week to do a competent job of it, Aunt Susan has bought me so many things.' And it wasn't just the armoire. There were two dressers and a chest full of stockings and shawls and gloves and dancing pumps dyed the exact shade of the trimmings on her ball gowns, not to mention various other accessories she hadn't possessed when she first came to London. 'I am never going to fit everything in my trunk, anyway.' Not that she wanted to, actually. Not considering how many of her earliest purchases had been such disasters.

'Mrs Trimble is having Fred fetch down a couple of bags from the attics you can use to put your essential items in, then we'll pack the rest of it and bring it on later.'

'Oh, yes. Very practical.'

'No, don't go looking at me like that, my lady,

we are all that sorry you are having to leave like this. It ain't—I mean,' she said, flushing, 'it isn't right, turning you out along with your mother, when you didn't have any choice in things.'

'I had already angered his lordship,' said Harriet, pulling open a drawer and wondering what she ought to consider essentials and put in the bags being brought to her for that purpose. 'He was just looking for an excuse to evict me.'

'Yes, and that's the other thing,' said Maud, coming to her side and pulling out a selection of undergarments that Harriet could see were exactly what she should have thought of herself. 'Once you leave this house, he won't be able to stop you asking about the theft of her ladyship's jewels, will he?'

'No.' Harriet lifted her chin. 'And if you've come to plead with me to stop, then I have to tell you—'

'No, it's just the opposite,' said Maud, rolling up a pair of stockings and reaching for another. 'We've been talking, below stairs, and have reached the same conclusion. We know it weren't any of us, but someone must have switched her ladyship's jewels, 'cos we can't none of us believe it was her. And, like you, we'd like to see her name cleared.'

'What?'

'You heard,' said Maud, with unusual pert-
ness. 'Now, listen, miss, 'cos we mayn't have
much time. I'm to tell you our suspicions and
what we've worked out so far, and then it's up to
you. We can trust you not to lay any blame on
any of us, can't we?'

'Yes!' Harriet's heart was beating so fast she
felt a little shaky. She hadn't dreamed her re-
newed determination to clear Aunt Susan's name
would have borne fruit so swiftly.

'Well, a few years back, in 1812, to be precise,
'cos Mrs Trimble looked it up in her journal,
there was this girl come to work as lady's maid.
Ever such a quiet little thing, she was. Would
barely talk to any of us. Well, at the time, we all
thought she was just shy. But now...' Maud shook
her head, lips pursed. 'Even the way she left was
suspicious, now we come to look back on it.'

'Suspicious? In what way?'

'Well, she *said* she was leaving on account
of she got a better offer. But she wouldn't tell us
where she was going. Nor she didn't ask for references neither. At the time, as I was saying, we
just thought it was all of a piece with the way she
was. But the thing is,' said Maud, going to the
armoire and taking a rapid inventory of its con-
tents before lifting down one of the day dresses
with the fewest ruffles and bows, and laying it

on the bed. 'Thing is, there's been no sign of her anywhere, ever since. Like she vanished off the face of the earth,' Maud finished as though she was reading aloud from some sensational story.

'We *did* think she must have gone back to Bogholt, the village where she said she come from, 'cos she certainly hasn't got work with anyone in London.'

'Do you mean that—have you in fact been looking for her?' Harriet lifted down her riding habit and tossed it on to the bed with the selection Maud was choosing for her.

'No, but see, footmen get together for a heavy wet down now and then. And butlers have their own watering holes. And they talk about…' She blushed and shrugged her shoulders. 'Well, what I mean is, if they get a new girl come to work for them, they talk about her. Whether she will… um…' Maud blushed.

'Let them kiss her?'

Maud nodded, clearly relieved not to have to explain the way footmen gossiped about the female staff they worked alongside. 'And if they are pretty, and so on. Now Jenny—that's the girl who come up from Norfolk—the footmen from here had all been talking about what a cold, starchy kind of girl she was. She gave Peter a real sharp set-down once or twice, apparently. And he reckons, if she'd gone to work anywhere else and someone else tried to flirt with her—not serious, mind, just in the way of having a bit of a laugh, for Mrs Trimble won't permit anything of that sort below stairs,' Maud put in hastily, as though Harriet might suspect the staff of doing nothing but flirting all day long, 'well, they'd have got the same reception. And they would have laughed about it over a heavy wet of an evening.'

Now *that* Harriet could believe. Young men, of whatever station, seemed to delight in making sport of young females and sharing their exploits with their peers appeared to be all part of it.

'So, you think she might have gone home? To Norfolk, was it you said?'

'Well, if she did that, why did she say she had got a better place? No,' Maud shook her head vigorously. 'We think she's gone to ground somewhere. With the proceeds from Lady Tarbrook's rubies. And you, miss, are the likeliest one to be able to find out where that somewhere is.'

Chapter Sixteen

Jack did a complete circuit of the ballroom on the pretext of exchanging a few pleasantries with all his old army cronies, as well as every single member of his club that he could spy. But eventually he could see he had no choice but to surrender to the necessity of approaching Lady Tarbrook. Who looked about as eager to speak to him as he had been to have to ask her the one question uppermost on his mind.

'Good evening,' he said, bowing over her hand. And coming straight to the point. 'Lady Harriet not here tonight? I was so hoping to be able to dance with her again.' Or, to be more precise, to *making* her dance with him again. It wasn't going to be enough, he'd decided about the time he was putting the finishing touches to his neckcloth earlier that evening, to simply flirt with other women. Or dance with other women. Since that was what she'd indicated she wanted. No, what would be a far more fitting revenge would be to challenge her and force her to choose. The rules governing the behaviour of young ladies were incredibly strict. If she refused to dance with a perfectly eligible man, then she could not dance with anyone else for the rest of the ball. Which would put her in bad odour with her aunt.

He'd been hoping to pitch her into a maelstrom somewhere between the devil and the deep blue sea. And now he felt cheated. How was he going to plague the life out of her if he couldn't even find her?

'Now that her own mother is in Town,' Lady Tarbrook said, with what looked like a forced smile, 'naturally she will be taking her about.'

'Yes, I noticed that she wasn't sitting with you. But surely you must have some idea whether she will be attending tonight? Did she not say?'

'I should perhaps explain,' she'd said, her smile growing even more strained, 'that my sister and niece have removed to Stone House. So I am no longer aware of what their plans may be.'

That all sounded plausible. And yet there was a touch of desperation lurking in Lady Tarbrook's eyes which convinced him she was not telling him the complete truth. And he recalled the way Harriet's uncle had called her out of the drawing room, with a face like an offended prune, for the purpose of giving her a trimming, if all the shouting he'd subsequently heard was any indication.

Whatever had the little minx been up to? Well, if she could sneak out of the house alone, at dawn, to indulge in an orgy of forbidden galloping, what other crimes might she not have contrived to commit?

He bowed over Lady Tarbrook's hand, murmuring all that was necessary to convince her that he accepted her version of events at face value. But inside he was whistling a jaunty air as he quit the ballroom, which no longer contained anything to hold his interest. He couldn't wait to find out what she'd done to provoke her uncle to wash his sanctimonious hands of her. Because that, he suspected, was what the old rascal had done.

So, next morning, early, he headed north towards Grosvenor Square where Archie was currently putting up with Zeus—probably in more ways than one.

'And to what,' said Zeus, laconically, 'do we owe the pleasure of your company?'

'I've come to collect Archie,' he said, with complete honesty. 'He said he wanted to call upon Lady Balderstone. The famous lady scientist.'

Zeus had, predictably, pulled a face and claimed a prior commitment. So it was only he and Archie who set off, on foot, for St James's Square a few minutes later.

'Now, you just give the butler your name and tell him you met her ladyship at that lecture we went to, and that she asked you to call whenever you liked.'

'B-but she didn't...'

'She meant to. I could tell from the way she was talking to you that she'd be glad to welcome you into her house whenever you chose to pay a visit.'

With any luck, she'd be so excited to hear Archie's name that she wouldn't bother enquiring who his friend was. So that Jack would be able to get into the house without Harriet hearing about it. It would be like a kind of ambush.

His heart beat in anticipation throughout the short walk to Stone House. For once they'd gained admittance to the drawing room, the two scientists would naturally draw apart from any other callers, as they launched into the kind of conversation that nobody outside the scientific community would understand. They would become so engrossed in their talk that they wouldn't notice anything going on around them, short of a grenade exploding, he shouldn't wonder. Archie would, in short, provide perfect cover for his sortie upon Lady Harriet.

His plans met with a check when they mounted the front steps only to find there was no knocker on the door.

'Are you sure Lady T-Tarbrook told you they'd c-come here?' Archie stepped back from under the roomy portico to peer up at the white-stuccoed façade. 'Don't look to m-me as though anyone is in residence.'

Jack's heart sank as he followed Archie's gaze and saw that all the blinds were half-drawn.

'Are you sure she didn't m-mean they'd gone b-back to the c-country?'

'No!' He rejected the notion with every fibre of his being. She couldn't have gone back to the country. Not before he'd had a chance to…to…

His stomach turning over, Jack stepped smartly up the front steps and pounded on the door with his clenched fist.

The sound echoed through what sounded like an empty hallway beyond. And, no matter how hard he pounded, there were no answering footsteps. No sign that anyone was coming to let him in.

No sign of anyone at all.

'So that's that, then,' said Archie gloomily.

It appeared so. For some reason, Lady Balderstone had not informed Lady Tarbrook of her plans. Or Lady Tarbrook might have said Stone House, when she meant Stone Court, he supposed. In either case, the result was the same. Lady Harriet was out of his reach. He could no longer pursue her.

Worse, he might never see her again.

In brooding silence, he escorted Archie back to Grosvenor Square where they parted company. And then he wandered the streets aimlessly for some time. Though part of him wanted to go to ground somewhere, somewhere quiet where he could lick his wounds in peace. However, the part of him that had seen him through so much of his life thus far refused to even admit that he *was* wounded. It made him greet every acquaintance with a cheerful smile and crack puerile jokes, and generally behave as though he hadn't a care in the world.

That evening, his determination to prove he had no interest at all in Lady Harriet's whereabouts saw him presiding over the most riotous table at Limmer's.

'Never a dull moment since you came to Town,' said Captain Challinor, clapping him on the back. 'What say you we repair to the Guards Club? Liven them up a bit?'

With a grin, he agreed. There was nothing he'd rather do, he decided on the spur of the moment, than shake up some of the stuffy set that presided over that place. He staggered along Bruton Street arm in arm with Captain Challinor, plotting various ways he could wreak havoc on the men who'd written him off as a clown and a fool, and a wastrel.

And then they reached Berkeley Square. And there was Tarbrook House. Where Lady Harriet wasn't living any longer. Lady Harriet, who also thought he was a clown and a fool, and a wastrel, he shouldn't wonder, else why would she have rebuffed him so forcefully?

And suddenly he no longer saw the point in making a nuisance of himself with the military set. It wasn't them he wanted to…shake.

'Just remembered, something I need to do,' he said.

Captain Challinor shrugged and set off south along the square, while Jack, having glared one last time at Tarbrook House, set off in a northerly direction.

The sun was just crawling sluggishly out of a bed of purplish clouds as he entered Hyde Park. He didn't know what good it would do to come and stand by the very tree under which he'd kissed her. Before he'd even known her name. And yet that was where he found himself standing. Gazing down at the ground. Remembering the taste of her. The feel of her coming alive in his arms. The moments he'd spent with her since. The way her little face came alive after only a moment or so of his teasing. The way her eyes flashed up at him as she sent him a stinging riposte.

'You really fell for her, didn't you?'

'Good God!' He whirled round at the sound of Zeus's laconic voice, emanating not five feet from behind him. 'Did you follow me here?' He hadn't noticed anyone following him. He hadn't thought there was anyone in the park at all, apart from a couple of sleepy park-keepers, either.

He clenched his fists. This was what his aimless existence had brought him to. This state of... dulled wits that rendered him vulnerable to ambush. If this had been northern Spain, he could well be dead.

'No. I did not follow you.'

'Then what the devil are you doing prowling around the park at this hour?'

'I could well ask you the same question,' said Zeus, glancing briefly at the spot on the grass where Lucifer had deposited him. 'But in your case, there is no need, is there?' He sighed. 'It is obvious that you are…in need of a friend.'

'Is it?' Jack gave a bitter laugh. 'I have it on good authority that there is never a dull moment while I am in Town.'

'That's as may be, but that doesn't mean you don't…hurt all the same.'

Hurt? He didn't hurt. He might be a touch disappointed that this…whatever it was with Lady Harriet had been nipped in the bud. But that was *all*.

'Damn you, Zeus!' Jack struggled with the urge to take a swing at him. 'You think you know everything…'

'No. Not everything,' he said with infuriating calm. 'But I do know what I saw when you were with her. You reminded me of a twelve-year-old boy, pulling the pigtails of a girl you liked, to try to get her attention. And now she's gone, perhaps *only* now she's gone, you are having to face the fact that she meant more to you than you knew. And also that your tactics were the worst you could possibly have employed.' He turned his head to gaze across the park, as though watching someone walking along the path, though Jack couldn't see anyone through the mist. 'Because the way you made her feel about you, the last time you spoke to her, means that you have no valid excuse for following after her and admitting what is really in your heart.' He uttered a strange, bitter kind of laugh. 'Even if you were to admit it, she now regards you with such suspicion that she won't believe a word you say. Not even should you demean yourself by grovelling. All you would do would be to make a complete cake of yourself.'

What? 'It's not as bad as that. Lady Harriet—'

'Who?' Zeus raised one hand to his head. It was only at this point that Jack began to wonder if Zeus was as foxed as himself. Only thing to account for him wandering about the park at this hour.

'Oh, her,' said Zeus. 'Yes, we were speaking of Lady Harriet, were we not?'

Jack wasn't at all sure any longer.

'You know what? You don't look quite the thing. I think you should go home.'

'Home. Hah.' His face contorted into a sneer. 'A great big house, that's all it is. Not a home.'

'Nevertheless, that's where I'm going to take you,' said Jack, going up to Zeus and taking him by the arm. He'd never seen his old friend reduced to such a state. Perversely, it made him feel a touch better to see proof that Zeus wasn't invincible after all. That a woman had managed to pierce what he'd thought was unshakeable belief in himself.

That Jack wasn't alone in his misery.

* * *

Jack slept most of the next day away. Awoke with gritty eyes and a sore head, and a determination to pull himself together. He could forgive himself one night of excess. But he was never going to get so drunk that people could creep up on him unawares again. Besides, it was ludicrous to permit one failed love affair to drive him to drink in the first place. If you could even classify it *as* a love affair. He hadn't actually declared himself to Lady Harriet and been repulsed, or anything near.

It was just that Lady Harriet's disappearance, coming on top of all the other blows he'd sustained of late, had been the last straw, that was all, he told himself as he went down to his study.

He was, slowly, making inroads into the mountain of paperwork he'd inherited from his supposedly magnificent predecessor. He glanced askance at himself as he passed the mirror placed strategically close to the desk. From what he'd been able to gather, George had caused it to be hung there when his father had first started looking as though he'd been given notice to quit. He must have imagined checking his appearance in it, before admitting callers. He could just see him standing there, stroking those magnificent moustaches, and giving a final flick to his neckcloth.

Though not actually sitting behind the desk. Not to judge from the utter chaos he'd found in here when he'd first inherited.

His father had put all his effort into training his oldest son, William. That was what had gone wrong. And George had spent most of his time hunting or whoring.

Jack resisted the urge to turn the mirror to the wall before sitting down at the desk. It was a good job he'd acquired a good training in administration during his time in the army. The success of campaigns depended on officers getting through a mountain of paperwork every single day. He might not cut an impressive figure swaggering about the estates, or leading the field in a hunt, but by God he could certainly keep the paperwork in order.

After a few minutes at work, he leaned back in his chair, and yielded to the temptation to put his feet up on the desk, twirling the pen in his ink-stained fingers. Perhaps it was time to return to Shropshire and throw his weight about a bit. Show them he wasn't the timid boy who'd gone, shivering, into the army the moment he left school. The tone of correspondence he was receiving from his father's steward was certainly becoming more respectful of late. Timmins no longer expressed surprise that he actually signed and returned the most urgent documents, anyway. Perhaps he should do as Zeus suggested and go down there, and take up the reins of his new life.

Zeus.

He growled, took his feet off the desk and pulled another document from the stack awaiting his attention. He was not going to do anything because Zeus bid him do it. He would go to Shropshire when he was good and ready.

And not a moment sooner.

The next morning he woke early, thanks to the fact that he'd spent so much of the previous day sleeping and had then passed the night entirely sober. Drinking to excess had never solved anyone's problems. It only dulled the brain, so that they no longer cared so much.

However, the prospect of spending the best part of the day indoors did not appeal. And even though this was only London, rather than somewhere more scenic, he decided to go out for a walk.

He could have gone in any direction. It must have been some perverse kind of desire to punish himself that sent him to St James's Square. Where he stood gazing forlornly up at the shuttered façade of Stone House for several minutes before shaking himself and striking out towards the Strand.

He'd walked along for several minutes before it struck him that the female hurrying along, several yards ahead of him, bore a marked resemblance to Lady Harriet.

Was it just wishful thinking? Was he so far gone that he was conjuring up likenesses to her in every stray woman he saw? Or did he actually recognise that bonnet? His heart speeded up. Surely, no two women in London could possibly have the same shade of hair as that single strand which had escaped from the confines of her bonnet and was trailing over her collar? And would any other woman manage to have all the pedestrians walking in the opposite direction move so swiftly out of her path?

Though she was walking very swiftly, his legs were longer. Nor was he hampered by skirts. Yet, for a few more minutes, he simply relished the sight of her. The way her hips swayed seductively with every step she took. The determined way she was gripping her umbrella in one hand and her reticule in the other, which made a fond smile kick up the corners of his mouth. If he'd been on horseback, at that moment, he would have clapped his heels into its flanks, and yelled 'View Halloo!'

Lady Harriet was still in London. And he had a second chance. This time, knowing what it felt like to imagine a life without her in it, he was going to be more careful with her. He was not going to let her slip through his fingers again.

Chapter Seventeen

The sun came out.

Or maybe it had already been shining and Jack simply hadn't noticed it before.

It took him but a moment to dodge his way through the traffic and reach a point on the pavement past which she'd have to go. And take up a position directly in her path.

'Why, Lady Harriet,' he said, risking the cut direct. 'What a pleasure to run across you today.'

'Is it?' She looked down her nose at him and made as if to step past him. He mirrored her move, blocking her way.

'Indeed it is,' he said. Had he ever seen anything so lovely as her narrowed, furious eyes? 'I was convinced you had left Town altogether and that I would never see you again.'

'And that would have been a tragedy, naturally,' she said in withering tones.

'It would indeed,' he said, smiting his breast. 'I do not know how I would have survived the loss.'

'Oh, I'm sure you would have found some other poor unfortunate female to make the butt of your jokes.'

He almost flinched. Zeus had been correct. He had *'pulled her pigtails'* once too often.

Time to rectify his error.

'I have no interest in any other lady,' he said with complete sincerity.

She made a very strange noise, for a lady. Something between a snarl and a mew.

'Kindly step aside,' she said, in a haughty voice quite unlike her own. 'I have pressing business to attend to.'

He stepped aside. But only to fall into step beside her when she set off again.

'What do you think you are doing?'

'Escorting you.'

'I have no need of your escort.'

'Tut, tut, Lady Harriet. Have you forgotten already how unwise it is to walk about without protection?'

'No, I haven't,' she said bitterly. 'London seems to be full of men who will take advantage of females who are out on their own.'

'Then what are you doing repeating your error? I took you for an intelligent female.'

'It is not a question of intelligence, but necessity. I no longer possess a footman and maid I can spare to traipse round after me when I'm out doing errands.'

'Indeed?' He looked down at her in concern. 'Has some misfortune befallen you? May I be of assistance in any way?'

'You?' She laughed.

He clenched his jaw on what had felt like a direct hit.

'You may think of me as a fool, but I can assure you, Lady Harriet, I am no such thing—'

'I don't think you are a fool,' she interrupted. He would have felt pleased to hear her say that, except that he had a feeling she had something else equally derogatory to say instead.

'You are too full of cunning and trickery to ever be mistaken for a fool.'

'Trickery? Whatever can you mean?'

'Oh, don't give me that. You told me yourself you are playing some kind of devious game. So why don't you go back to it rather than following me around?'

'Because I cannot leave you to wander about the streets, without protection. Since you say you have no footman, I can very easily fulfil that function for you today.'

'I cannot believe you wish to do any such

thing. You must have better things to do with your time than…follow round after me, just to annoy me.'

He almost said that he didn't and that, anyway, annoying her was much more fun than anything else he could be doing. But though it was true, telling her that wasn't going to produce the result he wanted. So he sighed. Adopted a mournful air.

'I'm afraid not. I have nothing better to do than loiter about the taverns and clubs, drinking my days away. Or gambling my fortune away. Don't you think it is positively your duty to save me from myself? Because at least if I was affording you some protection, I couldn't be getting into any mischief, now could I?'

'What utter nonsense! Besides, I have no need of your protection. See?' She lifted her umbrella and waved it under his nose. 'If anyone should importune me, I can defend myself.'

He demonstrated that she was in error, by taking it from her hand in a move so swift that she gasped. Then scowled.

'Hmmm,' he said, smacking the handle of it against his gloved palm. 'Yes, you could indeed do someone a nasty injury with this, should they have the effrontery to accost you. And having seen how well able you are to defend yourself, even when armed only with a riding crop, I have no doubt that you would set any number of villains running for their lives. But,' he said, handing her back the umbrella with an ironic bow, 'if I am at your side, the villains would not bother you in the first place. So I will be saving you from an embarrassing and possibly unpleasant scene.'

She made the noise again and started walking a bit faster.

'May I enquire where you are going?'

'What business is it of yours?'

'None whatsoever. I am just curious. We have already passed Ackermann's, which is the only place any person of fashion might consider visiting, along here.'

'Perhaps,' she said with a good deal of resentment, 'I am going to...to an employment agency, to hire a big, burly footman and a maid who enjoys going for walks.'

'Very sensible,' he said soothingly. And then, when she did no more than dart him a look loaded with resentment, saw that it was up to him to keep the conversation going. 'You mentioned lack of staff. Does that explain why there was nobody to answer the door when I called upon you yesterday?'

'You called upon me?'

'Yes. At least, I accompanied Archie, who was wishing to talk with your mother. I had planned to smile at you across the room as you refused to speak to me, just for the pleasure of baiting you.'

'Now that I can believe.'

'Archie and I were most disappointed to find the knocker removed from the door. We assumed you had gone back to the country.'

'No. We…' Lady Harriet paused at the corner of Catherine Street, looking distinctly harassed. 'I believe the, er…employment office is just up here,' she said. 'Please, I would rather you did not come any further.'

'If I didn't know any better, I would think you were intending to visit Bow Street!' He laughed as he made the suggestion, but Lady Harriet flinched and looked downright guilty. 'Good, God! You *are* heading for Bow Street.' A feeling came over him very similar to the one that had overtaken him when he'd seen her hangdog expression on emerging from her uncle's study. A rush of concern that was this time so overwhelming that he turned and, forgetting all notions of propriety, took hold of her by both shoulders. 'Are you in some sort of trouble? Are you sure hiring a Runner is the best course of action? Have you nobody else to advise you? Dammit, what is your mother thinking of, letting you run loose in London on such an errand?'

'Mama does not know I have come,' she said,

swiping to left and right with her umbrella to re-move his hands from her shoulders.

'Yes, but the Runners? Really? Are you sure?'

She chewed on her lower lip, suddenly look-ing very unsure and very vulnerable.

'Lady Harriet, if you are in some sort of fix, you'd do much better to let me help you out of it than trying to battle on alone. I didn't get the nickname of Ulysses at school for nothing.'

She looked up at him, as though perplexed. And then her expression closed up completely. 'You will have to forgive me, but I have not the slightest idea what you are talking about. I know nothing about Ulysses except that he was some character out of Ancient Greece.'

'Oh. Right.' He scratched his nose. 'Well, Ulysses was the most wily and...er...cunning of the generals fighting in the Trojan War. But it wasn't until he was on his way back from the wars that his talent for using those two weapons, against apparently insurmountable odds, were re-ally put to the test. For instance once, according to legend, he and his men were imprisoned in a cave by a one-eyed giant.'

'A giant?'

'Yes. And every night, this giant would eat one of his men for his supper.'

'Eurgh!' said Lady Harriet.

'Yes, but then one night Ulysses got the giant drunk and while he was asleep blinded him by poking him in the eye with a sharp stick.'

'He sounds perfectly horrid,' said Lady Harriet, wrinkling her nose.

'Well, it was a desperate situation. He couldn't sit back and let that giant eat his men, one by one, could he?'

She shrugged with one shoulder. 'I suppose not.'

'Well, the giant bellowed and his brothers came to find out what was the matter, and he shouted out—oh, I should perhaps have mentioned that Ulysses had already told the giant that his name was Nemo. Which means nobody, in Latin, do you see? So when the giant shouted, *"Nobody has blinded me"*, they all thought he'd got windmills in his head, and wandered off without helping him.'

'They must have been incredibly stupid.'

'Well, big fellows often are, I've found. But back to Ulysses and his men. The giant went off out to work, as he always did each day. He was a shepherd. And being a giant, his sheep were huge. Since he was blind, he ran his hands over the back of each sheep as he let it out of the cave to make sure it was a sheep and not one of the men who were getting out. But Ulysses got his men to cling to the underside of the sheep and so they all escaped.'

Lady Harriet frowned up at him. 'So your school friends named you after a man who told lies and blinded people?'

'You are missing the point. Ulysses used his brains instead of brute force to save both his own life and that of his men. And that was what I did, when I was at school. Used my brains to escape the attention of bullies, since I was too puny to fight back.'

'Puny?' She looked up at him. Glanced at his shoulders. Back up to his face.

'No,' he admitted, completely unable to stem a flush of pride at her assessment of his physique, 'I'm not puny now. But I was the youngest, and weakest, of three brothers. And the older two got a lot of pleasure from holding me face down in the mud, or by the ankles off a bridge, or what have you.'

'How very nasty of them.'

'They were brutes,' he agreed. 'And it was through them that I learned to dodge and weave my way through life. Or, if all else failed, when cornered, to come up with enough jokes or antics that they got more amusement from making me play the clown than roasting me over a fire. But this,' he said when she gasped, 'is getting beside the point. We are not here to discuss my past, but my ability to help you out of what I suspect is a fix. And don't give me that look,' he said when she pulled her lips into a mutinous line. 'You wouldn't be going to the Runners, all on your own, if you didn't need *somebody*'s help. And see here, Lady Harriet, I served in the army for the best part of ten years, after serving my apprenticeship in dodging trouble first at home and then at Eton. I know I appear in society like a bit of a…wastrel, but you have already told me you've seen through my disguise. The disguise I adopted when I was a boy, to make bullies think I didn't care, so there was no sport to be had from tormenting me.'

'Oh, are you in torment, then?'

She looked concerned. So he decided to strike while the iron was hot.

'I was, when I thought you had left Town and I might never see you again,' he said candidly. 'However,' he continued when she blushed and frowned, and looked as though she was about to voice an objection, 'we are not speaking of me. But you. And why you feel it necessary to visit the offices of Bow Street. Which, I give leave to inform you, is not at all the sort of place a virtuous young lady should venture, even with a footman in tow.'

'It is not,' she said, shifting from one foot to the other, 'something I can tell you.'

'Then it is something that is going on within your family.'

She gasped again. Telling him he'd hit the nail on the head.

'Hmm, well, that explains Lady Tarbrook's reluctance to speak of why your mother removed you from her care.'

She screwed her mouth up into a tight, resentful line.

'I was there, too, that day Lord Tarbrook stormed into the drawing room and hauled you out, in front of all the visitors, to give you a dressing down. At least, I heard him shouting and then saw your face when you came out of his study. Although I cannot see that a rift within your family circle would warrant a trip to Bow Street. Nor how you come to be at the centre of it.'

'Will you just stop this? This is not a guessing game. It is a very serious...' She pulled herself up. To her full height. And glared at him.

'Surely you know you can trust me,' he said gently. 'After all, I kept what happened between us, in the park, a secret, did I not?'

'Only because it was to your advantage,' she said mulishly. 'If anyone had known about it, you might have had to marry me.'

'Nonsense. I have told you that I am adept at escaping tricky situations. If I hadn't wanted to marry you, no amount of threats would have prevailed. I would have found a way to wriggle out of that particular snare, you may be sure. The reason I kept your secret was because…'

She looked up at him. Right in the eye. Which made him swallow.

'You are an innocent, that's why. If anyone had heard what you'd done, they might have placed an entirely different interpretation on events. And you didn't deserve that.'

'You maintain that you were protecting me?'

'I *was* protecting you.'

She didn't look convinced. So he stepped back and folded his arms across his chest.

'Now, look here Lady Harriet. You might as well accept the fact that I am going to find out what you are about, one way or another. Either you tell me, right now. Or I will come with you right into the offices and learn what is going on when you inform one of the Runners. Which is it to be?'

Chapter Eighteen

He wasn't going to budge. She could see it in his stance, in the set of his jaw, in the determined glint in his eyes.

So why didn't Harriet feel furious? Why was she instead tempted to unburden herself? To this man, of all people? The man who'd proved he could take nothing seriously?

It was partly because, the moment she'd set out that morning, she'd fallen prey to all sorts of disturbing thoughts. What if the men at Bow Street didn't believe her? What if they did believe her, but ignored her request for discretion and blundered in, frightening the servants again? After they'd *trusted* her to do the right thing. Or, worst of all, what if they discovered it was Uncle Hugo himself who'd had the jewels copied, because of amassing huge debts, somehow? That made so much sense, since she'd never believed a man so self-absorbed could really have been *that* concerned about the servants, that she then spent several minutes agonising over the consequences, should that prove to be the case.

She foresaw Kitty's Season coming to an ignominious end. The town house having to be sold. The entire family having to retreat to the countryside, which both Kitty *and* Aunt Susan would hate. And they'd hate her, too, for bringing it all down upon their heads. Because the one thing they would not do was blame Uncle Hugo, who, although it was his fault, had been taking steps to secure their future before anyone found out—

'Lady Harriet!'

She blinked out of her tangled web of conjecture to see Lord Becconsall still standing in her path, arms folded, expression stern.

'It…it isn't really my tale to tell,' she said, passing her umbrella from one hand to the other. 'Oh, dear, I really don't know what to do.'

'Is there nobody you can turn to for help?'

She shook her head. Mama didn't care. Papa was too far away. And nothing but the direst emergency would induce him to come up to Town anyway, since it was a place he heartily detested.

'Lady Harriet, I am here.' He spread his hands wide. 'Both willing and able to help you, no matter what it is that is troubling you so deeply.'

He looked so sincere. For a moment the temptation to unburden herself was so strong she almost confided in him.

But then she remembered why doing any such thing would be foolish in the extreme.

'Typical,' she said. 'The only person who has taken any notice of what I planned to do today had to be you.' She jabbed him in the stomach with her umbrella for emphasis. 'The one man I cannot trust with this…business.'

He rubbed his midsection ruefully.

'Of course you can trust me Lady Harriet. I swear, on my honour—'

'Honour? Hah!'

'That I will hold whatever you tell me in the strictest confidence.'

She wanted so badly to believe him it was almost enough to make her weep with vexation.

'Do you take me for a complete idiot? When you've just boasted about your cunning and your love of telling lies in one breath, you then ask me to trust you in the next. As if it were some kind of test of my gullibility. When I know full well that you already regard me as a joke.'

'What? How on earth do you come to that conclusion? Look, I may have teased you a bit, but—'

She stamped her foot. 'Don't think you can wriggle out of this one, *Ulysses*,' she spat out. 'I heard you with my own ears.' As though she could hear with anyone else's. This was what he'd reduced her to. Stamping her foot like a toddler and talking gibberish. 'You were laughing about me with your friends. About the wager you'd made.'

'You misunderstood—'

'No, I didn't.'

'Yes, you did.' He stepped forward. Leaned close and lowered his voice. 'I've just told you how I cover up my feelings by playing the fool. And that was what I did, after you'd left the park. When all I could think about was finding you again. But I didn't want to admit to my friends how much. So I made it seem like something I didn't care about at all.'

She'd planted her hands on her hips the moment he stepped forward. And it suddenly struck her how peculiar they must look, standing toe to toe the way they were. Right in the middle of the pavement so that other pedestrians were having to weave round them, like a stream of water dividing round a pile of rocks.

If anyone her aunt knew were to see her like this…

Only that wasn't very likely. Nobody from her aunt's circle was in the habit of getting up this early, she shouldn't think. Nor would fashionable people stray to this part of Town even if they did.

'I needed to find you, Harriet,' said Lord Becconsall. 'Needed to find out if, once I was sober, you were as perfect as you'd seemed when I was foxed. That the kiss we shared was as magical as I recalled, or merely a combination of drink and a blow to the head.'

Magical? He'd thought that kiss magical as well? She could feel herself leaning into him. Gazing at his mouth.

His lying, deceitful mouth.

She pulled herself up to her full height.

'Except that you didn't.'

'Didn't what?'

'Kiss me again. Nor even attempt to. Not at any point.'

He grabbed her by the upper arms. 'I can rectify *that* error right here, right now,' he said, leaning in and looking intently at her mouth.

'In the street?' Her voice came out as an indignant squeak. And she *was* indignant. Because that wasn't what she'd meant to say. What she ought to have said. Not at all. Because questioning the venue, rather than the action, would make him think that she wanted him to kiss her. And look, see? He was leaning in even closer. If she didn't do something, right now, then he would kiss her. And he was too close already for her to be able to jab him in the stomach with her umbrella again.

All she could do was pull her upper body as far back as she could and bring her umbrella down sharply on to his foot.

It had the desired effect. His face stopped looming inexorably closer. And he winced.

But he didn't let go of her arms.

'Your umbrella isn't going to keep me off,' he growled. 'I'm not a shower of rain.'

'But if you kiss me, here, in the street, it would cause a shocking scandal. You might even end up having to marry me.' There, if anything could frighten him off, the threat of marriage should do it.

Or so she would have thought. But to her surprise, it only made him smile, in a rather grim sort of way.

'At least if we were to marry I'd gain the right to come to your aid when you were in trouble. And you'd never have to walk about the streets unprotected, at the mercy of every rogue and rake in Town.'

'I...' Her breath seized in her throat. He really didn't seem that concerned about the prospect of marrying her. On the contrary, it was almost as though he'd relish the opportunity of getting more involved with her. She felt something melt inside. Something that had always been wound up tight, and hard, in the very centre of her being.

'It is a bit extreme,' she said breathily, 'don't you think? Marrying me, just to find out...what the difficulty is that I'm trying to solve?'

'That wouldn't be the only reason.'

'Oh?' The melty feeling expanded. Fluttered. Almost took on the shape of hope trying to spread its wings. 'What...what other reasons could there possibly be?' Her heart began to beat really fast.

'When I thought you'd left Town, when I thought I'd never see you again...' His hands were no longer gripping her hard. They were sliding up and down her arms in a positively caressing manner. 'I realised something.'

'Did you?'

'Yes, I—'

At that moment, a hawker carrying a massive pile of wicker baskets jostled them as he failed to find enough room on the pavement to avoid them, knocking Lord Becconsall's hat askew. Lord Becconsall scowled at him. Then straightened his hat. Then looked down at her as though he couldn't quite recall what he'd been about to say.

'This is not the place for this kind of discussion,' he said. With such a look in his eye that Harriet's burgeoning hope withered and died on the spot.

'Devil take it,' he snarled. Making her sure that he regretted all the soft words. All the hints that marrying her might not be such a dreadful fate after all.

'Where can a man and a woman go to discuss matters of this sort, without an audience?'

As he scowled at the ever-increasing stream of pedestrians going about their business, Harriet's spirits revived. Because he wanted to talk to her some more. About marriage.

'I know,' he said, seizing her hand and setting off back in the direction from which they'd come.

'Where are you taking me?' And why wasn't she putting up the slightest bit of a struggle?

'A coffee house,' he said, as he plunged down a side street. 'I know it isn't exactly the right place for a respectable young lady to go, on her own, with a young man. But can you imagine what would happen if we were to head for somewhere like Gunther's?'

She shuddered. Gunther's was practically on

Aunt Susan's doorstep. Plenty of society people went in there. Possibly even at this hour of the day. Someone would be bound to see them and carry the tale back to her aunt. And make it sound as scurrilous as they could, while they were at it.

'It isn't all that far,' said Lord Becconsall. 'But I suggest that you use the time until then thinking about how much you wish to tell me about your problem.'

Her problem? So…he wasn't taking her somewhere out of the way so he could speak to her about marriage?

Of course he wasn't. Foolish, hopeless, Harriet. He just couldn't stand being kept in the dark over a mystery.

'What,' she said with a touch of resentment, 'if I decide not to tell you anything about it?'

'Then I shall at least have had the pleasure of escorting you along the street and spending time with you, tête-à-tête, in a dark and private nook. But I give you fair warning…' He darted her a look loaded with laughter. 'Now that I know you are in some sort of trouble I shall be dogging your footsteps.'

'Must you?'

'I must. I would never forgive myself, you see, if any harm were to befall you.'

Something warm unfurled inside Harriet once more. Because nobody had ever cared enough to even say that they'd be unable to forgive themselves if something bad happened to her, even if they didn't really mean it.

He towed her across the narrow street and down an even narrower alley, before ducking into the doorway of an oak-beamed building that looked as though it really ought to have fallen down just after the Great Fire.

A couple of men were sitting at tables by the street windows, poring intently over newspapers. It was too dark, further in, for anyone to be able to see clearly enough to read. The place smelled of a mixture of roasting coffee, and stale tobacco smoke, and, strangely enough, something that reminded her of her father's hacking jacket when he'd been out in the rain.

Lord Becconsall strode without hesitation to a table stationed just behind one of the massive, blackened, oak pillars holding up the sooty ceiling.

'Now,' he said, removing his gloves and tossing them on to the table. 'Are you going to tell me how I can employ my low cunning to solve the problem you were considering taking to the Runners?'

She supposed she ought not to feel so disappointed that he looked so eager to talk about that, rather than continuing with the other thread of their conversation. The one that dealt with magical kisses and the world being empty when he thought she'd left Town. Or at least, that was what she hoped he'd been about to say before the basket seller had jostled him.

'It's not really my story to tell,' she began, leaning her umbrella against the table rim and laying her reticule in her lap.

He gave her a look that she thought might have been full of respect. Unless it was just yet more wishful thinking. Or a shadow flitting across his face from when the waiter had gone hurrying past.

'I tell you what,' he said, tilting his hat back to a ridiculous angle. 'Why don't you tell it to me as though it was…a story you have read in a book?'

'A what?'

'You do know what books are, don't you? Small square things, made of paper—'

She kicked him under the table.

He flinched, laughing. 'Come on. I've told you a legend from Ancient Greece. You could at least repay me by telling me a…fairy tale I've never heard before. And then, if anyone was to ask you what we were talking about all morning—if anyone should find out we've been together—you can tell them, with all honesty, that we told each other our favourite nursery tales. Because I have to say, Lady Harriet, that you don't look to me as though you are much good at telling lies.'

'I am not,' she said, lifting her chin.

'There you go, then.'

She sighed. Even now he was thinking of ways to explain away their meeting, ways that would get him out of a tight spot.

'My word, you are tricky,' she said resentfully. 'The inside of your head must be so tangled up with the intricate strategies you have to employ, just to get through a single day, that it must be like a nest of rats' tails.'

He made no reply to that. Because the waiter came over to take their order.

Even though she was sure the fellow couldn't possibly know her, Harriet ducked her head under the pretext of rummaging for something in her reticule. And didn't lift it again until he'd gone.

At which point Lord Becconsall cleared his throat.

'At the very least, if you tell the whole tale out loud, it might help you to get your thoughts clear and then you might know what line to take. Because at the moment, I have to say, you do not look at all as though you do.'

Which was perfectly true.

And anyway, she'd already pretty much made up her mind to tell him as much as she could. And his suggestion of presenting the facts as though they were a story out of a book was the perfect way of unburdening herself without actually breaking any of the promises she'd made about not speaking at all.

'And...and you will not tell anyone what I have told you?'

'I shall not.'

She wasn't sure whether it was because of the expression in his eyes, or simply because she so badly needed to confide in someone, but anyway, she decided to give him a chance. She was never going to find out if she could trust him, unless she took a leap of faith, was she? And if he did let her down, then at least she'd know she'd *tried*.

Chapter Nineteen

'Once upon a time...'

His face, never far from laughter, lit up as though she'd just given him a precious gift. 'Thank you,' he said. And then, after a glance round the murky room, as though to check whether anyone was attempting to eavesdrop, said in a louder voice, 'That's how all the best stories start.'

'There was a...a princess,' she continued, slowly removing her gloves. 'Who was going to a ball, where she was to choose a handsome prince to marry.'

'Did it have to be a prince?'

'I beg your pardon?'

'Couldn't it have been someone of more humble origin? A...viscount, say?'

'Absolutely not. Her father would not want her to marry anyone who wasn't of royal blood.'

His smile dimmed. He frowned at her hands.

'I had no idea he was so high in the instep.'

'Stop interrupting. Anyway, as I was saying, she was going to this ball and wanted to wear her finest jewels. Only when her father went to the… er…royal vault to fetch them, he discovered that they had been stolen. And glass beads left in the place where they were kept.'

'They'd been copied?'

'Yes. And the King was furious. So furious that he forbade anyone to speak of it, on pain of death.'

'That was a bit harsh.'

'He was a tyrant,' she said with feeling. 'I believe kings in fairy tales often are.'

Harriet had to pause in her narrative at that point since the waiter returned with their order and spent some time setting out the pots and cups on the surprisingly clean table.

Once he'd gone, Lord Becconsall leaned forward and murmured, 'Go on. I have a notion you are just getting to the interesting part.'

'Well, I don't know that it was more interesting than having the rubies switched for glass beads. But anyway, the King decided that it must have been the Queen who was guilty and had her put in the pillory! Which, of course, made the Princess very unhappy. And angered some of the courtiers, who loved the Queen and didn't like to see her humiliated in that fashion. So, anyway, one of them, who owed the Queen a very great debt,' she said, lowering her gaze and fiddling with the strings of her reticule, 'decided she would find out who had really stolen the rubies, so she could clear the Queen's name. The King was furious.' She glanced back up at Lord Becconsall. 'When he found out she had been asking questions, first of all he locked her in her room—'

Lord Becconsall stiffened. 'Locked you—I mean, her, in her room? How could he?'

'I did say he was a tyrant.'

'Yes, but—'

'And it wasn't as bad as all that. She only missed one meal. And the Queen brought her some books and things to read. And, actually, it did some good, you know, because it won her some favour with the servants. I mean,' she hastily corrected herself, 'the other courtiers. And it made them all want to help her clear the Queen's name.

'But then, when he found out that people were starting to flout his orders he—the King—um… banished her from court, and sent her to…er… Well, anyway, she found a place where she was safe from the King's wrath. Only…she still wanted to find out who had stolen those jewels, so she thought she'd hire some…er…'

'Wizards?' said Lord Becconsall, helpfully.

'Well, she did think they might be sort of magicians,' she admitted, thinking about the reputation of the Bow Street Runners. 'Only she wasn't sure if she could trust them. And she was a bit...' She lifted her spoon and stirred her chocolate, which Lord Becconsall had ordered for her. And how he'd managed to correctly guess exactly what she'd wanted, without even asking, was beyond her. 'A bit afraid of them, to be honest,' she admitted, fumbling her spoon into her saucer with a clatter.

'Well, those wizards probably lived in an enchanted forest, into which it was perilous to enter.'

'Yes, it was,' she said, grateful that he'd understood.

'What she needed was to find a soldier.'

'Did she?'

'Yes.' He reached across the table and laid his hand on top of the one that had just been occupied with her spoon. 'You know very often in those kinds of stories, the Princess comes across a ragged soldier, who turns out to be able to complete the quest on her behalf.'

'She isn't a princess,' Harriet pointed out.

'She looks like one to the raggedy soldier,' he said, running his fingers over the back of her knuckles.

Harriet flushed. All the way to her toes. It was a very strange feeling, having a man's bare hand caress her own bare hand. She couldn't think why it should be so, but it was having almost as much effect upon her as being held in his arms had done. 'Are we still talking about the…the story?'

'Do you want us to be?'

To her surprise, she rather did. It was far easier to talk about that, than what his light touch was doing to her insides. To admit she wished he would kiss her, the way he'd kissed her that morning. Besides, now that she'd started to tell him about the missing rubies, and what had been happening since she'd decided to find out where they'd gone, it was as though a great weight was sliding from her shoulders. And telling it half-concealed in the language of fairy tales was making it easier still.

However, her life was not a fairy tale. And if she wanted to get anywhere with her investigation, she was going to need practical help, not the laughing eyes of a born flirt distracting her from her purpose.

She pulled her hand out from under his and tucked it safely in her lap.

Lord Becconsall let her do so, but pushed his cup to one side, laid both elbows on the table, and leaned as far across the table as he could.

'Do you—I mean did the lady who was loyal to the Queen have any clues, perchance? It would make the soldier's quest much easier if she could give him, say, a map...'

'And a bottle of magic potion with which to send the dragons to sleep?'

Lord Becconsall chuckled. 'Just a map would be a start. With a map, and his own cunning, I reckon that soldier could find out who'd taken the jewels.'

'Oh, you do, do you? You are very sure of yourself.'

He quirked one eyebrow at her.

'I meant to say, of course, the soldier was very sure of himself. But, as it happens, I do have—I mean to say, the lady did have one clue, given to her by...the keeper of the royal vault.'

She couldn't have said that he moved, exactly, but something came over him. A sort of watchfulness. As though he was fully alert to whatever she might say next.

'Go on,' he said, when she paused.

'Yes, just as I, that is *she*, the courtier, was leaving the castle, the...um...keeper of the vault managed to whisper a name in her ear. It was the name of a person who had worked, for a very brief time, in the Queen's own chamber. And the name of the village from whence she came. And actually,' she said, putting her hand to the reticule in which she'd put the paper on which she'd written down everything Maud had told her, 'the name of the person who'd given her the reference to get the job in the first place. I would have thought, wouldn't you, that the person who'd sent Jenny to work for…um…the Queen, would be the one who now had the jewels, wouldn't you? The only problem is…'

'Is?'

'Well, she appears to be beyond reproach. I've already asked, discreetly, what kind of person she is,' she said, forgetting to hide the events behind the cloak of her fairy tale, 'and according to Mama she is an elderly recluse.'

'Don't you mean, a witch living in the centre of an enchanted forest?'

'No,' she said irritably. 'I can't keep up with all these fairy-tale analogies. And besides, haven't we already had an enchanted forest in this story?'

He chuckled. 'Indeed we have. So, would you prefer to let me give you time to think up a more original scenario? Or…'

'Or?'

'Or would you rather just forget all about kings and wizards and enchanted forests, and just tell me what is really going on?'

She sighed. 'I suppose I might as well. You've probably already worked out who the major characters in the story are.'

'They weren't exactly in heavy disguise.'

'No, well, I've never had to try to make my life sound like some kind of fairy tale before. And you didn't exactly give me much time to do so, did you? So...' She shrugged. 'Do you think you might be able to help me?'

'I'm sure I shall,' he said, boldly taking hold of both her hands this time. For a moment, she experienced a very strong urge to turn them over and cling to him. And never let go.

Which would be really stupid. She hardly knew him. And what she did know didn't encourage her to put her faith in him. Not in *that* way.

Oh, she could easily believe that he was intrigued by the notion of investigating a crime. His mind was so devious, and he had so little else to do, that she could see him finding unravelling what had gone on in Tarbrook House as entertaining as most people would find...doing an acrostic, say.

But as for truly wishing to marry her? No, she couldn't believe in that. He hadn't mentioned it at all once she'd got started on the mystery of the fake rubies. And so for the second time, she slid her hands out from beneath his and placed them on her lap.

He gave a wry smile. 'It's too soon, isn't it? I need to prove my worth. Demonstrate that I'm not just a cunning trickster, but a man upon whom you can depend. Will you permit me to do that, Harriet? Will you entrust me with this… quest?'

All of a sudden she felt breathless. Almost as though she'd been running. Because his words had answered her doubts with such uncanny accuracy. And it would help her to believe he was in earnest about her, if she allowed him to deal with the mystery of the missing rubies.

'Yes,' she admitted. 'I think… I rather think I will.'

His smile lit up his whole face. 'And you will tell me everything you've discovered now? In plain English?'

She nodded. Found she had to lower her head for just a second or two, because his delight was almost too much for her to resist. Only once she'd overcome the urge to grin back at him, like a besotted tavern wench when one of her striking brothers strode into view, did she raise her head and look at him again.

'Just before I left my uncle's house,' she said, 'one of the maids came to me and told me who the servants suspected had been the culprit. Although, I have to say, it would be very hard on that girl to have a Bow Street Runner set on her, if the worst she was guilty of was being rather shy and not very talkative. Or if she left service because she had an…ailing mother, or something of the sort.'

'There, you see? Hiring a Bow Street Runner would be the very worst thing to do. I can be far more discreet. I can go and investigate this servant's movements under pretext of…um, well of course that depends where she lives.'

'Well, the reference she gave says she comes from a village called Bogholt, which is in Norfolk.'

'Never heard of it. But I can soon locate it, if it exists.'

'Oh, it exists. I found it on the map. Though it took hours and hours.' But that was one of the benefits of not having to go to balls and pay morning calls or go shopping for fripperies she didn't need. It left her hours and hours and *hours* free to pore over maps. 'It is a tiny hamlet in Thetford Forest.'

'Thetford? Well, then, all I have to do is say I'm going to Newmarket for the races, next time there's a meet, and spend a day or so poking around in Thetford Forest to see what I can dig up. And there's no need to frown at me like that. I know how to reconnoitre behind enemy lines. Nobody will guess why I'm there, or what I'm about.'

'Then I fail to see how you will find out anything at all.'

'You do not need to see. Nor do I want you to see, because it will necessitate employing all sorts of underhanded methods which would no doubt give you a disgust of me. Which would rather defeat the object.'

'Would it?'

'You know it would,' he said with such a heated look that Harriet took refuge in taking a sip of her rapidly cooling chocolate.

'Now, you said you wanted to investigate the person who wrote the reference as well? But that you changed your mind, because she is beyond reproach.'

'So Mama informed me,' said Harriet, setting down her cup now that they were safely back to discussing crime, rather than his intention to impress her. 'The lady is, or was, at least, very well known at one time, although lately she seems to have become something of a recluse.'

'And where has she become a recluse? Somewhere in Norfolk, I take it?'

'No.' And then she gasped at what Lord Becconsall was implying. Just by looking at her in a particular manner. 'Dorset.'

He leaned back in his chair and grinned.

'So, how on earth did this shy little maidservant from a hamlet buried in the Forest of Thetford get a reference from an elderly recluse from Dorset?'

'I... I suppose there could be a perfectly innocent explanation...'

'You don't believe that any more than I do. No, what we need to do,' he said, sitting forward, placing both elbows on the table and clasping his hands over his coffee cup, 'is to look into that connection.'

'But that will take for ever!'

'Is time of the essence?'

'Yes. Because I have no idea how long Mama plans to stay in London. And once we go back to Stone Court I won't be able to...' She waved her hands in his direction. Then at herself.

'To direct operations,' he finished for her.

'Yes. That,' she agreed. Because there was no way she was going to admit she'd been about to say she'd no longer be able to meet with him like this. That there were no handy little coffee houses in Donnywich where nobody knew who she was. There was only the Black Swan. Into which she never ventured. And would never be able to come up with a plausible excuse for suddenly doing so to meet up with what they'd consider a fine London beau. For that's what they would think of Lord Becconsall, if he strolled into the public bar, dressed in the beautifully tailored, highly fashionable kind of outfit he was wearing today.

Actually, there was no plausible excuse for her to be sitting with him here, either, without any chaperon at all. If anyone she knew were to walk in and see her leaning over the table to hold a conversation with a man to whom she was not related, in heated whispers, they'd be bound to draw the worst conclusion.

She sat back, blushing. Lord Becconsall barely seemed to notice. He was frowning off into the distance, as though his mind was already fully occupied with the conundrum she'd set him, rather than proprieties.

'There's nothing for it,' he said after a moment or two, during which Harriet's levels of guilt grew to such a pitch that she couldn't help looking over her shoulder just in case one of the other customers might be someone she knew. 'We'll have to call in reinforcements.'

'What?'

'Get someone else to go to Dorset, while I'm prowling round Thetford Forest.'

'But you promised you wouldn't tell anyone!'

'I did. And I won't tell anyone without your permission. But you have to face facts, Lady Harriet. If you'd gone to Bow Street, you would have had to tell your tale to a lot of people. The mission might have been shared between many operatives, none of whom you would have known. Whereas if I enlist a couple of my friends, you may be sure they would handle your predicament with the utmost tact and discretion.'

'Your friends?' A solid lump of ice formed in her stomach as she saw what he intended. 'You mean, I take it, the ones I met in the park that morning?'

'That's it, you see—'

'The ones who have already made me the subject of a wager?'

'Ah.'

'Yes. Ah, indeed! If you think I am going to have them…interfering in my family business, after they've already made a…game of me…then I…' She got to her feet. Snatched up her gloves. Then her umbrella. 'This was a mistake. I should never have confided in you.' The moment she'd started to trust him, to believe he meant what he'd said, he'd shown his true colours. He saw nothing wrong with breaking a promise if it was expedient to do so. He saw nothing wrong with sharing what she'd told him, in the strictest confidence, with a group of men he must know were the very last people in the world she wished to know anything about her business at all.

'Lady Harriet—'

'Good day to you,' she said, turning on her heel and marching out of the shop.

Leaving him to pick up the bill.

Chapter Twenty

She hated him. Eight hours it had been since she'd stormed out of the coffee house and stalked home, alone, and during that time her initial hurt and mistrust had steadily grown to the point where it felt as if it was going to burst from her very fingertips in sheets of flame.

She wasn't quite sure how she managed to lay down her knife and fork so neatly across her plate when she'd finished eating dinner, rather than fling the plate across the room just for the pleasure of hearing breaking crockery, or stabbing the fork into the table so hard it stood upright, quivering.

'You are quite sure you do not wish to come with me, Harriet?'

Harriet met her mother's enquiry with a cold stare. There was nothing Mama wished for less than for her to suddenly change her mind and say that, yes, actually, she would love to come to the meeting at wherever it was to discuss whatever it was that had Mama so full of anticipation that she could hardly wait to get out the door. The very last thing Mama wanted was an unmarried daughter trailing round behind her, or worse, sitting in a secluded corner where she'd be at the mercy of every importunate rake—if indeed rakes attended meetings where scientists gathered to discuss the latest findings. Mama was just not cut out to take on the onerous duties of chaperon.

She patted her mouth with her napkin before putting Mama out of her misery by saying, 'No, thank you, Mama.'

True to form, Mama smiled at her in undisguised relief as she got to her feet and scurried across the room, leaving Harriet to thank Mrs Smethurst for providing the meal when the elderly woman eventually shuffled in to clear the table.

Mrs Smethurst grunted something that Harriet didn't quite catch above the noise of cutlery scraping and dishes rattling, but it didn't sound any more cheerful than Harriet felt.

She drifted out of the room, across the hall and into the drawing room, though why on earth she'd done so she couldn't imagine. The furniture was still shrouded in holland covers, and the grate stood empty. As empty as she'd felt when, contrary to all his protestations, Lord Becconsall had not pursued her from the coffee house. Not that she'd wanted him to. It was just that, if he'd been sincere, he would surely have attempted to explain. Or apologise. But, no. He hadn't. Which meant he didn't care about her. Not really.

He cared about his friends, though. So much that he'd attempted to conceal his interest in her from them by making it all out to be some kind of joke.

She rubbed her arms vigorously. If only she'd actually gone to an employment bureau this morning, while she'd been out, she might at least have been able to hire someone to light a few fires about the place. Though how hard could it be? The scullery maid who'd performed that office at Stone Court had been very young. As had the girl who'd come in to her room first thing at Tarbrook House. And right at the bottom of the hierarchy. If lighting a fire was such a menial task, she ought to be able to learn how to do it.

She went to the grate, gave the pile of dusty kindling and the empty coal scuttle a brief inspection, before deciding to go up to her room instead. There had been a fire in there earlier on, so that it wouldn't be so damp and smell so musty as it did down here. It wasn't as if she was expecting to receive visitors at this time of night. She could plan out her next move just as well at her dressing table, or curled up on her bed.

As she made her way up the stairs, she gave herself a stern talking-to. Running into Lord Becconsall earlier might have ended up being an infuriating and humiliating experience, but talking things through with him had given her a few ideas. To start with, if he could go to Thetford and make enquiries, then why shouldn't she? She could saddle her horse and...

Actually, no, she couldn't. Shadow was still stabled in the mews behind Tarbrook House. Uncle Hugo had drawn the line at condemning an innocent horse to potential neglect when he'd washed his hands of his female relatives. And she couldn't see him, or his head groom, releasing her mare to her without first making sure the animal was going to be properly cared for.

Besides, a girl couldn't turn up in a remote village, on horseback, without attendants, and expect locals to answer her questions in a helpful, or even respectful, manner. They'd think she was not a respectable person.

She strode to her bed and picked up the shawl she'd left lying there. Bother the rules that restricted the movements of females! Even a married woman couldn't get away with jumping on a horse and taking off like that, without raising eyebrows.

She wrapped the shawl round her shoulders and went to sit at her dressing table. Very well, it wouldn't be feasible to go to Thetford. But there was nothing to prevent her going to pay a visit to an elderly, female recluse, was there? She just had to come up with some pretext for the visit. To that end, she was going to have to—

At that point, her thoughts were interrupted by the sound of someone knocking on her bedroom door. Puzzled, she went to open it to see Mr Smethurst standing there, looking most put out.

'You have visitors, my lady,' he said accusingly.

'Visitors? I didn't hear anyone knock on the front door.'

'They didn't. Come round the back, they did,' he said indignantly, 'and was inside before I could rightly stop 'em.'

Once again Harriet felt guilty for not seeing to the hiring of extra staff to help the elderly couple who had been living here as caretakers. Especially as Mama had warned her, on the way here, that it was going to be her responsibility to see to the running of the house.

'Now, I am not going to berate you for falling

foul of Hugo,' she'd said. 'For what woman of spirit could fail to irritate a man with his tyrannical disposition? But you must see that though I support your stand against him, you cannot expect me to suddenly become domesticated. I had no intention of opening up Stone House when I came to London. And getting us thrown out of my sister's house is most inconvenient. You do see?'

'Yes, Mama,' she'd said meekly. And had vowed to see to everything. But first she'd spent those hours poring over maps to find out where Bogholt was and then had decided to visit Bow Street before the employment bureau. And finally, she'd been ambushed by Lord Becconsall. Which had left her so angry that she'd been in no fit state to do anything of a practical nature for the rest of the day.

With the result that she had no trained butler to deal with unexpected visitors, nor a burly footman to evict the kind that barged right in.

'Never mind, Smethurst,' she said. 'I'm sure you did your best.' Poor Mr Smethurst was only supposed to have the light duties of forwarding the mail and reporting to her father should the roof develop a leak, or something of that nature.

His expression became less troubled. 'Put 'em in the drawing room,' he said with a hint of malice. 'Told 'em it would be warmer in the kitchen, but they insisted they wanted somewhere more fitting.'

'You did quite right,' she said, thinking of the empty grate and the holland covers and the general air of disuse. They were not in a fit state to receive callers and if people insisted on coming in then it served them right.

'Who are they?'

Mr Smethurst looked blank.

'Didn't give no names.'

'Did they not give you their cards, either?'

He shook his head.

'Well, I'd better go and see what they want, I suppose. And…and you don't know who they are?'

He shook his head again.

She couldn't imagine what type of person would call at this hour of the night, unless it was someone looking for Mama. Oh, dear. She hadn't been paying very much attention earlier. Had she gone to the Institute of Enquiry into the Natural Sciences, or the Scientific Society of the… something else? The trouble with Mama's societies was that they all had names that used virtually the same words but in different orders. She was going to have to beg everyone's pardon and confess that she had no real idea where Mama was this evening, and invite them to return on another day. By which time she would have made the drawing room a bit more habitable. She descended the stairs with the sense of dread that always went before a potentially humiliating encounter, squared her shoulders as she crossed the hall and opened the door of the drawing room with her chin up.

Only to halt on the threshold in astonishment. For the callers who'd broken with convention by ignoring the lack of the knocker, going round to the back of the house and pushing past poor defenceless Mr Smethurst were none other than Lord Becconsall, Lord Rawcliffe, Captain Bretherton and Mr Kellett.

She might have known it. They were just the sort of men to dispense with decent manners and do exactly as they pleased.

'Very well, Mr Smethurst,' she said to the faithful man, who was still hovering nervously behind her. 'I can deal with this.' Looking relieved, Mr Smethurst turned away and ambled off in the direction of his nice warm kitchen.

Harriet stepped into the drawing room and shut the door behind her.

'You really ought not to be here at all, the four of you, not at this time of the evening,' she said.

'Yes, we know the proper time for paying calls

is far earlier in the day,' said Lord Becconsall, 'but this is not exactly a social call, is it?'

And they were here now. And she couldn't very well throw them all out.

Besides, part of her was intrigued by the fact that they'd all come. That Lord Becconsall had obliged them all to come. Even though she'd told him she didn't want them involved. And had walked away from him.

She'd been angry with him all day for not being persistent, but it looked as though his notion of persistency merely differed from hers. Which shouldn't have surprised her, given the complicated way his mind seemed to work.

'Very well,' she said. Because there was just the chance that he'd come here to plead for forgiveness. And more to the point, she'd have no peace if she turned him away without a hearing. 'Say what you have to say,' she said and folded her arms across her chest.

'Could we not sit somewhere where there is a fire? It is like an icehouse in here.'

He glanced at Atlas, then back at her, with a pleading expression.

'It is entirely your own fault. You would insist on coming in here.'

'Then it is clearly up to us to make the place more habitable,' said Lord Becconsall, going over to the fireplace, kneeling down, pulling a tinder box from a pocket and setting about lighting the fire.

'May I?' Captain Bretherton didn't await her reply before yanking the covers off a couple of chairs, rolling them up and tossing them into a corner.

Lord Rawcliffe prodded the upholstery of one of the uncovered chairs with the silver ferrule of his cane.

'Lord Becconsall informs us that we owe you an apology,' he said, turning to the other chair that Captain Bretherton had uncovered and giving it similar treatment. 'Over the matter of the wager.'

'Oh.' So that was why he'd brought them here.

'Yes. He is very angry with us. We have all, naturally, sworn that none of us have spoken out of turn, but he has remained adamant that we must all tender our apologies.' He shot Lord Becconsall's back a look of resentment.

'I don't see it is the slightest bit necessary for all of you to come here,' she said, becoming aware, suddenly, that there was a good deal of tension flickering between all four men.

'No, Ulysses is right,' said Captain Bretherton, his face creasing in concern. 'If you feel we have insulted you, then we do owe you an apology.'

'*If?*' She took a couple of paces into the room. 'You jolly well did insult me. Mocked me. I overheard you laughing about me. At Miss Roke—I think it was—her ball.'

'There, you see, Becconsall?' Lord Rawcliffe turned to where he was crouched on the hearthrug, blowing on to the wisps of kindling he'd managed so far to coax into sputtering out smoke. 'It was not one of us who spoke out of turn.'

'I never said it was,' said Lord Becconsall, between puffs. 'Can't you see, that's not the point,' he said, getting to his feet and wiping his hands on his coat tails.

'Then, what is the p-point?' asked Archie, looking totally bewildered.

'The point is,' said Lord Becconsall, approaching her with his hands held out as though in supplication, 'I need you to trust them all, Lady Harriet. You need help and I have no truer, finer friends than these three men.'

'Is that some kind of joke?' She took a step back. How dare he bring them here and practically demand she spill confidential family information to them, when he'd just confirmed the fact that they'd made a joke of the last predicament they'd found her in?

'The very last people I would trust with confidential family information is a bunch of men who make sport of defenceless females...'

'Hardly defenceless,' put in Lord Rawcliffe. 'I seem to recall you gave a very good account of yourself with that riding crop.'

'Nevertheless, you none of you behaved like gentlemen.'

'I helped you remount your horse,' Captain Bretherton objected.

'And then you made me the topic of a wager!'

'You know,' Lord Rawcliffe drawled, 'I believe Ulysses only did so as a pretext for tracking you down. He has been smitten from the very first.'

'Smitten? Hah!' Harriet tossed her head. Though even as she did so, she wondered if the gesture might be lacking in conviction. Because Lord Becconsall had already told her the very same thing, in the coffee house. 'A man who is smitten,' she continued, putting every ounce of indignation into her voice that she could muster, 'does not...hold the threat of exposure over a lady's head. And torment her with her less than exemplary conduct every time he meets her.'

'He does if he is behaving with the finesse of a boy of the age of twelve, who thinks the best way to attract the attention of a girl he likes is to pull her pigtails,' said Lord Becconsall, ruefully.

Was that what he'd been doing? Oh. Come to think of it, even when she'd warned him she would not admit him to her house, nor dance with him, he hadn't given up that teasing. On the contrary, he'd shown every indication of stepping up his campaign to annoy her.

There was a beat of silence while everyone stared at him. In varying degrees of shock. Well, everyone except Lord Rawcliffe, who wore his usual knowing, and faintly mocking expression.

'While you are setting the record straight, Ulysses,' said Lord Rawcliffe in a sarcastic drawl, 'why don't you explain the nature of the wager? She may well feel differently about the whole episode if she hears what the stakes were.'

'The stakes?' Lord Becconsall frowned. 'What difference will that make? It was not the stakes, but the fact that we were, apparently, bandying her name about as though we had no respect for her that she objected to.'

Harriet's heart leapt. He really did understand the nature of his offence. *That* was why he'd brought all his friends here. He could tell how badly he'd hurt her—how they'd all hurt her by treating her so lightly—and was genuinely sorry for doing something that had left her feeling humiliated. He also knew she needed to hear them *all* apologise.

And cared enough about her to make them do it.

He had broken the invisible bonds of male camaraderie that had made her feel so excluded when she'd seen them together before. To put her feelings first. To put *her* first.

'Just tell her,' Lord Rawcliffe insisted.

Lord Becconsall turned to her, looking shame-faced. 'You have to understand, we were all rather castaway. And I was trying to...'

She pulled herself up as tall as she could and looked down her nose at him, the way Mama was in the habit of looking at Uncle Hugo. She might be on the verge of forgiving him, but she had no intention of letting him off easily. He deserved to squirm, for the misery he'd put her through. 'You were trying to?'

'Well, never mind what I was trying to do. The point is, that night was the first time all four of us had been together since our schooldays. And we...well...' He ran his fingers through his hair. 'I think it was because we all started using the nicknames we had for each other at school. It made us all sort of slip back into the roles we had then. Zeus ordering us all around as though he was a god.' He shot Lord Rawcliffe a look of resentment. 'Atlas taking the burdens of the world on his shoulders...' He glanced over to where

Atlas had just slumped into one of the chairs he'd uncovered, looking like the last man able to shoulder any kind of burden. 'And Archie...'

'They called me Archimedes because they all thought I was so much cleverer than them,' said Mr Kellett mournfully. And subsided into the other chair, next to Atlas, even though she was still standing and hadn't given anyone permission to sit down. In other men, she would consider this a display of rank bad manners. And it was. But in the case of Atlas, he looked as though, if he hadn't sat down when he did, he might have fallen down. And Archie was just typical of the sort of men Mama often consorted with, who frequently forgot about inconsequential matters like etiquette when they were all fired up with weightier matters.

'Anyway, we argued about you,' Lord Becconsall continued, having shot Archie one exasperated glance. 'I maintained you were an innocent, who had no idea you were behaving improperly. Zeus swore you were no such thing. I wanted to clear your name,' he said, holding out his hands to her again, in that gesture of appeal for understanding.

And in a way, she did understand. After all, hadn't she infuriated Uncle Hugo, by the way she'd gone about trying to clear Aunt Susan's name? She'd been clumsy, and trampled all over lots of people's feelings. With the best of intentions.

'But at the same time, I'd only just found these fellows again, after years abroad, and… and other things, and it was so…' He spread his hands wide, as though lacking the words to explain himself properly. 'I didn't want to risk losing them again by letting it descend into a real quarrel. And so…'

'He turned it into a joke,' put in Lord Rawcliffe, giving Lord Becconsall a thoughtful look. 'The way he always did when he found himself in a tight corner.'

'A joke? I was a joke, then?'

'No! Not you. The wager. The wager was the joke. I declared that the stake should be what it always had been between us. It was an attempt to remind…all of us that we shared…well…' He floundered to a halt.

'Tell her what the stake was,' Lord Rawcliffe, insisted.

'It was a cream bun,' said Lord Becconsall in a voice barely above a whisper. 'That was what we always used to stake, at school.'

'You…made my reputation the topic of a wager? The winner to be bought a cream bun?'

'Yes.' Lord Becconsall hung his head.

For a moment Harriet stared at the four of them. Lord Rawcliffe somewhat defiant, his hands clasped tightly over the silver handle of his cane. Atlas slumped on one chair, looking too fragile to get up. Archie looking at her like a spaniel who'd been threatened with a bath after rolling in the midden. And Lord Becconsall, flushed, and staring at her with a mixture of defiance and embarrassment.

'Actually, if you want the whole truth,' said Lord Rawcliffe, 'by this stage we already had one wager behind us. Regarding Lucifer, my stallion, which he'd lost spectacularly.'

Lord Becconsall sighed. 'Yes. So we raised the stakes to double or quits.'

She stared at the defiant way Lord Rawcliffe was standing, the silver-topped cane clutched in his elegant fingers. And imagined him sitting down and happily devouring not one, but two cream buns. Like a greedy little schoolboy. The image was so incongruous that she started to giggle.

'C-cream b-buns. Oh, oh, lord!'

Well, she need no longer fear any of these four men would spill her family secrets. If it ever got out that Lord Rawcliffe, who, according to Aunt Susan, was just about the most elegant, hardened, philandering, sophisticated male of his generation, had taken part in a wager to win a cream bun, at the advanced age of thirty-five or whatever he was, he would never live it down.

And he knew it.

'So, now you know my deepest, darkest shame, Lady Harriet,' said Lord Rawcliffe, 'you can have no fear of trusting us with whatever it is that Ulysses wishes us to help you with. Our lips are, perforce, sealed.'

It was as though he'd been reading her mind.

'Yes. I qu-quite see th-that.' She giggled.

'Then you will let us help you?' Lord Becconsall took a pace towards her. 'You can see that they are men you can trust, can you not? After all, they never spoke a word about what you got up to in the park.'

'How ungentlemanly of you to remind me of that,' she said, pretending to be cross.

'Lady Harriet,' he said in a pleading tone.

'Well,' she said, pretending to think about it. 'I suppose…if they can keep the scandalous affair of the cream buns a secret, then they might very well be the type of men to entrust with the solving of the mystery of the fake rubies.'

Chapter Twenty-One

'Fake rubies?' Archie sprang to his feet as though he'd been jerked by invisible strings. 'Someone in your family has discovered they've g-got fake rubies, instead of the genuine article?'

'Yes,' said Harriet.

'By G-G-G…' He shook his head and swallowed. 'S-Same thing happened to us. That is m-my mother. That is, when she inherited g-g…' He swallowed again.

Lord Becconsall went to his side. 'Take a deep breath, Archie,' he said soothingly. 'No need to get so agitated,' he continued while Archie breathed in deeply a couple of times. 'I recall you telling us that your grandmother died recently and that you then discovered something disturbing about her that none of you had ever dreamed. Is this connected to Lady Harriet's case?'

'M-might be coincidence. B-but, see, her j-jewels—at least the rubies—t-turned out to be p-paste. C-Couldn't understand why she'd want to have them c-copied. No gaming habits. No d-debts my father c-could discover.'

'Oh!' Harriet sat down on a sofa that was still covered by a dusty dustsheet. 'And now everyone in your family is trying to keep it a secret, to protect her reputation.'

'That's ab-bout the size of it.'

'That is just what has happened to my aunt. At least…' she rubbed her brow with one finger as she tried to assemble the facts in an intelligible order '…it was Lord Tarbrook who discovered the rubies had been copied. When he took them to the jewellers for cleaning and re-setting against the day when Kitty would wear them at her betrothal ball. It's a sort of family tradition, apparently. And they were in such a horridly old-fashioned setting, Kitty said, that she wasn't surprised nobody wore them except when tradition demanded it. Anyway, when the jeweller told my uncle that the rubies were paste, he immediately assumed that my aunt had got into debt and raised the money to pay it off by having the rubies secretly copied, rather than owning up. And he still believes it, even though she swears she did no such thing.'

'And he didn't try to find out the truth?' Lord

Becconsall came to sit beside her on the sofa. Lord Rawcliffe chose to remain standing.

'No. He was determined to blame Aunt Susan,' she said indignantly. 'He was as mad as fire when I started to question the servants. Although, Aunt Susan said she could understand his attitude, because, you see, when he was a boy, his mother had accused a servant of stealing some of her jewellery, falsely, as it turned out, because the missing jewels turned up. But only after the servant had been condemned and hanged.'

Captain Bretherton and Archie both muttered imprecations. Lord Rawcliffe looked grim. Lord Becconsall shook his head.

'I know, it must have been terrible for him. But—' she turned to Lord Becconsall '—that would have given him the perfect reason for claiming he didn't want any sort of investigation if he'd been the one to have them copied, wouldn't it?'

'What makes you think he might have done that?'

'Well, he did cut up rough about some of the expenses Aunt Susan was running up this Season. And complained bitterly about bringing me out alongside her own daughter. So when he went all...medieval about the whole affair, I wondered if some of the bluster wasn't a sort of smoke-screen to cover up his own guilt.'

'No, I don't think that's it,' said Lord Becconsall at once. 'For one thing, if he was the one who'd had the jewels copied, he wouldn't have needed to say anything about it, would he?'

'Oh,' said Harriet, crestfallen. 'No, I suppose not.'

'Besides, now we know of a similar thing happening within Archie's family, it sounds much more like the work of a very sophisticated, highly organised, criminal gang.'

'Does it?'

'Yes—it's almost a perfect crime, isn't it?' His face took on a tinge of admiration. 'If jewels are just stolen, someone will raise a hue and cry at once. But stealing them this way, replacing them with good copies so that the crime isn't even noticed for some considerable time, makes tracing the people responsible almost impossible.'

'Oh.' Her spirits sank. 'You mean we are not going to be able to find out who took the rubies? And clear Aunt Susan's name?'

'I didn't say it was impossible. I said *almost* impossible. But look about you, Lady Harriet. We have here in this room four of the most capable men in England, each in their own way. If anyone can unmask the criminals, we can.'

Lady Harriet looked at his three friends in turn, trying to see what he could see in them. He'd kept insisting that Captain Bretherton was strong, but his sallow complexion and slightly shaky hands told a different tale. Likewise, Mr Kellett was supposed to be the cleverest man in England, but when agitated he could scarcely utter one intelligible word. And then there was Lord Rawcliffe, who believed in himself to such a degree that his friends referred to him as Zeus.

'Well, Ulysses, where do you suggest we start?'

To Harriet's surprise, it was Lord Rawcliffe who had spoken. He'd actually asked Lord Becconsall's opinion. She glanced from Lord Rawcliffe, to Lord Becconsall, who grinned at her expression of amazement. Lord Rawcliffe sniffed.

'I didn't give him the name of Ulysses for nothing. He has the kind of quick brain just suited to this kind of task. Even at school I could tell that most of his antics were designed to disguise his real nature. So that people would underestimate him.'

At her side, Lord Becconsall shifted in his seat, as though embarrassed.

'More to the point,' said Lord Becconsall, 'I have learned a lot about the habits of criminals from the men under my command. Not all of them, but rather a lot of them had cheated the gallows by joining up. And hardly a one of them reformed. Instead, they recreated the kind of network they'd been involved with in whatever town they'd come from. And set about flouting every rule ever devised by their superiors. They would have one man doing the thieving, another one watching out, another passing the goods to a fence—that is a receiver and handler of stolen goods. There were forgers and coiners, and confidence tricksters…'

'Oh! Forgers! Do you think that reference…?'

Lord Becconsall smiled at her. 'It is possible. Very possible.'

Lord Rawcliffe coughed. 'I hate to interrupt you, but the rest of us in this room have no idea what you are talking about.'

'I beg your pardon,' said Harriet. 'It is just that the girl suspected of being the jewel thief in our household was given a reference by an elderly lady who never sets foot from her home in Dorset. And the girl herself came from Norfolk. So how could they possibly have met?'

'Not in itself conclusive evidence a forgery has been employed.'

'No, but…' She sighed in exasperation. 'I am not explaining this very clearly. You see, at first, when I started asking the servants what they knew, they all got very annoyed with me. But then, when Lord Tarbrook had me shut in my room, they began to relent.'

At her side, on the sofa, she was aware of Lord Becconsall stiffening. If it was because she'd just said Lord Tarbrook had shut her in her room, then he wasn't as bright as everyone thought, for she'd told him, by way of her story, about being shut in. She glanced at him to see he was gazing at her with what looked like admiration, though why on earth he should do any such thing, at this point in her narrative, she couldn't imagine.

'Anyway,' she continued informing the others, 'by the time he threw us out—me and Mama, that is—they were beginning to see that all I wanted was to clear Aunt Susan's name, not send one of them, wrongfully, to the gallows. And they'd all been talking amongst themselves, and remembered this girl who'd worked for Lady Tarbrook for only a few weeks, a couple of years ago.'

'Two years ago? Then…the criminals must have been running this rig—which is what they call deceiving their victims,' Lord Becconsall explained, 'for some considerable time.'

'My grandmother,' put in Archie, 'died six months ago.'

'I wonder how many other thefts there have been in the interim,' Lord Becconsall pondered. 'Because I cannot see them leaving a great gap between one operation and the next, not if the method had such a successful outcome.'

'You are assuming the theft of the Kellett rubies took place only six months ago,' pointed out Lord Rawcliffe. 'Your jewel thief may have taken them at the same time as she took the Tarbrook parure. Each theft was only discovered upon the event of an impending betrothal, or burial,' he said, as though either fate was an equally horrid one.

'Well, I don't suppose we'll ever know,' Harriet answered. 'Because nobody will talk about the copying of jewels, will they? Because they will think that it means someone in their family is concealing debts.'

'My word, but whoever thought this up must be brilliant,' said Lord Becconsall. 'First they have the jewels copied, to delay discovery, and then they relied on the people concerned bickering amongst themselves about who may be responsible, rather than reporting it as theft at all. Hiding their crime under two layers of concealment.'

'They might have been doing this for years…' breathed Harriet.

'Until you believed in the innocence of one of their victims,' said Lord Becconsall with a look in his eyes that she could not mistake this time. He really did look as though he admired her.

'Come,' he said. 'Tell us everything you have managed to discover.'

'Well, not much more than I've already told you. Maud only had the time it took us to pack my things to tell me what the servants suspected, because Lord Tarbrook wanted us out of his house almost as quickly as Mama wished to leave. Maud only managed to tell me that they became suspicious about this one particular girl because although she said she was leaving because she'd got a better place, to their knowledge she wasn't actually in service anywhere any longer.'

'The better offer might have come from a man,' Lord Rawcliffe put in.

'I suppose it might,' Harriet conceded. 'Except that even in that case, somebody would have caught sight of her, wouldn't they? Parading about the park in her new finery? And also, she wasn't very attractive. Nor flirtatious. A little mouse, was the way Maud described her. Which makes her sound like the perfect person to creep into my aunt's house and sneak out again as soon as she'd accomplished what she'd set out to do.

Oh, dear,' she added. 'I sound as if I've found her guilty already. Just because she didn't fit in with the other servants and she didn't bother to tell any of them where she intended to go when she left. For whatever reason.'

'Well, isn't that another reason not to employ Bow Street Runners? They would be more concerned about appearing to apprehend a culprit, than finding out the truth.'

Harriet sighed. 'Yes, I suppose so. I certainly want to find her and make her answer a few questions. Even if she isn't involved, directly, she might know something...'

'We shall find her, Lady Harriet,' said Lord Becconsall gently. 'But we won't apprehend her unless we are sure she is guilty. You have my word.'

'And how are we to find her,' said Lord Rawcliffe witheringly, 'when the servants claim to have no idea where she has gone?'

'Well, we could start looking in the village where she came from. It's called Bogholt—'

Lord Rawcliffe let out a bark of laughter. 'If there is really any such place I shall be very surprised.'

'Well, be surprised then,' Harriet retorted, 'because I found it on a map. Somebody there is bound to know of her, if she really came from there, because it is only a tiny hamlet. In the Forest of Thetford.'

Lord Rawcliffe inclined his head in her direction. 'I stand corrected. Please, do tell us what else you believe you know.'

Harriet glared at him. And then proceeded to tell the others what she knew.

'Her name is Jenny Wren—'

'An alias if ever I heard one,' muttered Lord Rawcliffe.

'And she was given the job on the recommendation of the Dowager Lady Buntingford.'

'Lady B-B...' Archie began.

'Buntingford,' Lord Rawcliffe finished on his behalf. 'Why, is there some special significance to that name, in your case as well?'

'Yes. She was one of Grandmama's friends. C-Came out together, wrote to each other all the time. Asked her to b-be my own mother's godmother. Lives in Lesser Peeving, now, as I recall.'

'Is that in Dorset?'

'Y-yes.'

'Then there we have a clear connection.'

'Do you seriously mean to tell me,' said Harriet in disbelief, 'that you suspect this elderly lady of persuading her former friends to employ a jewel thief in the guise of a lady's maid? So that she can…hoard them all up like some kind of elderly demented magpie?'

'Perhaps that is why she has become a recluse,' suggested Lord Rawcliffe. 'Perhaps her family have her safely locked away on one of their estates so that she cannot wander about in society embarrassing everyone by helping herself to other people's gewgaws.'

'But she is thwarting them all by sending out an experienced jewel thief in her stead? No, I don't think that will fadge,' said Lord Becconsall. 'For one thing, how did she meet the thief? If she is being kept locked away?'

'What about forgery?' said Captain Bretherton, making Harriet jump because he'd been so quiet since he'd slumped down on his chair that she'd suspected he'd dozed off. 'Probably easy enough to forge the writing of an elderly lady. I've seen men forge my own signature,' he said bitterly, 'in such a convincing manner that I was half-persuaded I'd signed the docket myself.'

'I suppose,' said Lord Becconsall, 'that if a criminal gang can employ a girl to slip into houses under the guise of a maid and make her disappear afterwards, and can think of a crime that is damn near unnoticeable, then they would be bound to have access to a forger. And a fence.'

'But that doesn't explain why it's always rubies,' said Harriet. 'I mean, I can see a demented elderly lady wanting to pile them all up, in secret. But not for a professional criminal to only steal one kind of jewels. Why didn't he go for the Tarbrook diamonds? They must be worth a lot more than that old set of rubies that hardly anyone ever wore.'

'We have no evidence that the thieves have only ever stolen rubies,' said Lord Rawcliffe. 'We only know of two cases, after all. It may be coincidence that both crimes feature rubies.'

'According to my men,' said Lord Becconsall, 'some thefts are done to order.'

'You mean,' said Harriet incredulously, 'people say, I'd like a ruby necklace, and a thief just goes out and steals one?'

'Not quite that cut and dried, but someone with a particular demand will let it be known in certain quarters that a suitable reward will be offered for the right kind of goods. That sort of thing.'

'Goodness.'

'Yes, but I think you have also given us another very good reason why this particular criminal has targeted the jewels in question. The Tarbrook diamonds are famous and popular. The rubies were not.'

'That's true. Aunt Susan kept them shut away and nobody wore them except on special occasions because they were so hideous.'

'Another layer of insurance to ensure the theft wasn't detected. The gang only stole jewels that were not going to be missed in a hurry. Though they might well have had a specific buyer in mind, all the same,' said Lord Becconsall, as though reluctant to relinquish his theory about why there were two sets of rubies that had been copied.

'It m-makes you w-wonder how a thief w-would know ab-bout them, then. If the ladies hardly ever wore them.'

There was a beat of silence. 'They do appear in several portraits, apparently,' said Harriet. 'Painted whenever one of the Tarbrook ladies became betrothed. There is one hanging in the London house, of Lord Tarbrook's sister, done many years ago. Kitty pointed it out to me to prove how hideous they were.'

'Ah! It's the same with the K-Kellett Set. Show up in p-portraits going back hundreds of years. Starting in Elizab-bethan t-times. Only reason I knew a-bout them as I've never seen my mother actually wear them. C-couldn't have done, of c-course,' he added with a frown, 'since they were in m-my g-grandmother's p-possession until she d-died.'

Lord Becconsall whistled low. 'Whoever is running this particular rig must have had access to the homes of families from the *haut ton* and seen the jewels he planned to steal depicted in portraits, since the ladies in both these cases were reluctant to actually wear them in public.'

'Or she,' pointed out Lord Rawcliffe. 'There is some merit in Lady Harriet's theory of the elderly demented magpie, in my opinion.'

Harriet would have preened had she not detected a hint of cynicism in Lord Rawcliffe's voice that made her fear he was actually mocking her.

'It would be much simpler to assume that she sent a lady's maid into the houses to steal jewels she had her eye on, rather than to have someone go to all the trouble of employing a forger to fake those references. She also knows the families intimately and would therefore have known that it would be possible to steal and copy jewels that weren't very often on show. And given the maid clear instructions as to how to go about it.'

'Oh, that's a very good point,' said Harriet, grudgingly, for she wasn't at all sure she wanted to be thinking along the same lines as Lord Rawcliffe. 'For Maud said none of the servants could see how a burglar could have got in and stolen the jewels, then replaced them with copies before anyone noticed they'd even gone missing. Which made me think that there must have been somebody who knew the family, and their habits, and all about the jewels, too.'

'It would also explain,' said Lord Becconsall, 'as you said earlier, Rawcliffe, why her family keep her shut away, nowadays, if she is in the habit of helping herself to shiny things that don't belong to her.'

'Lesser Peeving,' said Lord Rawcliffe, as though he hadn't been paying attention to the last few moments of conversation. 'Why does that place sound familiar? I am certain I can never have visited the place. But I have heard it mentioned. Somewhere.'

'It will come to you,' said Lord Becconsall. 'Probably when you are thinking about something else.'

'I feel sure you must be right,' he said in such a condescending tone that Harriet felt a bit indignant on Lord Becconsall's behalf.

'Well, then,' said Lord Becconsall, without appearing to have taken the slightest bit of offence. 'Now all we have to do is come up with a plan of campaign.' He got to his feet, as though eager to get started.

'I have already told Lady Harriet that I am willing to go to this Bogholt place to find out what I can about the servant girl,' he said, 'under pretext of attending the next meeting at New-market.'

'Do you not think it would be better,' said Lord Rawcliffe, 'if I were to do that? I attend the races regularly. Whereas you do not have the reputation of being much of a gamester.'

'Except when it comes to cream buns, apparently,' Harriet couldn't resist saying.

Lord Rawcliffe gave her a cold stare.

'I hope I am not going to regret admitting you into my confidence.'

'Never mind the cream buns,' said Lord Becconsall, planting his fists on his hips. 'We need to focus on the rubies. And finding out who took them. And I already have things all planned out in my head regarding the trip to Bogholt. I can mingle with the locals and win their trust far more easily than you, Zeus. You'll go striding in there as though you are God and set up everyone's backs, I shouldn't wonder.'

Lord Rawcliffe raised one eyebrow. 'You are seriously considering leaving Town, just when Lady Harriet is beginning to soften towards you?'

Lord Becconsall turned to look at Harriet, who

felt as if she'd just been stripped naked by that percipient remark. Which wasn't a very helpful feeling to have, just when Lord Becconsall was looking at her so intently.

For a moment, they just stood there, staring at each other. And though Harriet was blushing, she couldn't drag her eyes from Lord Becconsall's face. Because it bore such a look of wonder, and hope, that her initial feeling of vulnerability faded with each breath she took.

'I have something to prove to Lady Harriet,' said Lord Becconsall to Lord Rawcliffe, though he hadn't taken his eyes off her. 'My trip to Bogholt will be in the nature of a quest.'

'I don't think that will be necessary,' Lord Rawcliffe drawled. 'Or advisable. You would do far better to stay here and court her in form. As she deserves. Ladies, so I have found, prefer a man to be near them, dancing attendance, not haring off on ridiculous quests which they will decide you have undertaken as much for your own amusement as to impress them.'

'Is that so?' Again, although he was speaking to Lord Rawcliffe, he was looking intently at her face. 'Lady Harriet?' He took a half-step closer to her and gazed down into her face. Whatever he saw there appeared to help him come to a decision.

'You go to Bogholt, then,' he said to Lord Rawcliffe airily, 'and find out what you can. I will stay here with Lady Harriet and—'

'Give her daily reports of progress with the investigation,' said Lord Rawcliffe smoothly.

'And I will go to Lesser P-Peeving,' said Archie. 'P-pay a visit to my mother's g-godmother. See if she is hoarding rubies in her chamber p-pot, or something of that nature.'

'Or if she's taken a skilled forger into her employ,' put in Captain Bretherton, who appeared to have forgers on the brain. Not surprising if he'd had his own signature faked, she supposed. 'Do you happen to have a role mapped out for me?'

'I should think Ulysses will, in due course, be in need of a groomsman. And who better to stand up with him than you?'

Both Captain Bretherton and Lord Becconsall shot Lord Rawcliffe identical looks of indignation. And Harriet was pretty certain a similar sort of expression showed on her own face. It was all very well his friends calling him Zeus, and letting him manage their lives, but he had no right to subject her to the same kind of treatment.

'Ah. It has just come to me,' he said, as though oblivious to the hostile glances being aimed in his direction. 'Lesser Peeving. Oh, lord, how ironic,' he said with a shake of his head.

'Are you going to enlighten us?'

Lord Rawcliffe regarded the head of his cane for a moment or two. 'I do not think it has any bearing on the case. At least, I hope it does not have any bearing on the case. It is just that I happen to know of a clergyman who was sent to a parish there, a few years ago. His father is the incumbent of the parish nearest to Kelsham Park, so naturally I hear news of his offspring, from time to time.'

'Well, that's one mystery solved,' said Lord Becconsall, with heavy irony.

'Which, gentlemen, brings the proceedings here to a conclusion. I will take my leave of you, Lady Harriet,' said Lord Rawcliffe, bowing over her hand and kissing it. And darting her a look from a pair of heavy-lidded eyes that would, she was sure, have made the hearts of many society misses skip a beat.

Apart from one whose heart had already been given to another.

'Come, Atlas, Archie,' he said, jerking his head to the other two men, who immediately sprang to their feet.

Only Lord Becconsall remained exactly where he was. Even when his friends had left the room, shutting the door behind them.

And he was looking at her in such a way that

her heart began to thump against her chest. For she was alone, in a virtually empty house, with a man who was gazing at her as though he wanted to devour her.

Chapter Twenty-Two

'**Y**our hands are absolutely freezing,' said Lord Becconsall.

She looked down to discover that at some point he'd taken hold of them in his own.

He cleared his throat. 'At least the fire is beginning to put out a little heat now, along with the smoke.'

Harriet could not believe her ears. He'd led her to believe he was about to propose, but now all he could talk about was the smoking fire.

'I…we…that is…' He took a deep breath. And she suddenly perceived he was as nervous as she was. 'Hang it, you know we should not really be alone like this.'

'No.' She looked up at him shyly. 'It is highly improper.'

Whatever he saw in her face must have reassured him, for he grinned.

'What I am about to do next is even more improper,' he said. 'At least, people would say so, if they ever found out, but you were the one to point out that it was something I should have done already.'

She could tell from the burning look in his eyes that he was going to kiss her. That was what he meant. She supposed a properly brought-up young lady should have protested. Laid her hand upon his chest as he loomed closer, as though to prevent him having his way.

But Harriet hadn't been 'properly' brought up. So she clung on to his hands very tightly and lifted her face to make it easier for him to gain access to her lips.

She'd expected him to kiss her the way he'd kissed her in the park, since he'd told her he wanted to find out if it really had been as splendid as he'd thought. But instead, he gently touched his lips to hers, with what felt almost like reverence.

And yet that scarcely-there brush of his mouth sent rivers of pleasure cascading through her body all the same. And made her utter a little hum of pleasure.

'Zeus was right, wasn't he?' he said, breaking off to gaze down into her face. 'You are softening towards me.'

'If I wasn't, I'd have reached for the poker long before this,' she said, looping her arms round his neck. 'And brained you with it.'

His breath hitched. He leaned in and kissed her again, this time with more confidence, and for considerably longer. By the time he broke off, they were both breathing heavily and Harriet's heart was pounding thickly, making her blood course hotly through her veins.

'I have been longing to do that ever since that morning in the park. I have dreamed of your lips. Your hair,' he said, reaching up one hand to stroke an errant strand that had come untucked from its pins. 'The feel of you...' he breathed, sliding one arm round her waist and pulling her closer.

'It wasn't just the park, though, was it? Or the blow to the head, or—'

He stopped her mouth with another kiss. Pulled her tight to his body, so that they were melded together from breast to knee.

'It was you, Harriet...' he breathed. 'The magic all came from you. How did I get to be so lucky?' He gazed down at her as though he'd never seen anything quite so lovely.

'You mean, if you hadn't fallen off that horse at my feet...'

'No. That was just how we met. I meant that

I cannot believe I have been lucky enough to be here, with you in my arms like this, after doing everything wrong. I should have courted you, instead of teasing and tormenting you. Only...'

'Only what?'

'It was too important, that was what it was,' he said reflectively. 'If you hadn't liked me as much as I liked you, to start with, then it would have hurt. Very much.'

'Much safer to test the waters, first?'

'Something like that. God, what a coward I am.'

'No. Not you,' she said, twirling a strand of his hair between her fingers. 'You are just...a bit like me, I think. And that is why I understand the way you've behaved, better than another woman would. You have never had anyone love you very much, have you? Which has left you feeling as if perhaps you are not very lovable.'

He started. 'You feel the same way?'

She pressed her lips together in a rueful way. 'Most girls, I have observed, seem to find it easy to let men know when advances would be welcome. They have the confidence to believe that it is worthwhile giving their favourite a hint, you see. Only I always thought that if I did something like that, I would just be making a fool of myself...'

'We are a matched pair, are we not?' He gripped her hands again, as though what he was about to say was really important. 'I felt that, you know, right from the start. As though I recognised you, somehow. Does that sound very foolish?'

She shook her head. Nothing he was saying sounded foolish to her eager ears.

'I sometimes felt as though you saw me as well. The real me. The one who hides beneath all the layers of artifice and jocularity. The only other person who has ever appeared to see anything of value in me has been Zeus. It is largely because he believed in me at a time when I was at my most vulnerable that I forgive him so much else… Lord, listen to me! These are not exactly words of courtship, are they?'

'Actually, I feel as though they are,' she said. 'Because you are allowing me to see your very deepest self. The part of you that you conceal from everyone else.'

'I never want to be anything but totally honest with you, Harriet. I wish I had been from the start. That I'd laid my feelings bare and courted you properly.'

'I probably wouldn't have believed you were in earnest, anyway. I'm not exactly the kind of girl men fall in love with at first sight, am I?'

'Who has made you feel like that,' he said indignantly. 'Your aunt?'

She shook her head.

'Your uncle? Hauling you out of the drawing room in front of everyone the way he did and locking you in your room…'

'No, no, I don't care what he thinks of me.'

'Hmmph,' he said. 'So if it wasn't them, then who was it? Your mother? That's it, isn't it? I have often wondered why she isn't the one bringing you out.'

'It isn't because she thinks I'm not marriageable. It's more because—oh, dear, this isn't very easy to explain. Especially as for years and years I thought she simply didn't care about me at all.'

'Why is that?'

'Well, she has some very…er…modern ideas about educating females, apparently. But also, well, to be perfectly frank, she is one of the most self-absorbed people you are ever likely to meet. And Papa is a dear, but…'

'But?'

'Well, I'm not a boy.'

'I had noticed,' he said with a wicked grin. 'And I thank God for it.'

She blushed, but persisted. 'Yes, but you see, Papa has always had to spend a lot of time with my oldest brother, Charles.'

'His heir,' he said, with a tinge of bitterness.

'Yes, his heir.'

'And they spend all day, riding round the estates. So that he can teach him all about the land he will one day have to manage.'

'Yes. That's only natural.' She looked up into his face with concern.

'Oh, yes, it's natural, right enough. One day Charles will have to fill your father's shoes. And should something happen to him, he still has the magnificent George ready to take up the reins.'

'And also, there is William. He takes after Mama in his mania for the natural sciences. Papa is proud of him for being so intrepid—he's off in South America, hunting for plants. And Mama dotes on him, too, because of all the fascinating things he writes to her about from his travels.'

'Ah. Your father has some pride in *his* youngest son, does he?'

'Did not yours?' she asked, finally understanding the source of his bitterness as they were discussing her older brothers.

'No. I told you, did I not, that I was always regarded as the runt of the litter.'

'At least I was just…merely a girl,' said Harriet with feeling. 'And an afterthought. I always thought nobody quite knew what to do with me, but they never made me feel…'

'Oh, I think they did, though, didn't they? That is why, at bottom, we understand each other so well.'

'Oh, oh…' She pulled up short. 'I cannot keep calling you Lord Becconsall. And I absolutely will not call you Ulysses.'

He grinned. 'My name is Jack. When we are making love, you can call me that.'

'Oh, Jack.' She sighed, raising her face hopefully.

And, since he wasn't a stupid man, he did exactly as she hoped. He kissed her, long and thoroughly.

And somehow, whilst doing so, he managed to direct both of them to the sofa and get them both sitting down. And then almost lying down, with him half over her. And her hands found their way under his waistcoat. And his hands traced the shape of her legs through her thin cotton gown.

'We should stop this,' said Jack, rearing back and sucking in a ragged breath.

'Must we? I have never felt like this before. Never so good.'

'Yes, I know, but we shouldn't. Not before we are married.'

'Oh. Are we going to be married then?'

'Yes. Definitely.'

'But I thought you didn't want to get married.'

'I didn't. Not until I met you, anyway,' he growled.

'Don't you think you should ask me, then?'

'No. If I'm going to do the thing correctly, the person I should ask is your father.'

She thumped him.

He laughed.

And then he kissed her some more.

'Mmm…no…' he breathed. 'Really must stop. I was about to say something important when you distracted me.'

'*I* distracted *you*? I didn't do anything!'

'Yes, you did. You looked at me all dewy-eyed and breathed my name as though it was a prayer.'

It had felt like one.

'No, now, don't start looking at me like that again,' he said. 'I have remembered, I was going to make all sorts of promises, about mending my ways and such.'

'Oh. Do you have to?' She ran one finger round his top waistcoat button. Pushed at it, experimentally. And smiled when it popped through the buttonhole.

'Yes, I do,' he said, catching hold of her hand. 'And it isn't going to help if you start undressing me.'

'Oh, very well,' she said, lying back and rais-

ing both arms above her head, as though in surrender.

'You…' His eyes flicked down over her body,
to where their legs were tangled together in a
muddle of holland covers. 'Now, see here, Harriet, I mean to do better with my life than I have
done of late. I told you about my father not spar-
ing me a thought, didn't I? Well, what I didn't
tell you was that he wept when he knew it was
I who would take his title and not one of my far
more magnificent brothers.'

'Oh, Jack!' She stopped trying to be seductive.
Reached up and laid one palm against his cheek.
'How horrid for you.'

'Yes, well…' He shifted position slightly. So
that she could sit up. Which she did.

'And how very stupid of him,' she continued.

'What do you mean?'

'Well, for heaven's sake, you'd been a major
in the army. There is a huge amount of work to
do, running a brigade. Or so George is always
saying. Mountains of paperwork, as well as han-
dling the men under your command. And Papa
is always telling *him* that there's hardly any better training for running a large estate.'

'No wonder I love you,' he breathed. 'But,' he
said, his expression turning serious, 'it wasn't
just him. The others, the trustees and so forth,

advised me to come to Town and find a wife. As if they thought all I was good for was passing on the name to the next generation.'

'Then—oh! That's why you behaved so badly that even Aunt Susan warned me that you weren't good marriage material.'

'Did she? And yet you still lit up like a candle whenever I walked into the room.'

'Well,' she said, darting him a look from under her eyelashes, 'you'd already kissed me, hadn't you? So nothing anyone could say could influence the way you made me feel.'

His face fell again. 'Are you hinting that I should not have been influenced by what the trustees said? That I should have stayed in Shropshire and made everyone take me seriously, rather than coming to London and living down to their expectations of me?'

'No, of course not, I never meant—'

'It wasn't just that, you know. It was the memories that leapt out at me from behind every bush, every damn locked door…' He hung his head, his eyes briefly closed. 'I felt like a small, scared boy too often for my peace of mind.'

'Do you want to stay in London then, after we're married?'

He lifted his head, a grin spreading slowly across his face.

'I haven't asked you yet, you forward wench.'

'Yes, but you will do. *Eventually*,' she said drily. 'So, if you want to carry on living in London, living down to everyone's expectations, I shan't mind,' she said stoically.

'That's very noble of you, but, no. That is what I have been trying to tell you. It is high time I went and claimed my estates. Started running them the way I wish. Unless...do you prefer to stay in Town?' She could see him struggling to be generous as he made the offer. 'I know a lot of ladies like all the social whirl. The balls and picnics and such.'

'No.' She shook her head. 'I thought I would love all that sort of thing. Aunt Susan and Kitty made it sound so exciting. But I wasn't here long before I discovered that I *much* prefer the country, Jack. Which you know, really, deep down, don't you? Else why would I have been galloping about the park, at dawn, when it isn't the done thing?'

He smiled at her with evident relief.

'And while we are talking about going to your estates, and laying claim to them, may I make a suggestion?'

'Of course!' His eyes flew wide as though surprised. 'I don't want you to feel you have to tiptoe round me.'

She smiled. He clearly wasn't going to be the kind of husband who would stop her saying, or doing, whatever she wished.

'Well, when you *eventually* get round to going to visit my father and asking permission to pay your addresses to me…'

He chuckled.

'…why don't you ask him to visit your estates with you and give his advice? He lives and breathes land management. And…actually, he is very well respected in certain farming circles.'

'So…if I were to get him on my side, you mean, then I won't have any more trouble with my steward?'

She nodded, hoping he wouldn't take offence at her suggestion.

He looked thoughtful. 'Do you think he would be willing to do that? And…if he did, would he cut up rough if I were to ignore everything he said and did it my own way?'

'I think he would be delighted to have a son-in-law who had a mind of his own. He copes splendidly with Mama, after all, who very rarely agrees with *any*one. But, seriously, he would also love to go exploring round someone else's estates and give them the benefit of his own opinion. He does it all the time. The only thing is…'

'Mmm?'

'Well, if he enjoys himself too much, we might never get rid of him. I have been the one to keep Stone Court running smoothly, you see, because Mama is simply not interested.'

'So he does value you, then?'

'He certainly values my housekeeping skills. But the moment Charles marries and brings another woman in to take over my duties, he will be perfectly happy to never see me again.'

Jack frowned and looked as though he was about to say something derogatory about her father. But then he bit it back. 'Then I fervently hope Charles marries very soon, so that I may have you, and your excellent housewifely skills, all to myself.'

'That was exactly the right thing to say,' she said. 'You clever, clever man.'

'And do I deserve a reward?'

'Oh, yes,' she said. And took his dear face between her hands and kissed him, just to prove she could understand what he wanted of her as cleverly as he'd just understood her need for him not to criticise Papa.

She was just starting to gently subside beneath the pressure of his answering kiss when the door flew open, causing them to spring guiltily apart. In the doorway stood her mother, the strings of her bonnet untied and half the buttons of her coat undone.

'Harriet,' she said. 'Do you know where my set of Napier's bones may be? I know I had them in my trunk when I came to Town, but in the move from your Aunt Susan's house they seem to have gone astray.'

At her side, Jack sat frozen, as though, if he kept still enough, his presence might go unnoticed.

'And I must have them,' Mama was complaining. 'The calculations Mr Swann put up on the blackboard tonight made no sense whatever. I need to go over them again, myself.'

'I placed them in the top drawer of your desk when I unpacked, Mama,' said Harriet, surreptitiously encouraging her skirts, which seemed to have risen up her legs, back to their proper place.

'Whatever did you put them there for?'

'Well, I thought you might need them.'

'Then you should have placed them on top of my desk, not hidden them away in a drawer. Honestly, Harriet, I despair of you sometimes, I really do.' Then she turned and flounced out of the room, slamming the door behind her.

Jack made a low growling noise. 'Did she even notice that I was here?'

'Probably not. She has just come in from some talk or other that clearly has her all fired up.'

'I couldn't really believe it when you said they wouldn't miss you, but that…' he pointed to the door through which Mama had just gone. '…that does it. Even if I hadn't decided to make an honest woman of you, I'd have to marry you now.'

'Because my mother found us together in a compromising position?'

'Because the blasted woman didn't even notice. She should be taking far better care of you. But she never has done, has she?'

'No, but only think, Jack. If she'd been a strict parent, then we would never have met, would we? Because she would have taught me to behave properly and I would never have gone riding in the park.'

'Yes, there is that,' he conceded. 'But…to leave you alone in the room, with me just now. I mean, I could be anybody. I could be a…an evil seducer, intent on having my wicked way with you!'

'I was rather hoping you were.'

He gave her a stern frown. Which didn't fool her one bit, since he hadn't managed to prevent his eyes from twinkling. 'Young lady, if you cannot tell the difference between a rake who is intent only upon his own pleasure and a man who is making love to the woman he intends to marry and spend the rest of his life with, then…'

'Then?'

'Then I had better show you.'

'Ooh…' She sighed. 'Please do.'

Epilogue

'But, Harriet, I really don't understand...' Aunt Susan twisted the strings of her reticule. 'I thought you wished me to help you purchase bride clothes, not—'

'Well, yes, I do want your help with that.' And it had been the one thing guaranteed to soften Uncle Hugo's stance on their associating with each other. When Harriet had written to tell him she had become engaged and needed her aunt's help with shopping for the wedding, his reply had been swift, and tinged, predictably, with a touch of gloating that she felt obliged to ask her aunt to perform that office, rather than be able to rely on her own mother. 'Just not today,' Harriet explained. 'Or perhaps, later on. After,' she said, wriggling across the seat of the carriage in preparation for getting out, 'we have finished with Lord Rawcliffe.'

Getting out of the carriage did the trick. Her aunt, who'd been displaying such reluctance to be seen anywhere near the house which took up such a large slice of Grosvenor Square, girded up her mental loins and set out after her niece.

'It is most inappropriate for you to be calling upon such a man,' she said in an urgent undertone. 'Even if he is a close friend of your betrothed.'

Her curiosity piqued, Harriet delayed informing her aunt that her betrothed would also be at the meeting he'd arranged. She'd always wondered what it was about Lord Rawcliffe that set her aunt against him as a matrimonial prospect for Kitty. And there was no better time to find out than now.

'What do you mean, *such a man*? He seems perfectly respectable to me.'

'Oh, it is not a question of that,' said Aunt Susan, panting up the front steps after her. 'It is just that he has a reputation with…that is, I have lost count of the number of hopeful females who have dashed themselves to pieces against the hardness of his heart.'

'You mean, women throw themselves at him? Whatever for?'

'Because he is a matrimonial prize. Or at least, he was considered so, when he was younger. And he still is, in many respects,' said Aunt Susan, jerking her head at the imposing façade of his house in a meaningful way. 'It is just that careful mothers keep their daughters away from him. He won't marry anyone who looks the slightest bit...'

'Desperate?' When her aunt merely pursed her lips and shook her head as though words failed her, Harriet tried another one. 'Fast?'

'I think,' said Aunt Susan slowly, as though choosing her words with care, 'it is more likely that when he does marry, it will be a woman of his own choosing, rather than one who has thrown herself at him. Well, you saw the way Lord Lensborough reacted when those silly girls threw themselves at his head, at the picnic.'

'At his feet, don't you mean?'

'Harriet,' Aunt Susan said repressively. 'The point is, men who are as high in the instep as Lensborough, or Rawcliffe, only ever marry girls of good character, with an impeccable lineage and a fortune to match their own.'

He would remain a bachelor for the rest of his life then. Not that she could say as much, when the front door was being opened by exactly the kind of butler she would guess a man as full of his own consequence as *Zeus* would employ.

In spite of telling Harriet that setting foot inside Lord Rawcliffe's house was tantamount to committing some sort of social faux pas, Aunt Susan's eyes flicked round, taking in every inch of the immense hall, the portraits on the walls, the moulding round the doors, the little tables set at strategic points to display their collection of probably priceless urns and dishes, during the short walk across the hall behind the butler.

'Lady Tarbrook, Lady Harriet Inskip,' said the butler, as he opened the door, before stepping aside and making the slightest inclination of his head to let them know they should go in.

'Harriet!' Jack had been lounging against the mantelpiece, but the moment he saw her, his face lit up with such obvious pleasure it was impossible not to smile back. Especially since he flew to her side and seized her hands as though he meant to haul her close and kiss her.

She squeezed his hands back, then tilted her head sideways, to remind him that her aunt was standing right there.

'And Lady Tarbrook,' said Jack, finally recalling his manners. 'Thank you both for coming.'

'I...well, not at all,' said Aunt Susan, clearly bewildered, but determined not to let on that Harriet had virtually ambushed her.

'Please, do take a seat,' said Lord Rawcliffe, gesturing to a sofa set at a slight angle to the fireplace. He had been standing right next to Jack, Harriet realised, though she hadn't really noticed him before. As Aunt Susan did as she'd been told, Harriet dropped a brief curtsy to acknowledge her host, then she and Jack gravitated to the sofa opposite her aunt's and sat down together, still holding hands.

'You know Mr Kellett,' said Lord Rawcliffe, indicating Archie, who was sitting on a chair by one of the windows overlooking the rear to the house, his hands clasped in his lap.

Aunt Susan accorded him a regal nod.

'Then, I shall ring for tea,' said Lord Rawcliffe, going across to the bell pull by the fireplace.

There then followed a short interlude, during which Lord Rawcliffe kept the conversation at the most banal of levels, whilst they ordered, then waited for the refreshments to arrive. Aunt Susan did her best to look as though it was perfectly normal to pay a morning call upon an unmarried gentleman. But Harriet noticed how uneasy she was from the way she twined the strings of her reticule round her fingers so tightly that when it came time to remove her gloves, she was hard pressed to untangle them.

But at length, the moment that Harriet had been waiting for finally arrived. Just as they were all on their second cup of tea and the cakes had been reduced to crumbs, she heard the sound of the final, and most important guest of all, knock on the front door.

Only seconds later, Lord Rawcliffe's butler opened the door again, and, as all eyes swung to look at him, he announced, 'Lord Tarbrook.'

Aunt Susan started and dropped her teaspoon into her saucer with a tinkle. Fortunately, nobody but Harriet noticed this, because at the exact same moment, Lord Tarbrook was saying, 'Cannot imagine what business you have with me that you consider so urgent, Rawcliffe. Good God. Susan!'

By now, Aunt Susan had composed herself and was able to greet his incredulity at finding her there with the mere raising of one eyebrow, as if to convey she had every right to be there.

'What the devil is going on here?' said Lord Tarbrook, darting dagger glances round the room.

'Would you care for some tea?' Lord Rawcliffe asked mildly.

'The devil take your tea. What I want is an explanation.'

'And you shall have it,' said Lord Rawcliffe, waving a slender hand to another chair, inviting the latest arrival to sit on it.

Lord Tarbrook drew his brows down and leaned on his cane, as though declaring his refusal to accept the hospitality of a man who had engineered a meeting with his wife in such an underhand manner.

'As you wish,' said Lord Rawcliffe as though he perfectly understood. 'Becconsall, perhaps you would like to conduct the next part of this meeting?'

'Yes. Absolutely,' said Jack, getting to his feet. 'It's like this, my lord. Harriet, that is, Lady Harriet, my betrothed, has naturally confided in me about the rift that occurred between you over the matter of the missing jewels.'

'She did what?' Lord Tarbrook turned his attention to her. And threw her his most repressive glare.

'And it turns out that there has been a similar case in the family of our mutual friend, Mr Kellett,' said Jack, drawing Lord Tarbrook's attention to the figure sitting mute by the window.

'What?' Lord Tarbrook looked from one man to the other in confusion.

'Yes,' said Archie, finally getting to his feet. 'When my g-grandmother died, my father found that some of her jewels were not the genuine article. C-couldn't find any trace of gambling debts.

Thought it must have been a private wager. Had them c-copied to raise the blunt. Hushed it up.'

'What!'

'Then, when we heard about the same thing happening in your own family, started wondering if…'

'You heard about… How did you… Harriet!' Lord Tarbrook whirled on her, his fury pouring off him in waves.

'Started asking a few qu-questions,' carried on Archie, ignoring Lord Tarbrook's outburst. 'T-turned out she had a maid with her during her last illness who matched the description of one employed by Lady Tarbrook.'

'What?' Now it was Lady Tarbrook's turn to express shock.

'More to the point, she'd c-come to my g-grandmother's notice through an old friend of hers. Lady B-Buntingford.'

'Oh!' Aunt Susan clapped a hand to her chest. 'I took on a girl recommended to me by Lady Buntingford. As a favour. But that must have been…well, it was a few years ago.'

'We believe,' said Jack, 'that is when the switch of your rubies must have taken place.'

'You mean…' Aunt Susan was heaving for breath.

'Yes. We believe you have been the victim of a very cleverly orchestrated crime.'

'Lady Buntingford?' Aunt Susan was shaking her head. 'No. I cannot believe it. She would not...'

'All we know so far,' said Jack, 'is that she has been the link between the families who have had jewels switched and the girl who appears to have done the switching. We will need to investigate further to discover—'

'No!' Uncle Hugo thumped his cane on the floor. 'No investigation. I will not have my family's reputation dragged through the mire.'

'There will be no need for that,' said Lord Rawcliffe repressively. 'Archie will be going to Dorset on a visit to Lady Buntingford, who is his mother's godmother, to discreetly ask her a few questions. It won't arouse any suspicion outside our own circle. Nothing more natural for a man in his position to spend part of his holidays visiting such a woman. Particularly not when she happens to live in such a beautiful part of the country.'

'And what part, pray, do you play in all of this? What makes you think you have the right to become so busy in my family affairs?'

'I will be pursuing the girl who appears to have done the actual thieving,' said Lord Rawcliffe. 'Since I plan to go to the area from which we have reason to believe she hales, in a few days in any case, my own movements should not alert anyone to the fact that there is an investigation taking place.'

'I don't like it,' grumbled Uncle Hugo.

'That is what the thieves want, though, isn't it?' put in Harriet. 'For everyone to be so determined to cover up the crime that they get away with it. And we can't let them get away with it. We can't!'

'You don't seriously expect to apprehend the culprits, do you? After all this time? And as for thinking you will ever be able to recover the jewels...' He shook his head.

'It isn't a question of recovering the jewels,' said Harriet. 'But of seeing justice done. Of clearing Aunt Susan's name. Proving her innocent!'

'Hugo,' said Aunt Susan. 'What these gentlemen have just told us...the lengths to which they are prepared to go...well, you know what this means, don't you?' She got to her feet.

'What does it mean?' he replied testily.

'It means,' she said coldly, 'that you owe me an apology.'

Everyone in the room held their breath, or at least that was how it seemed to Harriet. Everyone except Uncle Hugo, who was glaring down at the head of his cane and heaving in great heavy breaths as though they were all sorely trying his patience. He rapped the cane on the floor once or twice, his face working.

Harriet braced herself for an explosion.

But then he sighed. Raised his head to look at Aunt Susan. 'Yes,' he said. 'Yes, I do.'

Aunt Susan, who clearly hadn't expected him to admit any such thing, especially not so quickly, sat down rather abruptly.

'I...overreacted, I suppose that is what you all think. But...' he glared defiantly round the room '... I saw it as evidence.'

'Evidence?' Aunt Susan was glaring right back at him. 'Of what?'

He sighed again. And shrugged, in a rather sulky sort of way. 'Well, you only married me because our parents pushed you into it. And you never gave me any sign that...' He trailed off, going rather red about the ears.

'That what?'

'No matter what I did you never...cared.' He straightened up, almost defiantly, and focused intently on his wife. 'You never gave any indication that you returned my feelings.'

'Your feelings?'

As the middle-aged couple stared at each other, Harriet could see a maelstrom of emotion playing across their faces. And she recalled the list of grievances her aunt had poured forth about Uncle Hugo's behaviour, over the breakfast table.

And wondered if he'd been doing exactly what Jack had done to her. Acted badly, to try to get her attention.

Well, Uncle Hugo had certainly got Aunt Susan's attention now. The pair of them were looking at each other as though they'd completely forgotten anyone else was in the room.

Lord Rawcliffe cleared his throat, and, when Harriet looked his way, saw that he was gesturing to the door.

With a smile tugging at her lips, Harriet took Jack's arm, and followed Lord Rawcliffe and Archie out. Neither her aunt nor her uncle appeared to notice they were leaving, though neither of them had said anything, yet. Not that they needed to. Everything they were thinking was plain for anyone to see.

'I wonder,' said Jack, as Lord Rawcliffe shut the door behind them, 'which of them will be the first to break down and admit they've been secretly in love with the other for years.'

'I think it might well be Uncle Hugo,' said Harriet. 'After all, he almost went too far this time, the way he treated my aunt. He has a lot of apologising to do, and I dare say even he will have worked out, by now, that the best way to gain forgiveness is to admit that he loves her. And after that, she will admit that she loves him, too, and then—'

'Please, no more,' said Lord Rawcliffe with a shudder. 'I may never be able to look at that particular sofa with anything but revulsion again. In fact,' he said, pushing open the door to another room, which looked as though it might be his private study, 'I may well simply throw it out and get a new one.'

The thought of what he suspected Uncle Hugo and Aunt Susan of being about to get up to on his sofa, that would make him wish to destroy it, seemed to amuse Jack no end.

But Harriet thought it was rather sweet.

'I hope,' she whispered up to Jack, while Lord Rawcliffe was busy pouring himself a drink from a decanter that stood on a side table, 'that we are still as much in love as they are, when we reach their age.'

'You can count on it,' Jack replied, giving her waist a squeeze. 'Though I shan't be such a nod-cock as to leave you ignorant of my own feelings for so many years.'

'No?'

'No. I plan to tell you, at least once every day,

that you are the light of my life and that I love you more than…'

'More than what?'

'More than anything, of course.'

Harriet sighed with pure contentment. At last, she mattered to someone.

More than anything.

* * * * *

*If you enjoyed this story, you won't want to
miss these other great reads
from Annie Burrows*

*A MISTRESS FOR MAJOR BARTLETT
THE CAPTAIN'S CHRISTMAS BRIDE
IN BED WITH THE DUKE
THE DEBUTANTE'S SHOCKING PROPOSAL*

MILLS & BOON®

HISTORICAL

AWAKEN THE ROMANCE OF THE PAST

A sneak peek at next month's titles...

In stores from 5th October 2017:

- **Courting Danger with Mr Dyer** – Georgie Lee
- **His Mistletoe Wager** – Virginia Heath
- **An Innocent Maid for the Duke** – Ann Lethbridge
- **The Viking Warrior's Bride** – Harper St. George
- **Scandal and Miss Markham** – Janice Preston
- **Western Christmas Brides** – Lauri Robinson, Lynna Banning *and* Carol Arens

---

Just can't wait?
Buy our books online before they hit the shops!
www.millsandboon.co.uk

Also available as eBooks.

MILLS & BOON®

EXCLUSIVE EXTRACT

Spy Bartholomew Dyer is forced to enlist the help of Moira, Lady Rexford, who jilted him five years ago. He's determined not to succumb to her charms *again*, because Bart suspects it's not just their lives at risk— it's their hearts…

Read on for a sneak preview of
COURTING DANGER WITH MR DYER

Bart longed to slide across the squabs and sit beside Moira, to slip his hands around her waist and claim her lips, but he remained where he was. If he could give her all the things the far-off look in her eyes said she wanted, he would, but he wasn't a man for marriage and children. To take her into his arms would be to lead her into a lie. Deception was too much a part of his life already and he refused to deceive her. 'I'm sure you'll find a man worthy of your heart.'

'I hope so, but sometimes it's difficult to imagine, especially when I see all the other young ladies.' She picked at the embroidery on her dress. 'I don't have their daring, or their ability to flirt and make a spectacle out of myself to catch a man's eye.'

'You may not make a spectacle of yourself, but you certainly have their daring and a courage worthy of any soldier on the battlefield.'

This brought a smile to her face, but it was one of embarrassment. She tilted her head down and looked up at him through her eyelashes, innocent and alluring all at the same time. 'Now I see why they only allow male judges on the bench. No female judge could withstand your flattery.'

'Perhaps, but a man is as easy to flatter as a woman, one just has to do it a little differently.'

She leaned forward, her green eyes sparkling with a wit he wished to see more of. 'And how does one flatter you, Bart?'

He leaned forward, resting his elbow on his thigh and bringing his face achingly close to hers. He could wipe the playful smirk off her lips with a kiss, taste again her sensual mouth and the heady excitement of desire he'd experienced with her five years ago. Except he was no longer young and thoughtless and neither was she. He'd experienced the consequences of forgetting himself with her once before. He had no desire to repeat the mistake again, no matter how tempting it might be. There was a great deal more at stake this time than his heart.

Don't miss
COURTING DANGER WITH MR DYER
By Georgie Lee

Available October 2017
www.millsandboon.co.uk

MILLS & BOON®

Why shop at millsandboon.co.uk?

Each year, thousands of romance readers find their perfect read at millsandboon.co.uk. That's because we're passionate about bringing you the very best romantic fiction. Here are some of the advantages of shopping at www.millsandboon.co.uk:

* **Get new books first**—you'll be able to buy your favourite books one month before they hit the shops

* **Get exclusive discounts**—you'll also be able to buy our specially created monthly collections, with up to 50% off the RRP

* **Find your favourite authors**—latest news, interviews and new releases for all your favourite authors and series on our website, plus ideas for what to try next

* **Join in**—once you've bought your favourite books, don't forget to register with us to rate, review and join in the discussions

Visit **www.millsandboon.co.uk** for all this and more today!

Join Britain's BIGGES
Romance Book Club

- **EXCLUSIVE offers** every month

- **FREE delivery dire** to your door

- **NEVER MISS a titl**

- **EARN Bonus Bool** points

Call Customer Services
0844 844 1358*

or visit
millsandboon.co.uk/subscriptio